THE CAT STAR CHRONICLES

WARRIOR

THE CAT STAR CHRONICLES

WARRIOR

CHERYL BROOKS

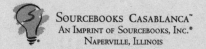

SOURCEBOOKS CASABLANCA™
AN IMPRINT OF SOURCEBOOKS, INC.®
NAPERVILLE, ILLINOIS

Copyright © 2008 by Cheryl Brooks
Cover and internal design © 2008 by Sourcebooks, Inc.
Cover photos © Fotolia.com, Mario Bruno; Dreamstime.com,
Argus 456
Cover design by Anne Cain
Sourcebooks and the colophon are registered trademarks of
Sourcebooks, Inc.

The characters and events portrayed in this book are fictitious or
are used fictitiously. Any similarity to real persons, living or dead,
is purely coincidental and not intended by the author.

Published by Sourcebooks Casablanca, an imprint of
Sourcebooks, Inc.
P.O. Box 4410, Naperville, Illinois 60567-4410
(630) 961-3900
FAX: (630) 961-2168
www.sourcebooks.com

Library of Congress Cataloging-in-Publication Data
Brooks, Cheryl
Warrior / by Cheryl Brooks.
p. cm. — (Cat Star Chronicles)
ISBN-13: 978-1-4022-1440-0
ISBN-10: 1-4022-1440-5
I. Title.
PS3602.R64425W37 2008
813'.6—dc22
2008014861

Printed and bound in the United States of America
QW 10 9 8 7 6 5 4 3 2

For that little bit of witch in all of us…
and every witch needs her cat…

Chapter 1

HE CAME TO ME IN THE DEAD OF WINTER, HIS BODY burning with fever. Even before he arrived on my doorstep, bound, beaten, and unconscious, I knew my quiet life was about to change forever. And I was ready.

As I stirred my potion, I heard the creak of saddle leather and the muffled thud of a body falling into the snow outside my isolated cottage, followed by Rafe's grunt of effort as he dragged the unconscious offworlder through the drifts. With a gust of cold air and a swirling cloud of snowflakes, he pushed my door open and burst inside without so much as a knock.

The evening had begun tranquilly enough. I had just brought in extra wood from the shed, but it was snowing so hard, I decided to go back out into the wintry darkness for more. I can conjure up fire better than any other witch I've heard of, but it helps to have some fuel. Besides, I love the cozy warmth and smell of a wood fire.

From her place by the fire, Desdemona gazed up at me with narrowed eyes, nodding her agreement. I trusted her feline intuition to alert me to danger, but Desdemona had given me no warning. Yawning, she stretched and let out a loud purr before curling up once more.

Reassured, I pushed open the heavy wooden door and peered out into the thickly falling snow. Big, fluffy flakes drifted by in the beam of light, floating gently but inexorably to the ground. It was already a hand-span in depth and more was on the way. But there was something else in the air tonight—a strange feeling, heralding something altogether new and unexpected. Not a feeling of dread or fear, but something that whispered of the fulfillment of a promise. It hung there, on the edge of awareness, teasing me with its elusive aura. Just what—or who—it was, only time would tell. Time and the gods.

My woodshed was only a few paces from the door, though with the snow it seemed farther than usual. Treading softly, I sank into the snow with each step, feeling my way through the darkness. The door to the shed creaked open on its rusty hinges and I glanced up at the lantern, shooting fire into the wick, instantly illuminating the interior with a warm glow.

I had plenty of wood stored there for the winter; the people of the forest saw to that. I was too important to their well-being for them to ever let me freeze or starve, and offerings appeared almost daily on my doorstep—sometimes openly, sometimes covertly, but still they came without fail. I reminded myself frequently that one day they might not, and was, therefore, frugal with whatever I had. I knew full well that my honored status could vanish on a whim, and I wouldn't have been the first of the chosen ones to be cast out to starve. It was a tenuous existence, to be sure, but one for which I had been born and bred.

Stacking the new logs on my arm, I made my way carefully back through the snow to my house. Although the right to own property was denied most women on this world, it was *my* house and had been my mother's before me, and her mother's before her, time out of mind—never once having a male to claim ownership. Our children had fathers, of course, but we seldom married—at least, not in the traditional sense—and therefore traced our lineage through the female line. The one child we were granted was of the utmost importance, for it was she who would continue our work and our traditions—and that child was always female. Always.

Desdemona purred her greeting as I came back inside and dumped the logs by the fire. I had three days' worth of wood there already, but the snow was deepening quickly, so I thought I might as well bring in more. Pausing by the door, I listened. There was barely any wind, and the snow fell silently until, just on the fringes of my hearing, I was at last able to hear what I'd been waiting for: hooves in the snow, and heavily laden, by the sound of them. A rider was coming, but that was not all.

I could hear the effort the horse was making as he strained to climb. He was coming from the east, and I could place him now. It was Sinjar; I sent a greeting of thought out to him and heard him nicker in reply. We knew each other well, for his master, Rafe, had been my lover once. Too arrogant now to trouble with the likes of me, he'd been charming enough in his youth. I'd known that Rafe wasn't the one—had always known, even from the beginning—but loneliness sometimes drives one to seek out solace in places where happiness can never be found. It had been over for many years; Rafe had a wife and sons now and had never once strayed back to my bed. That it was for the best, I was well aware, because he had become too powerful and had too much to lose by consorting with a witch.

Sinjar's thoughts reached into my mind. *"I'm tired and hungry,"* he said. *"They are heavy."*

"They?" I asked.

"The master and another," he replied. *"Sick and hurt. A slave, I think. He is...strange. An offworlder."*

"I'll have food and water waiting for you, Sinjar," I promised.

"Good. It's not far now. I'll be glad to see you again, Tisana."

"And I, you."

Returning to the shed, I gathered up buckets and feed and carried them back to the house, filling one of them with water from the pump by my door. Rafe might want food and drink as much as his horse did, but he would have to ask for it when he arrived.

Rafe and I had not parted company on the best of terms, though he did use my talents when it served his purpose. He must need my help very badly to come out on a night like this—and for a slave, no less. An offworlder, which didn't bode well, for my skills and medicines were sometimes useless with other species. My knowledge had grown with time, but there were still those whose physiology was too different to respond to my treatments. Many of the basic principles were the same, but they were usually strangers, and often didn't trust me completely, which was half the battle. This one might already be beyond my aid, for I could sense something ominous about him, a life-force on the wane. Rafe may have been too late.

I set Sinjar's food and water down and went inside, leaving the door unlatched, and gathered what herbs I thought I might need. Water was already hot in the kettle hanging from a hook over the fire, and I mixed the pungent potion in an earthenware bowl on a heavy wooden table that was probably as old as the cottage itself. Powdered comfrey root mixed with sage and rosemary tea would help to heal his battered body, but an infusion of thyme, lavender, rosemary, and vervain would help restore the will to live, which I could tell even from a distance was the chief problem afflicting my newest client. I doubted that many slaves would prefer death to slavery, but some might. Rafe was a stern man and could be an exacting master. On the other hand, Rafe would presumably have paid good money for him, and see him as an investment to be protected. He wouldn't be coming at such a time if it didn't matter to him.

Putting my fingertips to my temples, I wished for perhaps the millionth time that I could read the thoughts of humans as well as those of animals. My grandmother had had that gift. My mother had had both, though to a lesser degree, but I could read only the beasts of the forest and farm. It was a useful skill, for very few others could ask their horse which foot was hurting them, or if the girth was pulled too tight. I always knew where to find the juiciest berries and the lushest patches of wild rosemary, because the rabbits knew, and their minds were much occupied with these matters. Animals had a feel for weather, too, and were a much more reliable source of information than your typical village sage.

Still, with sick or injured humans, you can ask what the trouble is—if they're conscious enough to reply— but it's a given that they will sometimes embellish upon the truth. Rafe had lied to me—many times. I sometimes let him think I believed him, but I wasn't fooled.

Taking a deep breath, I put my thoughts of Rafe firmly aside. I couldn't afford to let them, or anything else, interfere, because I knew this one would require all of my concentration.

And so, as I gathered my powers and my resolve, Rafe came bursting through the door with his usual lack of ceremony.

"See what you can do for him, Tisana," he said, dropping his burden upon the rough wooden floor, and stepping past the inert form to warm himself by the fire. "Seems my wife covets him for some reason, though I couldn't tell you why—at least, not from the look of him. Said he was an oddity, and it would bring us added prestige to have him as a slave, although I think she's a bit touched in the head, myself. He doesn't even look to be worth the little dab I paid for him." I saw Rafe's nostrils flare as he took in the aroma of the herbs, and his eyes narrowed in suspicion. "You knew we were coming," he said flatly. "How?"

"How not?" I asked, unperturbed. "You make such a racket, even in the snow. I heard you coming a mile away."

"But how could you know *why* I was coming?" he countered, indicating the steaming bowl on the table.

"Why else would you come, Rafe?" I retorted. "It's long past the time when you came seeking my company."

A bushy eyebrow went up. "I may surprise you someday, Tisana." Rafe was a big man, with broad, heavy shoulders, curly, dark red hair and beard, and dark, flashing eyes—eyes which now swept over me from head to toe with a slow, assessing look. "You're still quite beautiful, you know. I just might…"

Another lie. I wasn't nearly as beautiful as his wife, Carnita, and never had been. His attraction to me had nothing to do with beauty, and everything to do with seeking power. I'd been an experiment—a youthful folly, if you will—which, as it turned out, had paid him nothing in the long run. His wife had given him something that I never could; she had given him sons, which meant that she was worth far more than I, and Rafe knew that every bit as well as I did myself.

The women of my family could love where we wished, but the choice of the man to father our single daughter was with the gods. Conception could occur only with the right one and at the right time. Rafe had not been destined to be the father of my child, and I suspected that fact still rankled. I'd been waiting many years and had taken several lovers, but had not yet found the one. In such a remote area, I didn't meet very many new people, unless there was a need for my services— a traveler, perhaps, ill or injured on his journey. And so, through the long years, I had continued on with my work and waited for the one who would ensure the succession.

Ignoring Rafe's remark, I gestured toward my patient. "What else can you tell me about him?"

"Offworlder," he said shortly. "Like a cat in many ways. Reportedly a good fighter, hunter, and tracker. I have no idea where he came from or how he got here. Looks to have had it rough, but Carnita wanted him, anyway, and insisted that I bring him to you for healing. Said no one else had such a slave, and it would be good for our standing in the cartel. I believe at the last conclave she was belittled by some of the other women for not having any that were more remarkable."

"Why, Rafe!" I exclaimed in mock surprise. "I had no idea that social standing meant so much to you!"

"Just heal him, Tisana," he said, glowering at me. "Don't plague me with needless chatter."

As he turned to go, I heard Sinjar protest, *"Keep him talking! I'm not finished yet! If he'd taken this cursed bridle off I could eat faster, but no-o-o!" You know, he can be a real horse's ass sometimes!"*

"What if I can't save him?" I asked Rafe, barely suppressing a smile. Sinjar had more personality than most humans, and I thought he was the funniest horse I'd ever met. In comparison, my own mare, Morgana, had absolutely no sense of humor whatsoever.

Rafe shrugged insolently. "He dies, then. Really, Tisana! I paid very little for him. Whether he lives or dies is with the gods."

I looked upon my latest charge with a doubtful eye, hoping that the gods were feeling benevolent toward him—though it was fairly obvious they hadn't done much for him in the recent past. This slave would need not only my skill, but also their help if he was to recover. "Come back for him in a month," I suggested. "I'll send word if he fails to survive."

"That would be very kind of you," he said simply, starting again for the door, just as Sinjar licked the last of the grain out of the bucket and raised his head.

"'That would be very kind of you,'" Sinjar mimicked. *"Sure isn't very kind to anyone else! I wouldn't bother if I were you, except that it might save me a trip."*

Smiling to myself, I asked Sinjar, *"If you hate him so much, then why don't you leave him?"*

"Well, the food's good, and I do have a very nice stable and a pretty girl to take care of me. It could be worse."

"True. You've been much better treated than this slave."

"He looks pretty bad, doesn't he?" agreed Sinjar. *"Well, if anyone can save him, it's you, Tisana! You're the best healer there is."*

"Oh, you're only saying that because I cured that abscess in your hoof," I chided him.

"Yes, but no one else could find it," Sinjar reminded me. *"You did."*

"Only because you told me where to look," I responded modestly, following Rafe to the door.

Sinjar's attention returned to his master as Rafe put a foot in the stirrup to mount.

"In a month," Rafe reiterated, swinging up into the saddle. He glanced past me to the inert body lying in the middle of my floor. "Though it might take longer."

"I'll let you know," I promised. I didn't want Rafe coming around any more than was absolutely necessary. His visits were…unsettling. "Have a safe journey, and may the gods be with you."

Rafe snorted his thanks. I received a nicer acknowledgment from his horse.

"Good luck with him," Sinjar said as they started off into the snowy night. *"You're gonna need it!"*

I watched the horse and rider disappear into the night before returning to attend to my latest charge. "Might at least have helped me get him onto a pallet," I grumbled.

"But no-o-o!" I said, mimicking Sinjar. "That would have been *much* too considerate of him!"

I dragged the pallet out from beneath my bed and took the blankets outside to shake the worst of the dust from them. I hadn't had anyone remain in my care for quite some time now, and it would be strange having someone there with me again. I'd grown so used to the solitude; just the sound of another person's breathing would be an intrusion.

The first step would be to burn the rags he was wearing and wash him, for he smelled of filth, sweat, and sickness. There was some festering infection there, perhaps on his skin, perhaps in his lungs, or perhaps both. Wherever it was, I could smell it and knew it for what it was. I rolled him over onto his stomach to undress him, unfastening the cords at his neck and waist before I did so. The best I could tell, he had no broken bones, but I could feel the fever in him even through the rough fabric of his tunic.

As I began to strip the clothing from his body, the stench was so strong, I decided that washing him before even laying him on the pallet would be the best course. Peeling his tunic from a back crisscrossed with sores—presumably lashes from a whip—I considered it fortunate for him that he was unconscious.

I rolled up the rug that covered a place in the floor where the spaces between the boards were open and, after tossing his shirt into the fire, drenched his upper body with hot, soapy water, which steamed with the aroma of the herbs, letting it run down through the boards in the floor. I'd done this before with others, as no doubt all of my ancestors had done. I distinctly remembered my mother doing it with one woman she had cared for, and she'd cautioned me to never fill in the chinks in the floor, but to cover them with the rug, instead, to keep out the drafts.

The man had long, light brown hair which, if clean, might have hung in attractive spirals but was now little more than a matted rat's nest and was undoubtedly infested with vermin. I had a cure for that, and though it might have been simpler to shave his head, I didn't do it, simply because the thought of cutting such luxuriant locks appalled me. Combing out his tangles would take a considerable amount of time, but it would give me something to do while I sat with him. I washed his hair with a strong soap and then worked oils of rosemary, lavender, and geranium into it, which would kill any parasites harbored there. After washing his back and applying a soothing comfrey and sage ointment, I covered it with a clean cloth before rolling him over.

Rafe had said he was catlike, but I'd had no idea what to expect. His ears were pointed—that much I had seen when I did his hair—but he had other feline characteristics as well. Upon examining the inside of his mouth, I discovered surprisingly strong, white—and extremely sharp—teeth, with fanglike canines. He had full lips, a prominent nose, and golden brows which swept gracefully upward toward his temples. With some trepidation, I lifted an eyelid to reveal an eye which shone forth with a soft glow through a vertical slit of a pupil, surrounded by an iris that put me in mind of the uneven landscape of an old gold coin.

As I washed the grime from his face, I noted that he seemed to have no beard whatsoever—not even a stubble—and found old scars along with several more recent scrapes and bruises. What could he possibly have done to deserve such punishment? I began to fear what dangers might lurk within him when he awakened. If he chose to escape, I had no doubt that he could overpower me when he recovered, for his chest and arms were well muscled, though not with the heavy power Rafe possessed. No, this man's muscles were hard, but leaner and more sinewy, like those of a hunting cat, and even covered with scabs and bruises, he looked strong.

Having treated the wounds on his chest, I undressed his lower body—and got the surprise of my life! What I found there was unlike anything I'd ever seen on any humanoid, from this world or any other. Flaccid at first, his penis simply appeared to be long and thick, but when I washed it, it blossomed like a rose, the head putting out a wide corona with a scalloped edge.

I tried not to stare as I finished washing his legs, but it was the sort of thing that couldn't help but draw your eye and make you wonder what it would feel like to…but, no, I wouldn't be doing that. Not with him—not unless he was prone to rape, and with a penis like that, he could probably rip the insides out of any woman he chose to assault. And then, of course, there were those *teeth*…

I wondered briefly if Carnita had seen his genitals, and if that was why she had wanted him. If so, she probably already suspected that this man could outperform Rafe with one arm tied behind his back—maybe even both arms. Rafe was the sort who was interested only in his own pleasure, whereas this man looked as though he could satisfy even the most uninterested partner imaginable—with some supplemental lubrication, perhaps—without even trying. Then I noticed something else, which was that he already had plenty of lubrication dripping from the starlike points of the corona. And this was all happening while he was unconscious!

Or was he? He could have been feigning a comatose state for all I knew, but this wasn't the first erection I'd ever seen on a male who was merely sleeping. Then he did something else that made me suspicious. He began to purr.

Now, the average cat does not purr when it is truly asleep, but this one did—or seemed to. I sent a thought to Desdemona.

"No," was her firm reply. *"He's awake. It requires a conscious effort to purr—if that's what he's really doing."*

"Why pretend then?" I wondered.

"Who knows?" she said. *"Maybe it's his way of protecting himself from further harm."*

"But what I've been doing to him had to hurt!" I protested. *"And he never even flinched!"*

*"Maybe you only woke him up when you washed that enormous…*thing *of his,"* she suggested.

Since this was apparently true, all I could do was nod. Then another thought occurred to me. *"What do you suppose it would take to get it to go back down?"*

Her laugh sounded a bit like a wheeze. *"Well, if you don't know the answer to that by now, Tisana, there's no hope for you!"*

I made a face at her. "Oh, you know what I mean!" I grumbled aloud. "I just—"

"Who are you speaking to?"

His question was so unexpected that I nearly bit my tongue. "My cat, Desdemona," I replied in an unsteady voice. "She said you were awake."

Seeming to ignore the oddity of a woman who could converse with a cat, he went on to ask, "Would you be able to sleep if a male was washing you?"

"That would depend on how tired I was," I said reasonably. "Besides," I added accusingly, "you weren't just asleep; you were unconscious!"

"I am awake now," he stated firmly.

"Do you want me to stop?"

As sick and injured as he was, I wouldn't have believed him to be capable of smiling, but I'll swear he did just then, for I saw the flash of those sharp teeth, and his purring began again, even more loudly than before.

In response to my own question, I muttered, "Guess not," under my breath. "Can you turn over?"

He shifted to one side, moving with surprising quickness, but I would never have guessed that his penis would have folded *down* between his legs instead of up toward his stomach. He never touched it, but it moved, seemingly of its own accord, to fit neatly between his testicles. It was still dripping onto the floor as I washed the back of his legs and his buttocks and pulsed when I inadvertently dripped water on it, causing a flood of clear fluid to gush from the corona, as well as from the slit in the head. I decided that this guy would never have to use force with anyone—he'd simply have to display his showy cock and all the women in his vicinity would scramble to line up and take their turn. It made me wonder if he hadn't been beaten within an inch of his life and then sold into slavery by a jealous husband, something

Rafe might also wind up doing if Carnita ever got wind of what she was missing. I couldn't imagine any woman kicking this particular man out of her bed—unless she was totally against sexual pleasure in any form.

Obviously, Desdemona was listening to my thoughts, for I heard her snickering at me from her perch by the fire.

"Oh, be quiet!" I admonished her.

"I did not speak," my patient said quietly.

"I wasn't talking to you," I said. "I was talking to Desdemona. She's been eavesdropping on my thoughts."

"Must have been amusing thoughts," he commented. "I do not believe I have ever heard an animal laugh before."

"Oh, she does it all the time," I grumbled. "Mostly to annoy me, I think. There's a squirrel living nearby who's a real joker, too. He throws nuts at me whenever I walk under the tree he happens to be in."

"And he does not fear being killed for food?"

"Oh, I never hunt them," I replied. "Although sometimes I think maybe I should, just to keep them in line! Other people bring me food, but they're careful not to hunt near my house. They don't actually know that I can communicate with the animals, but it's always been one of those unspoken rules about bringing offerings to the local witch—and was in my mother's time, as well."

"You keep it secret, then, this talking with animals?"

"Yes," I replied. "I also have other…talents…that I don't advertise. Some of the locals frighten easily, and knowing what I can do might make them…uncomfortable, and forgive me if I don't care for the idea of people coming after me with ropes and pitchforks."

"Then why are you telling me?"

I had no reply to that. "I really don't know," I said,

a bit surprised that I had somehow managed to reveal one of my most closely guarded secrets to a complete stranger. "I suppose I shouldn't be. Desdemona could probably come up with a reason for you, though. She's very wise."

Which got another snicker out of her.

"She truly does understand you?"

"All too well," I replied with a wry smile. "It's impossible to keep secrets from her."

"You must be very lonely to talk to a cat," he observed.

"I suppose I am," I agreed. "But, unlike other people who talk to their cats, mine can talk back to me."

"Is that why you would buy a slave?" he asked curiously. "Because you are lonely?"

The notion that I would purchase a slave, even for so innocuous a reason, hit me like a slap in the face. "I didn't buy you," I said shortly. "Someone else did. I'm just supposed to get you well enough to be able to work."

"Doing what?" he inquired.

"I have no idea," I replied, "though I got the impression you were a trophy of sorts. I have no way of knowing what your duties will be." I could just imagine him as Carnita's personal slave. She would have *plenty* for him to do...

"And how will you keep me from escaping?" he asked with a sly smile.

"Fear," I said, smiling right back at him. He was going to give me trouble, I could tell.

"Of what you can do that I do not know about?"

I nodded. "It keeps most people in line when they deal with me. They don't really know what I'm capable of—and most of them don't want to find out. It's not wise to anger a witch, you know."

"A witch," he mused. I saw his eyes flash, and the golden light from his pupils grew brighter. "I believe I would like to please a witch, not anger her," he purred. "Especially such a beautiful witch."

"Oh, is that right?" I commented witheringly. "I suppose you think that if you sweet-talk me enough, I'll smuggle you out of here, and you won't have to be a slave anymore."

His purr stopped abruptly. "I believe I have lost all hope there," he said quietly.

"But wouldn't you like to go home?"

"I have no home."

He said it with such an air of finality that I left it at that, not wanting to upset him by questioning him further. The fact that he had no home to go back to made me wonder if his family had sold him into slavery to settle a debt—perhaps even when he was a child. If that were the case, he might have been bitter enough to want to go almost anywhere but home.

He went back to purring again after that. I wondered at his change of mood, but the fact that I was still absently washing his ass—massaging it, in fact—might have had something to do with it. I suppose I should have stopped, but found that I didn't want to. He felt quite delightful beneath my hands, and it made me want to massage his entire body—not simply wash and dry it. He was making me hot in a way I hadn't experienced for quite a while. For a man who'd appeared to be close to death not long before, he seemed to have made a miraculous, if not instantaneous, recovery.

"So, tell me, how is it that you were near death when Rafe brought you here, and already seem so much better?"

"The touch of a female hand is very healing to me," he replied. "It is something that I have not felt for many years."

Must have been owned only by men, I decided, because I couldn't imagine any woman owning him and not looking for excuses to touch him all the time! I mean, he'd only been there with me for a short while, and I was already regretting having to give him back to Rafe. Perhaps I would simply tell Rafe that he had died. I somehow doubted that he would ever demand to see the body—or even offer to help me bury him...

I stopped short with those thoughts before Desdemona had a chance to comment. She would have been right if she had, of course, because I knew I shouldn't get attached to him. He was my patient, he was a slave, and on top of that, he belonged to Rafe, of all people.

"What do they call you?" he asked.

"Tisana," I replied absently. "And you?"

"I am called Leccarian."

"That's quite a mouthful," I commented. "Have you another name?"

"Banadänsk."

"Well, now, that's certainly an improvement!" I said with a sardonic smile. I tried again. "What do they call you for short?"

"You may call me anything you like," he replied with a purr. "I will always answer."

"Ooo, that is one smooth-talking cat!" Desdemona said. *"You'd better watch your step with him."*

As I gazed at him, taking in the vision of his raw,

leonine power, I was reminded that while leonine was an ancient word and there were few now who could recall the animal from which it was derived, it was still an apt description of him. I had heard tales of them from old Earth: big, powerful, tawny cats with thick manes, sharp teeth, and rippling muscles, similar to those that this man possessed. Lions, they were called.

"What if I were to just call you Leo?" I inquired carefully. "Would that bother you?"

I didn't want to belittle him, or treat him too much like a slave—calling him any name I chose with no regard to his feelings on the subject. As far as I was concerned, during his stay with me, he wasn't a slave, and I certainly didn't intend to treat him like one.

His breath went out in the loudest purr yet. "Not if you keep doing that whenever you speak to me."

For a moment, I didn't catch his meaning, but as soon as I realized that I had unconsciously resumed the butt massage, the reason was perfectly obvious.

"I enjoy listening to the sound of your voice," he went on. "And the touch of your hand is very soothing."

The sound of *his* voice was lulling me into a daze, and it made me wonder what it would be like to have his hands on me in that fashion. I had a month—even longer if I sent word to Rafe. A month with Leo…until he saw his chance to escape and took it, that is. I reminded myself that while *I* might not choose to think of him as a slave, *he* certainly knew the difference and would not simply stay here waiting for his master to return to take possession of him. I couldn't blame him for that, because I knew that if our roles were reversed, I would take advantage of any opportunity to escape. I wished I had told Rafe to take care of him himself. Should never have agreed to this—but then, that's what I *do*…

Leo turned just then, and suddenly my fingers were massaging not his back side, but his front side, instead. That remarkable cock of his snapped up, bumping into my hand in what seemed to be a random movement—until he began to stroke my arm with it. He had amazing control—never once touching it with his hand—but seemed to be moving it with a set of highly specialized muscles which, normally, only a four-legged animal might have possessed.

I stared at it, suddenly stricken with an astonishing hunger. It was clean—I knew it was, because I'd just washed it myself—and there was no infection there, for the fluid pouring forth from it was as clear as spring water. I could taste him and suffer no ill effects—I was certain of that. Reminding myself that I could take any lover I wished, I was sorely tempted, for I knew that while not one of my lovers would conceive a child in me unless he was the one chosen for me by the gods, for all I knew, this man might have been the one. The gods may have brought him here from a world that only they would know of—and for this sole purpose. There was no way to be sure, but I also knew that there were many things that must simply be taken on faith.

He didn't smell bad anymore—and it wasn't only due to the soap. There was something else about him, an aura that seemed to fill the air about him like a cloud. Whatever it was, it was intoxicating and pervasive, sending my senses reeling. This time, when I touched his cock, it wasn't to wash it, but to caress it. Thick and hard in my grasp, it felt hot and slick, and I could no more have ignored it than I could ignore the way I wanted to devour it—or the way his purring intensified with my touch. He wanted it every bit as much as I…

When I leaned down and took him in my mouth, he tasted delightful, but it was a flavor with which I was unfamiliar. Warm and creamy. I sucked him for perhaps thirty seconds before an orgasm hit me, flooring me with its intensity.

I let go of him, gasping, "Gods alive! What was that?"

Leo smiled and pushed my head back down. "It will get even better," he promised. "Continue, Tisana, my lovely witch, and I will give you joy unlike any you have ever known."

My head was spinning, but all I could think of was that if this wasn't already joy, then joy would probably be the death of me, for he was certainly more potent than any drug or potion I had ever conjured up. Delirious with need, I went down on him again.

My orgasms were so strong, so continuous, I could barely tell where one ended and another began. It was terrifying to lose control in such a manner—he could have throttled me, and I wouldn't have known the difference, would never have fought back or lifted so much as a finger to save myself.

Then I realized that his goal would not be murder, but escape. He would simply leave me lying there on the floor sleeping it off and disappear into the woods. I could explain to Rafe that he'd died of his wounds, but I had a sneaking suspicion that I would probably die without him, could almost feel my body becoming addicted to him and whatever drug it was that he was pumping into my system. It had to be that coronal fluid,

I thought wildly. There was something in it, some chemical whose sole purpose was to drive women insane…

He pumped against me, sliding that big cock in and out of my mouth—I couldn't stop him and didn't want to. Finally, I just lay there with my head on his stomach and let him do as he pleased, since I was helpless to prevent him. His hands were tangled in my hair, and my body was tied up in knots of helpless ecstasy. When at last he groaned and erupted, filling my mouth with his warm, sweet cream, I understood what he'd meant when he said he would give me joy unlike any I had ever known, for there was simply no other way to describe the feeling of unbelievable euphoria—and all I'd done was suck him!

Then, with a satisfied purr, he withdrew himself, and darkness took me.

Chapter 2

When I awoke, I fully expected Leo to be long gone—and he didn't disappoint me. It was stupid of him, for not only was there the snow to slow him down—and make his trail easy to follow—but I seriously doubted that he had anywhere else to go, no safe haven to which he could retreat. Shaking off the aftereffects of the night before, I called to my mare, Morgana, and we soon found him buried in a snowdrift less than a mile off, as cold and still as death.

Dragging him from the snowdrift, I focused carefully and sent in enough heat to warm him up, hoping to at least keep him alive long enough to get him back to my cottage.

"Stupid male," Morgana snorted. *"If they'd just use their brains once in a while, they'd be much better off."*

Which was what I had been thinking, myself, but somehow, in his case, I knew there was more to it than mere stupidity and couldn't help but defend him.

"Well, what did you expect him to do, Morgana? He's a slave! His last master nearly killed him—who could blame him for running? Granted, it was stupid, but it's probably what I would have done, myself. He may not have known he had a month before Rafe would come back for him. It would have been nice if he'd been

able to trust me, but I can see where trusting anyone would be difficult for him."

"It was still stupid," Morgana insisted. "*They all are.*"

Pulling the poles to the sling down from the saddle, I peered at her out of the corner of my eye. "*Oh, by the way, Morgana, I forgot to tell you: Sinjar was here last night. He's the one who brought Leo and Rafe. Sorry you missed him.*"

She curled her neck around and gave me *such* a look! "*As if I care,*" she said haughtily.

"*Aw, don't be so mareish,*" I said. "*You'd like him well enough, if he'd ever come around when you were in season.*"

As I might have expected, she made no reply. Smiling to myself, I rolled Leo's inert form onto the sling, then slid the poles through the sides of it and hitched them to the saddle. Mounting quickly, I sent Morgana off at a steady trot, and we were back home a short time later, though Morgana grumbled the whole way about how heavy he was.

Hauling him inside, I noted that stripping him and burning his clothes hadn't hindered his escape, for, being a resourceful fellow, he'd simply stolen some of mine. Of course, they didn't fit him particularly well, and he'd had to split a few seams to get them on. He was wearing his own boots, which was my mistake. I should have burned them along with his clothes—and I seriously considered it—though I hoped he would realize now that running away was not his best choice.

Delirium was the most logical reason for such an ill-advised attempt, and though he'd seemed lucid enough earlier when first roused by my touch, it was possible that he'd suffered a relapse during the night while I was oblivious. It must have looked like a golden opportunity—though I wondered why he wasn't deterred by the depth of the snow. On the other hand, I'd known cats to bolt in conditions that would definitely have made me think twice.

Stripping him down again, I placed him on his pallet by the fire with a hot brick at his feet and bundled him up with warm blankets. The tisane I'd prepared the night before still sat on the table, and I heated it with a glance before soaking a cloth in it to lay across his chest and neck to allow the volatile herbs to be inhaled as well as absorbed through his skin. It would have worked much more quickly if he'd been able to drink it, but while my great-grandmother had possessed the gift of a form of mind control, I didn't inherit that one, and therefore couldn't make him swallow just because I wanted him to. I chuckled to myself, thinking that it would have been handy, because then I might have been able to put the notion into his head to stay put.

I might have missed out on many other useful powers, but being able to heat things up just by looking at them in a certain way was one that, to the best of my knowledge, none of my ancestors had possessed. It was also a power that I was very careful not to use in anyone else's presence—at least, not if they were paying attention—because it had enormous potential for misuse, and I didn't ever want to be accused of setting someone on fire or roasting them alive. Besides, I had learned early that it was useful to have some secrets,

I had discovered my gift quite by accident when, as a

child, I realized that I could ripen fruit just by looking at it. This was a useful skill in and of itself, but I continued to experiment, finally reaching the point where I could make dried grasses smolder by focusing my gaze on them, and the power continued to grow and develop until, in time, I managed to acquire a fairly precise control of it. I can't explain the actual power involved any more than I can explain any other innate capability, such as the instincts that animals have to guide their migratory behavior—or my ability to communicate with them. These things simply exist in nature, having been put there by the gods.

Just as Leo had been put there—so far from his home, and so completely and utterly alone. Where would he have gone if his escape attempt had been successful? What would he have done? He had no means to provide for himself; he would either have had to steal or work for someone else—though it was a given that as a hired hand, he would be treated more kindly than he had been as a slave. I still didn't know how he'd come to be in such a state, for I hadn't, as yet, had the opportunity to ask him. Promising myself to do that later, I swept his body with another heated glance to warm him, and then fixed a pot of porridge, hoping at least to get some food into him before he ran off again—if he ever regained consciousness at all.

By midmorning, the animals had all been fed, and I had finished my own breakfast, but Leo had not yet begun to stir. As I'd intended before, I pulled him back to the unsealed part of the floor and washed and combed his hair, separating it into long, spiraling strands. It was every bit as beautiful as I'd imagined it would be—thick and shining and soft to the touch—and even the feel of it was intoxicating, just like everything else about him. It was as if the gods had designed him with that sole purpose in mind.

As I washed and redressed his wounds, I noted that, while they were not yet healed, at least the poison was gone, and the tissues already seemed healthier. But still, he did not awaken.

Desdemona purred from her perch on the hearth. *"Given up hope yet?"* she asked gently.

"No, should I have?" Despair *had* been creeping into my mind, and Desdemona must have sensed it, though I hadn't admitted it to myself as yet.

"Not necessarily," she replied. *"Cats have nine lives, you know."*

"I think this one must have more than your average cat," I remarked. *"Just think what he must have been through in his life! All the places he's been, the people he's seen, the horrors he's had to endure. It's enough to break your heart just thinking about it!"*

"His heart isn't broken, though," Desdemona pointed out. *"Nor is his spirit."*

Given his earlier behavior, I was forced to agree. *"Must be getting close to it, though,"* I said. *"Everyone has their breaking point. I mean, why else would he run off into a snowstorm?"*

When she didn't reply, I peered at her curiously, my head slowly tipping to one side. *"You knew when he left, didn't you? Why didn't you wake me?"*

Desdemona stretched a hind leg up into the air and licked it, seeming to ignore my question.

"Mona!" I said sharply. *"Answer me!"*

Cats are adept at withdrawing into their own little world, and this cat was no exception. However, her total lack of interest seemed to indicate quite the opposite. She was hiding something. *"You're jealous, aren't you?"* I accused her. *"You're afraid he's going to replace you as the witch's cat!"*

Still, she said nothing, but continued to groom herself as though I didn't exist.

"Come on, Mona!" I urged. *"Talk to me!"*

One thing that can be said about a cat—*any* cat—is that if she doesn't want to talk, you can't very well make her. Grumbling to myself, I gave up.

"Great! Now I have *two* cats, and neither one of them will talk! I may have to go out and talk to Morgana!" Except Morgana would probably just want to tell me more crap about how worthless men were, and granted, many of them were, but I, for one, was getting tired of hearing it! I mean, I thought Sinjar was a great guy, but she wouldn't give him the time of day! Of course, she *was* right about Rafe…

I sat there a while longer, combing my fingers through Leo's hair, searching my memory for the right combination of herbs and magic that might revive him. Then I remembered what had brought him out of his stupor the day before.

"Oh, surely not!" I muttered. "That would be *much* too simple!" But I figured it was worth a try—and while it would be for his own good, *I* wouldn't exactly mind, either…Then, perhaps, I could get some food and medicine into him before he ran off again. I reached under the blankets.

"Oh, not again!" Desdemona groaned, breaking her

silence at last. *"Do you have to do that while I'm sitting here watching?"*

"Well, no," I said nastily. *"You don't have to sit there and watch, you can go out and catch some mice! I'm sure there are plenty of them in the shed."*

Turning ever so slightly to peer disdainfully at me over her shoulder, she again made no reply, but resumed her morning ablutions as though I hadn't spoken. Frustrating creature. I opted for a bit of verbal sparring.

"Yes, there are plenty of them out there," I told her. *"I've heard them. They have this delightful little song they like to sing. Would you like to hear it? Oh, of course you would!"* I went on, giving her no opportunity to reply. *"It goes like this:*

Desdemona, the witch's cat,
Desdemona, the lazy rat!
Sits all day on the hearth by the fire
Wouldn't lift a paw if we ran right by 'er
We're out here feasting in the grain
With no one but herself to blame
While horses starve and mice get fatter
And no one sleeps for all our chatter
Desdemona sits and purrs—"

"Enough!" Mona hissed.

"And thinks that the whole world is hers!" I finished with fiendish glee.

"Charming," she sneered and stalked off with her tail held high.

Chuckling wickedly, I glanced down just in time to catch the faint smirk on Leo's face. Since I had my hand wrapped around his cock at the time, I gave it a quick squeeze.

"Morning, sleepyhead! It's about time you woke up!" I took a firmer grip on his stiffening shaft and asked, "Mind telling me just what possessed you to run off like that?"

His eyes flew open as my fingers tightened. "It was a momentary fit of madness, I believe, and I was weaker than I realized."

"Hmph!" I snorted. "A likely story! I tell you, there's no justice—or gratitude—in this world! I suck myself into an orgasmic coma, and then you steal my clothes and sneak out on me! *Not* a very nice thing to do, and you must know it's not wise to anger a witch. After all, I might turn you into a toad!"

Leo smiled up at me. "Are you able to do that?"

"Well, no," I admitted, "but I might try it anyway. Of course, I'd probably botch the spell and turn you into something really disgusting, like a slug or a roach." I paused for a moment to consider the notion. "Do you know, I believe the idea has merit! I *should* turn you into a slug, because then you wouldn't be stupid enough to go running off into the snow! I mean, even slugs know better than to do anything so idiotic!"

"You are angry with me," Leo observed.

"You bet I'm angry with you!" I said hotly, giving his penis a yank. "You get me hooked on your orgasmic cock syrup and then you run off! What were you thinking? Do you *want* to die?"

"That was not my intention."

"Well, then why? Rafe isn't coming back for another month! You can be as free as you like until then—or you can escape if you want to, but please, just promise me you'll wait for better weather!"

Leo seemed to be digesting this information. "You are concerned for my welfare?"

I rolled my eyes in frustration. "It's what I *do*, Leo! I'm a healer, and I don't appreciate you wasting all of my efforts to keep you alive by running off into a blizzard! I do not—and I repeat, do *not!*—want to have to drag you out of a snowdrift ever again! Besides," I added, giving his penis an affectionate pat and reluctantly letting go, "I happen to like this thing. I wouldn't want it to get frostbitten."

"That would not happen," he said in a tone that brooked no argument. "My species is capable of sleeping in the cold and slowing our body functions down to a very slow rate."

"You can hibernate?" I asked with genuine surprise. "That's quite remarkable, but were you planning to stay there until spring? I mean, I can just imagine you lying there all curled up in your snowdrift and then having it melt all around you while you were still dead to the world. Then Rafe would find you and beat you to within an inch of your life the way your last master must have done, and we'd be right back where we started!" I stopped to take an exasperated breath before saying, "Look, Leo, if you'll just trust me, maybe we can figure something out—some way to set you free without killing you in the process."

"You would do that for me?" he asked. I couldn't blame him for being skeptical, but it saddened me that he thought I wouldn't help him.

"Yes, I would," I replied earnestly. "Though I'll admit, I'd much rather keep you, myself. Desdemona has good reason to be jealous. You're addicting, you know."

His response to that was a slow, sensuous blink, after which, he began purring again. Oh, yes! He knew just exactly how addicting he was, and he was using that knowledge quite ruthlessly.

"Manipulative, too, I see. So, tell me, Leo. What should I do with you?"

His response to that was another loud, insistent purr.

"You certainly seem to have your mind fixed on sexual matters," I commented. "But if you really wanted that, you shouldn't have tried to run away."

"Slaves always look for opportunities to escape," he said solemnly, "but I will not attempt it again." Something in the way he said that made me believe him, though I couldn't have said why, exactly. It might have been truth and honesty shining out from his eyes or something of that nature—who knows? "Tell me about this person, Rafe," he went on. "Do you know him well?"

"A little too well, I'm afraid," I said ruefully. "Rafe isn't a bad sort, really, he's just—" I hesitated, searching for the right words to describe him. It was difficult. "Rafe just doesn't care very much about anyone but himself— and if he ever does seem to care, there's usually a self-serving motive involved somehow."

"He was your lover?"

Honestly, he was as bad as Desdemona! Must be a trait among cats, I decided, this insight into other people's minds. "Good guess, Leo, but how did you know that?"

"I have seen much in my lifetime."

"Learned a few things, have you?" I said with a grimace. "Yes, he was my lover, but there was no future in it—for either of us, actually. It died a natural, though painful, death. I was very young, and though my mother was still here to remind me of my future duties, I thought I might somehow manage to escape my own destiny by teaming up with Rafe. I wanted to be free to pursue my own life, the way *I* wanted to live it." And I still did, but I remembered that time, as well as the anguish and despair I'd felt when I realized without a doubt that I had no choice, my life's path having been determined from the moment I was conceived. It simply took twenty-five years or more for me to realize it. "Of course it didn't happen, and when my mother died several years later, it was left to me to take up the responsibility of caring for those within my domain."

Leo seemed surprised by this. "She died so young?"

I nodded. "She grew sick and knew she couldn't be saved. I sometimes wonder if she told me that only to absolve me of any guilt associated with her death—though having raised her successor, she may have felt that her life as one of the chosen was already fulfilled."

"That is what you are, then? One of the chosen?"

I nodded. "And we may bear only one child, a daughter, but not just any man can father her, he must be chosen by the gods. That was why Rafe cast me off in favor of another woman—one who could give him sons." It surprised me to find that there was still pain associated with that old wound, though I wouldn't have thought it possible after so many years. But it was still there, making my heart ache and my eyes sting with unshed tears.

"He knew this even before you were lovers?"

"Yes, he knew," I replied with a tight-lipped smile. "And so did I. It was a…a mistake. I believe he simply wanted to see if he could be the one." I sighed deeply, remembering my own disappointment, and also Rafe's inevitable reaction. "It angered him when he found that he was not." I leaned back, away from Leo, crossing my arms over my chest, as if doing so might stop the pain and loneliness from reaching my heart—to shield it in some way—but it was useless. Turning away from him, I closed my eyes, sending tears coursing down my cheeks.

"You were more than lovers, then," Leo said gently. "You loved him."

"Yes," I admitted. "—Or at least I thought I did. Either way, it amounts to the same thing."

"He was your only lover?"

I shook my head. "No," I replied. "No, he was only the first. There have been others, but I haven't given my heart to any of them. My experience with Rafe taught me that much."

"But to love is a great gift," Leo disagreed. "I have loved before, and though I have lost each one, I believe it to be worth the pain, and I think of them when there is no love to be found."

Remembering how he'd been mistreated and abused by his latest owner, I hoped that, for his sake, his good memories were strong ones. Poor Leo! I'd saved him twice now, had kept him alive, only to be owned and possibly tortured again by someone else. His tenacious hold on life must seem like a curse at times—times when death might be welcomed, if for no other reason than to set him free.

A log settled in the fireplace, sending sparks soaring up the chimney to seek the open air and freedom, even though they would burn away to nothing long before they ever reached the sky. I was reminded then that although Leo's chains might have been more real, he was not the only slave, not the only one who suffered, not the only one who longed for freedom.

I myself had always envied the birds their ability to go soaring through the skies, but even they had to return to the ground eventually, seeking food or respite. But those moments of flight for the sheer joy of it; how I envied them that feeling! That spreading of the wings to leave everything else behind, if only for the briefest time. I wanted to fly, to feel joy and laughter, to feel alive and free. Free to go where I wished and love whom I pleased, without fear, and without reservation. Just once.

But I knew that these growing desires were very selfish of me, especially when someone for whom real chains were both heavy and painful lay there before me with the scars to prove it.

Staring into the fire, I watched the flames leap higher and higher until the heat grew too intense even for Desdemona, who had returned to her perch while Leo and I were talking.

"Tisana!" she complained. *"Stop that! It's too hot!"*

"Sorry," I whispered. Blinking and turning away from the heat, I found Leo regarding me curiously.

"What are you thinking?" he asked.

"Nothing specific," I replied. "Only random thoughts."

He nodded and let it go at that, but something in his expression suggested that he wasn't convinced. Reaching out, he took my hand and said, "But those thoughts trouble you."

"Yes, they do," I said quietly. "They trouble me a great deal." I tried to shake off the clinging remnants of self-pity and focus on the care of him instead. "But I shouldn't be thinking about such things, especially when you need to eat."

Getting to my feet, I took the bowl of porridge from the table and, with my back toward him, stared at it, stirring it with the spoon until steam began to rise from the surface. Leo accepted it gratefully from my hand, and if he thought it odd that it should be so hot after so long away from the fire, he made no comment.

I glanced over at Desdemona, now curled comfortably on the hearth. She had probably been listening in on my thoughts, only breaking into them when she deemed it necessary, but what she thought of them was a mystery. She was my companion and had been for many years, but she could still be as secretive as any other cat. Oh, she might know what I was thinking at any given time—effectively reading my mind, and sometimes even correctly interpreting my speech—but her thoughts were her own unless she directed them at me. Cats were peculiar in that respect, for while I often picked up on other conversations—I heard the mice chattering among themselves all the time—I had never been able to eavesdrop on one of hers. Having told me before that she wasn't always listening, I could hope that she hadn't been, but it was difficult to tell.

I wondered what price Leo would pay for his freedom. He'd been willing enough to risk his life for it, but at the same time he seemed so philosophical about it. I seriously doubted that I would have felt that way in his situation. He'd made his attempt to escape, and it had failed—as, quite obviously, his every other attempt had done. I suppose he'd simply keep on trying at intervals, just to see if the impossible might actually occur someday. He might even hope that someone would buy him, only to set him free. It must be the one dream that all slaves share: to finally be bought by the one master who would be a gift from the gods and the answer to all of his prayers—the one who granted him his freedom.

Unfortunately, I strongly doubted that having Rafe as a master could ever be such a gift. No, Leo's best chance at freedom from Rafe was either to feign his own death or to hope that Rafe's own life was short and that his heirs didn't survive him. Rafe had two young sons—the sons that I couldn't have given him—who were a bane to anyone seeking any of his property—property that now included Leo.

The men of our world might love their daughters dearly, but their sons were the ones who would inherit their property when they died. I was unique in that respect, for there were never any male children in my family, so no one could take my house, but I had seen it happen before; had seen marriages forced upon unwilling widows, just to enable them to go on living in their own homes. It occurred to me then that, out of all the women in this little corner of our world, I was, quite possibly, the one who enjoyed the *most* freedom. I should remember that more often, I decided, and spend less time envying the birds.

Leo had finished eating by then, and I showed him where the "facilities" were. My house was very old, which was possibly why no one had ever tried to take it from me, though it might also have been the fear of an angry witch that kept anyone from making the attempt. Although indoor plumbing had been installed at some point, it *was* primitive. However, it had the virtue of rarely failing and required no power other than your own in order to work. All that was required was to obtain a bucket of water from the well via the hand pump by the door and then use it to flush the stool into the septic pool below.

I'd often heard tales of remarkable power sources that kept lights burning and wheels turning and sent ships flying through space, but the denizens of my planet considered them abhorrent, as well as damaging to the environment, and had left them behind when they migrated from Earth to establish the original colony. I myself found it peculiar that such conveniences could be considered abhorrent, while the concept of slavery was not. I suppose that having slaves to attend to such mundane matters made it all possible, but, in my opinion, slavery was wrong in and of itself. That slaves didn't exist on most other worlds was a well-known fact, but here on the planet Utopia, well, let's just say that no one was willing to give an inch when it came to relinquishing property.

I had never traveled offworld and, while some aliens did visit us from time to time, Utopia didn't have what you'd call a thriving tourist industry. We were too backward for most people; adhering to an old standard of ways that some people might have found quaint, though primitive, and so, for the most part, very few were able to see any attraction. Utopia didn't produce any products that weren't readily available on a hundred other worlds, though we did produce some very fine pottery. Anything remotely resembling modern technology had to be obtained offworld—which included anything but the most rudimentary implements such as cookware, farming tools, as well as, I'm sorry to say, the occasional sword—but interplanetary trade wasn't terribly common, and technological marvels tended to be shunned.

There was much more excitement to be had on other worlds that had no qualms about using their technological abilities to the maximum extent, though we did receive the occasional visit from beings who longed for a more simple and peaceful existence—which was part of the reason for our colony to begin with. Space travel was remarkable in and of itself, and even in our culture we knew it existed, for it was as a result of such marvels that we had been able to colonize this planet with any degree of success.

Ironically, there were still some who refused to believe in such things, but I had seen enough to know it was true even before I'd met Leo; in fact, the chosen ones existed solely because of those other worlds. We witches were hybrids—the result of the mating of women skilled in the ways of herbal medicine with alien beings who possessed seemingly magical powers—though those matings had occurred many generations in the past. I wasn't sure how many other witches were out there at any given time, or exactly how our powers varied. The sisterhood was scattered far and wide, and rarely trespassed into each other's domains.

Leo, himself, was more living proof that those other worlds existed. I had seen species even stranger than Leo—but none that were more attractive. Just watching him walk back into the room made me fight to keep from gasping aloud. Everything about him made you want to sit and stare at him, even the way he moved, and this was especially true now that he wasn't wearing a stitch of clothing.

He seemed to possess some remarkable recuperative powers, as well. When I'd suggested to Rafe that he return for him in a month, I'd been skeptical because, at the time, I hadn't been certain that Leo would even survive, let alone improve so quickly. Perhaps what I'd sensed when I felt his life force waning was simply his way of shutting down in order to heal himself. It wasn't the first instance I'd encountered of a species that was able to do that, so I had no reason not to believe it.

Of course, if every species were capable of self-healing, I'd be out of a job—which, the more I thought about it, might not be such a bad thing, because then I would be free to do something different with my life. Perhaps I could simply be a normal person, as opposed to one of the chosen.

But I *was* one of the chosen, and, as such, had certain duties to perform. With that in mind, I busied myself with brewing a pot of alowa bark tea, which would not only help him to rest, but would also aid his body in fighting infection.

My intentions were good—and I'll admit I had made

it fairly strong—but if his wrinkled nose was any indication, he didn't care for it.

"What's the matter?" I asked. "Don't like the taste?"

"It is…bitter," he replied, stifling a sneeze.

"Some people just can't take their medicine," I teased, though without much feeling. "I'll put some spearmint in it the next time." Taking the cup from him with a forced smile, I realized I wasn't feeling particularly chipper myself. Perhaps I needed to take some of my own medicine. After adding some powdered stevia root, I handed it back to him. "Try it now."

Taking a cautious sip, he nodded his limited approval before going back to his pallet by the fire to drink it. I went on preparing another tisane when, after a bit, I realized that he was simply lying there, watching me.

"What are you looking at?" I asked finally.

"You," he replied. "What do you do here all alone?"

"Just things," I said, somewhat defensively. "Taking care of my animals and anyone else who comes to me for help. In summer, I keep pretty busy planting and gathering the herbs I need for healing—and food to eat, of course. It's much…quieter in winter. I read a lot." I, for one, welcomed the restful time of winter, when the simple chores of keeping myself warm and fed were what occupied most of my time—the cozy warmth of a wood fire and hot food had a regenerative effect, preparing me for the hard work of the warmer months. I loved studying the ancient lore in the leather-bound volumes that lined the shelves of my cottage. Some revealed medical techniques that dated back to old Earth, and I longed for a day when my skills would be truly challenged.

I wondered briefly if the kind of technique to which Leo seemed to respond so well would be applicable to the males of other species, but I couldn't quite see myself trying it out. I struggled unsuccessfully to get my mind off his unique attributes and could only be grateful that he couldn't read my mind as well as Desdemona.

"You are alone much of the time, then?"

I nodded. "Mostly. I like it that way." Or I had, until recently.

"Perhaps you *should* buy a slave," he remarked, his lips curling into a smile. "Then you would not be so alone."

Ignoring the implication that I should buy this particular slave for myself, I said, "It takes money to buy a slave, Leo, and, unfortunately, I rarely get paid in currency. I'd have to trade something, and the only thing I have that might be worth the price of a slave is my horse, but since I don't truly own her, I can never sell her, either."

He gazed at me with those golden eyes as if he would peer into my soul. "Perhaps you prefer to be alone," he observed. "I am here with you now, and yet you continue to work and to stare into the fire as though I were not."

"I'm just thinking, Leo!" I sputtered, still a bit on the defensive. "I'm not trying to be antisocial!"

"But I believe you are."

"No, I'm not!" I insisted. "Why would you think that?"

"I am here on my bed before the fire, wishing very much to mate with you, and yet you pretend that I am not here."

"Hey, now!" I protested. "I spent a very cold morning looking for you, pulling you out of a snow-drift, and then sat here with you for hours! I can't help it if you slept through it! I combed your hair, kept you warm, put ointment on your back—all those things! I'm not pretending you aren't here! Believe me, you've kept me busy all day!"

He made no further comment, but simply yawned and stretched before lying back to lounge by the fire, the flickering light from the flames illuminating his body and casting warm highlights on his tawny hair. But though he seemed to relax, his gaze never wavered. I went on with my various chores, but I could feel his eyes upon me, no matter where I was, or what I was doing. I tried not to look at him, and in that respect, I suppose he was right—I *was* avoiding him. He'd been right about other things, too, for I was alone much of the time—and usually preferred it so—but I knew that if I let him, Leo could become too much a part of my life, and then, just when I knew I wouldn't ever want to part with him, Rafe would come to take him back.

Still, Leo was nothing if not persistent, and, finally, I couldn't take it anymore.

"Besides," I went on, snappishly, "I prefer to 'mate' with people I know. You're a…stranger to me."

"No, I am not," he disagreed. "You know me very well. But you are afraid."

"Afraid?" I echoed. "I wouldn't say that. You aren't *that* scary! And I don't know you well at all!" I *had* been fairly intimate with him, but it wasn't my fault he'd sprung the cursed thing on me and drugged me with it. It was almost as if he had cast a spell on me, causing me to crave him. I'd managed to justify it that much, for I'd never done such a thing with anyone before—and certainly not with someone I was supposed to be healing!

And, yes, I'd gone in search of him, but not only because I'd wanted him back. When you are treating someone, there's a certain obligation not to misplace them in the process.

"I did not say that you were afraid of *me,*" he said. "You have other fears."

"And you don't know as much as you think you do," I countered.

"You think not?" he asked with a wry smile. "I have seen, and I have learned." For some reason, the way he said it took the smugness out of his remarks—it was simply a fact, not a boast.

"What am I afraid of, then?" I asked. "Tell me."

"You are afraid of finding something you want more than this life you lead, and that it will make you feel discontented when you do find it."

It was almost as if he *had* been reading my mind, or had been engaged in some sort of a cat-to-cat mental exchange with Desdemona. Of course he, of all people, should know a thing or two about how it felt to be discontented. The odd thing was that, despite his status as a slave and his unsuccessful escape attempt, he seemed to be the most contented man I'd ever met. Of course, all the purring he was doing might have had something to do with why I felt that way.

The trouble was, his purring was much louder than that of your typical house cat, and, as such, was difficult to ignore. He wasn't nagging at me, precisely, but was simply refusing to lie there and be ignored. I busied myself by chopping up meat and vegetables for a stew, turning my back to him, and doing my best to drown out his purring with the sound of my knife pounding on the wooden board.

I was so intent on making noise that I didn't notice when his purring ceased, enabling him to steal silently across the room to come up behind me, unannounced and unnoticed. Startling me just a bit as he threaded his arms around my waist, he leaned down to lick at my ear, biting it gently, sending thrills of intense desire flying over my skin, nearly making my hair stand on end.

Fortunately, I was finished making the stew and had only to hang the pot over the fireplace, or we wouldn't have gotten anything to eat that night, because Leo's scent, or aura, or presence—or whatever it was about him which made him so irresistible—threatened to overcome me. He wasn't holding anything back or being coy about it. He wanted to mate, as he put it, and it was becoming perfectly obvious that he wasn't going to leave me be until he did just that.

"If this is your way of trying to send me into another stupor so you can escape again," I muttered as I hung the stew pot above the flames, "you can forget about me coming to your rescue. I've pulled you out of a snow-drift for the last time."

"I will not attempt to escape again," he said, with a slow, sensuous sweep of his tongue on my neck. "Now that I know I have time to be with you, I will stay to—" he paused, letting out a long, loud purr "—enjoy it."

The feel of his hot, wet tongue on my skin sent waves of desire flaming down into the depths of my body to boil there until I simply gave up, leaning back into him, feeling the warmth of his body against my back, letting it envelop me with the need for him.

And I *did* need him! Though I hadn't had a lover in quite some time, the need was still there; I hadn't lost it, I'd only forgotten what it was.

I let him take me then, sweeping me down onto the pallet by the fire. Leo's long tresses lured my hands to them, seeking only to delve into their soft, swirling mass. I heard his purr getting closer as he leaned down to pull at my lips. I still felt myself to be falling, for the floor seemed to move away from me as I sank further into it. Leo's purr was roaring in my ears; I could feel the vibrations in my chest, almost as though I were the one purring myself.

I felt his hands on me. What was he doing? Oh, yes, I thought feebly. My clothes. He was taking them off. Perhaps I should have stopped him, but I didn't care. His lips were soft and wet against my own, melting into me, and I didn't care—about anything. Except him.

I knew what he could do to me, had at least some small inkling of how he could make me feel, but he was right, because I *was* afraid—if only just a little—that nothing in the rest of my whole life would even begin to compare with what I could have with him. It seemed as though I were standing at the edge of a cliff, waiting to take the plunge and knowing that beyond this point, everything—all that I knew, and all that I would ever know—would change.

Leo had nothing to lose and nothing to gain by it. He was a slave, and would undoubtedly remain so whether he did this with me or not. He was simply responding to a drive inherent within him. It may have meant nothing more to him than pleasure, but it was also possible that he might be able to remember these moments someday when faced with the horrors of slavery. He could remember, and it would help him to endure those times—as it would help me to endure my own isolation. This could be a memory to review with fondness when loneliness threatened to overwhelm me—and there was also the possibility that he could be the one...

My mother had once told me about finding my father. He'd been a stranger, she said, and had a lame horse he'd brought to her for treatment on the advice of someone in the town. She told me that the moment she laid eyes on him, she knew he was the one. I wasn't quite so sure with Leo, but I did know that I felt a stronger attraction to him than I ever had with anyone else. Perhaps that was why. Of course, there was only one way to find out for sure...

I don't know if Leo felt it or not, that moment when I relinquished control, but he seemed to accept it for what it was. Consent. That moment when a woman decides that, yes, this one—out of perhaps a dozen men clamoring for her attention or her hand—*this* one, I will choose. The reasons didn't matter in the slightest, what mattered was the choice—and I made it.

Leo might have been the first alien being I'd ever lain with—and I had no idea whether or not he'd ever had a human female before—but he seemed to know exactly what he was doing.

Purring softly, he delved inside my mouth, stroking my tongue in a sensuous dance, swirling his fingertips on my skin, heating me with his touch. Something in the way he held me made me feel rare and precious, as though he felt privileged to be able to lay a hand on me. The deep, sensual massage I'd given him before was repeated, but this time, I was the recipient, and I felt beautiful, alive, and heated to the point of combustion with passionate desire. Suckling at my breasts as if he would draw strength from them, as if the taste of me was something he craved, he brought me teetering to the edge of ecstasy, and then with one last, solid swipe of his tongue, sent me soaring off into infinity.

His cock was in full bloom, dripping moisture from the points of the corona as he nudged my thighs apart and began to caress me with it. The fluid he produced worked every bit as well there as it had in my mouth— sending a piercing note of sensation driving in full force to penetrate me to the core, drawing my womb into a tight, burning mass which then burst forth into flame.

Teasing me with the head of his cock, I found out something else about that fluid; it made me more sensitive, for my clitoris swelled forcefully as though it, too, might burst into bloom, just as his cock had done. Using both chemical and manual stimulation, he drove me to near insanity with it, and for what came next, there is no adequate description—ecstasy is too weak, orgasm imprecise, and climax seems, well, anti-climactic— but, whatever you choose to call it, it built steadily to a peak deep inside me before erupting from my lips with a piercing cry. Leo's purr softened to become a self-satisfied sigh. Rubbing his face against my neck, I felt his hair, teasingly soft against my skin, and his weight on me began to increase, as though he were somehow melting and becoming a part of me. Pushing, pulsing, penetrating, he came inside, opening me with the blunt head, slowly pulling back to fan out the corona and rake my inner walls, making me delirious with pleasure.

That it was bringing him joy, as well, was clearly evident. I looked up at him, his feline features illuminated by the fire, and saw that his softly glowing pupils were now huge and completely round, and his purr had become a soft groan which coincided with each thrust. His cockhead was flexible, but the shaft was as thick and strong as the trunk of a tree, and from time to time he paused, pushing in deeply to swirl the passion within as he rotated it inside me, much as you would use a wooden spoon to stir a pot of stew.

Though my orgasms continued without any sign of abatement, after a while, they seemed to become purely mental, as though huge doses of erotic sensation were pulsing through my mind.

Picking up speed, he drove into me with a force that I was surprised I was able to tolerate, given the size of him, but it didn't hurt in the slightest, and, instead, raked a place inside me to a fever pitch before slowly ramping back down only to be pushed upward once more. At last, with a deep, guttural growl, he lurched forward, spilling his semen into me with a force that seemed to focus on my deepest, most sensitive spot, hitting it with a spurt of fluid that had me crying out once again.

With a deep, purring sigh, Leo relaxed on me, but that penis of his never seemed to stop. I could still feel something moving deep inside and realized that it was the coronal points, moving in a slow, undulating wave, continuing to stimulate me until I couldn't even think anymore, was just one big, raw nerve ending—fully exposed and stimulated to the maximum level.

Then, just when I'd thought it was over, I felt something else welling up inside me. It wasn't an ecstatic burst this time, but was, instead, a soothing warmth which suffused my entire body, reaching steadily outward from my center toward the tips of my fingers and toes, making my scalp feel for all the world as though my hair were curling into spirals as tight as his own.

What was it he had said? That he would give me joy unlike any I had ever known? He had put it far too mildly, but I'd been right about one thing, for I was definitely changed by it. I can't explain how, but it was as though I'd been altered in some way, and at a level so deep, so basic, that the change would be both elemental and everlasting. Just what that change would mean, however, remained to be seen.

Chapter 3

ONE THING WAS CERTAIN, THAT LAST, LONG MONTH OF winter wasn't a lonely one—not by anyone's definition of the word. Leo was always there with me and was fairly talkative much of the time, telling me stories—the amusing ones—about his life and the places he'd seen. I had never ventured much beyond the fringes of my domain, but through him I was able to travel to worlds that I hadn't previously known existed. In addition to having a wealth of fascinating stories, he was a good storyteller and was possessed of a very dry sense of humor. His style of speech made many things seem more amusing than they might have been otherwise.

Leo told me that he came from a large family, and while he was one of many, it was plain that there had been strong bonds among them. He knew of no family members who had survived the destruction of his homeworld of Zetith, but he and the other warriors of his unit had been a close-knit group, and he missed them very much.

Captured at the end of the war, he and the other members of his unit had faced execution, but had been sold as slaves instead. According to Leo, the man who had sold them had been acting against orders—and not for any noble reason, but for his own personal gain. Leo spoke fondly of his comrades, for they had been more like brothers than mere cohorts. One pair actually *were* brothers, but they were nothing alike, he reported. Tragonathan had been raised by an uncle on a space freighter and had seen more of life beyond Zetith than any of the others. He was cocky and a bit on the wild side, while his brother, Tycharian, sounded to me like a ladies' man. "It made no difference what he wanted from a woman," Leo said with frank admiration. "He would smile and flatter them, and they would give him anything—which always irritated his brother, Trag." Leo smiled. "Trag always complained that everyone liked Tychar best—which was not true, though we frequently reminded him of it." He spoke fondly of Carkdacund, who had been their leader and the one they all looked up to, and also of one called Lynxsander.

"He was the youngest," Leo said, "and worked very hard at his assigned tasks—given enough time, he could repair any type of machine—but spoke very little. I have no idea what happened to him—or to any of the others. They might all be dead by now, though I hope very much that they are not." It didn't seem to trouble Leo to think about the past, though it might have been disturbing for others in his situation. He was philosophical about it, saying that at some point, if they still lived, their fortunes were bound to improve. "As my own have done," he said slyly.

For the first few days he merely seemed to recuperate, lying before the fire with Desdemona while I worked, but, unlike her, he couldn't remain idle for long. Soon, he was helping me with the household chores and had stitched a new tunic and breeches for himself out of some fabric that I had laid by.

As a result of his help, I had more free time than usual, and Leo, as you may imagine, had some definite ideas about what to do with that time. Actually, I was beginning to see his help around the house as having an ulterior motive since, with his assistance, I would always finish more quickly and would, therefore, have more time for him.

This was no hardship for me, for I was at a point where I truly believe I could have lived on love alone—if it could be called that. Leo had a way of seeming to blend in with my life. Being in his arms made me feel more alive, and just resting my eyes upon him lifted my spirits. I suppose I was in love, though I'd never experienced anything quite like this and had no point of reference. One thing I could say for certain, he was nothing like any of the other men I'd been with.

Perhaps it was from having been a slave—or it may have been a common trait of his kind—but he seemed to have no overwhelming sense of pride. He was who he was, and he did as he pleased, not making any outward attempts to impress or influence me in any way. When he'd said that he would give me joy, it was a statement of fact, not an idle promise. He was, perhaps for the first time in many years, free to do as he wished, and for the most part, it seemed as though pleasing me was his current mission in life. What made it seem odd was that, while I was the one who was supposed to be healing him, quite often it seemed to be the other way around.

The realization that I would have to give him up soon nagged at me, but as I awoke one morning after a night spent making love, it occurred to me that perhaps it might not be such a bad thing if Rafe did take Leo away from me. I wasn't sure I'd be able to take so much ecstasy when I got a little older, and I had an idea that one day I would simply die in his arms. It also occurred to me that I was, perhaps, not the only one to feel that way about one of these men of Zetith.

Leo had told me that the people of his planet had been introduced to space travel as a technology brought to them by others. They hadn't minded using it, however, and had somehow managed to get into a few wars because of it. He was a little vague as to the reasons for those conflicts, but it was clear that he had fought more than a few battles, and the fact that he had ended up as a slave was an indication that the outcome of those battles had not been in the Zetithians' favor.

His having come from such a faraway planet made me wonder just how Leo had ended up here—unless slave traders throughout the galaxy knew that we still adhered to that ancient custom. My own personal views on slavery notwithstanding, there were plenty of other Utopians who felt that we simply couldn't function without them. What that really meant was that those with a hold on the currency would have to give up more of it to pay free men to work for them. Wars had been fought and civilizations had been destroyed over the issue of slavery in the past, but still, we persisted. I was of the opinion that we could manage to live in perfect harmony with nature without resorting to forcing slaves to do most of the manual labor—but my opinions were rarely considered when it came to policy-making within the cartel.

On the other hand, Rafe's opinions were often consulted. He was powerful enough to make changes if he wanted to, but trying to convince him that he didn't need slaves was pointless, for he would never willingly give up anything he felt to be rightfully his. Leo would therefore remain a slave, and if I wanted him, I would have to buy him. Unfortunately, I had no money and nothing of value. I tried to resign myself to the fact that Leo and I were simply not meant to be together forever, but it was difficult—especially when I was looking into his golden eyes.

It took a week or so for all traces of Leo's wounds to disappear, which was remarkable given their severity. He normally healed quickly, he said, but was also of the opinion that my treatment of him had hastened the process. The smile that accompanied that comment made me fairly certain that he hadn't been referring to my herbs or medicines. With regard to my own sense of having been healed, it wasn't just that he'd been helping with the chores. No, what he had done for me went deeper than that, for I was genuinely happy, perhaps for the first time in my life, though I still felt some… reservations.

During that time, I noticed that the offerings on my doorstep increased, almost as though it had become common knowledge that I now had another mouth to feed. I had no idea how anyone might have known, although I suppose Rafe might have mentioned it, or it was possible that Leo had been seen. Either way, I was grateful for the extra provisions. Of course, keeping it a secret that he was almost fully recovered might prove difficult if he were out and about, so, by an unspoken, but mutual agreement, he stayed close to the house, rarely venturing outside.

Even this was no guarantee that our little secret would remain undiscovered, and, fortunately, when a local woman came by seeking medicine for her sick child, Leo was napping on his pallet by the fire and at least appeared still to be in need of my care. I had no doubt that if word reached Rafe that Leo was well, our time together would be cut short.

After she'd gone, Leo smiled up at me with an expression I was beginning to know well. "Do I appear ill?"

"No," I replied. "Not in the slightest, but I don't think she suspected. It's a good thing you were lying down, though."

"I will moan the next time someone comes," he said, obviously understanding the need for a bit of subterfuge. "And be…irritable."

"A show of delirium might be a nice touch, too," I suggested. "You know, call out or mutter in your sleep—in a different language would be best."

"I will remember that," he said, uncurling from his pallet to get to his feet. No, he didn't appear to be even slightly under the weather, and, except for the scars, he looked absolutely perfect. The man was simply designed and built to be alluring to women; he even *tasted* good! Coming closer, I could hear him purring. "Tisana," he murmured, "it is time for my bath."

As I had bathed him every afternoon since his arrival, his suggestion wasn't out of line. I had, by this time, made love with him many times, but I still felt a certain reserve, almost as though he were some forbidden well or spring from which I knew I shouldn't drink. This strange show of reluctance on my part was getting worse as the end of the month loomed closer.

"Well, heat up some water, then," I said briskly, as though the prospect of bathing him was of no interest to me. "In case you hadn't noticed, I'm busy fixing dinner. Besides, I think you're well enough to do your own bath now."

"But I am in your care," he said, still purring seductively. "You would not wish me to suffer a relapse."

"That's not very likely," I said, rolling my eyes. "You look disgustingly healthy to me, and I doubt that a little dirt would kill you, anyway." Leo had a tendency to get amorous while I was cooking, so he must have found domesticity appealing—either that, or he was attracted to knife-wielding women. Added to the fact that he had been asleep for a while—another thing which seemed to get him in the mood—I suppose I should have expected it, though we had begun the day in each other's embrace. The time of day didn't seem to matter to Leo. But for some reason, even knowing what he could do to me, I was reluctant to drop whatever I happened to be doing. I had never been particularly reticent with my other lovers, so such behavior wasn't typical for me.

Maybe it was the sneaking suspicion that Leo was only interested in me because I was the one who happened to be there. I reminded myself once again that he was a slave and, as such, couldn't afford to be too choosy when it came to women, but, like any woman, I still wanted to feel as though he wanted me for myself. I had no cause to complain, because he had a way of focusing his attention on me that was unsurpassed by anyone I'd ever known. I'd spent time with other men, but there were always times when, even while I was in the same room with them, I'd felt alone. Leo never ignored me, but was continually interacting with me. His earlier comment that I knew him well was probably truer than it had been with others whom I'd known for many years.

No, the real trouble was that I knew I wouldn't be able to be with him for years—or even months. We *both* knew it, and perhaps that was why everything had moved so quickly between us. No matter what happened, we would be parted from one another much too soon—unless we ran away together, and I'll admit, I was beginning to consider this possibility. If only we could simply pack up and disappear. I doubted that we would get very far, since my lack of currency would have slowed us down considerably. I suppose that never having any money was part of what kept a witch secure within her domain, and it was possible that somewhere along the line, someone had decided that bartering with the witch, rather than paying her, would keep her from straying—which made some sense, because there weren't very many of us.

It was tough having to remain a permanent fixture when you happened to come down with a bad case of wanderlust. I considered telling Rafe that if he (and everyone else in the region) wanted me to continue on as their healer, I wanted Leo as payment. It seemed fair enough to me, especially since Rafe had remarked that Leo hadn't been terribly expensive. Of course, now that I'd fixed him up, Leo was probably worth much more and could be resold at a profit, although the fact that it had been Carnita who'd wanted to buy him in the first place might make a difference. If she ever found out even half of what I knew, she'd refuse to ever sell him, much less hand him over to me.

Besides, Carnita didn't need a man; she had Rafe. Come to think of it, perhaps she *did* need one. I'd spent enough time with Rafe to know that Leo was a decided improvement, and if Carnita ever (literally) got a taste of Leo, she would probably feel the same way. Selling Leo or giving him to me was probably Rafe's best course of action. He could simply tell Carnita that Leo had died—which would work out just fine until Carnita paid me a visit—and she'd been known to do that from time to time, as everyone else did.

The truth was, I didn't know *what* to do with him! I wanted nothing more than to spend the rest of my life in his arms, but I also knew that it couldn't happen—not without several major upheavals in the process, that is. I kept telling myself to simply take it on faith and enjoy the time I had with him, but it's difficult to do that when you've been raised as I was. My mother had always told me that nothing was as simple as it seemed, and more often than not, she was right. I wondered what she would have said about Leo. Probably pretty much the same as she had when I was falling in love with Rafe—to be careful what I wished for. It was times such as these when I most regretted her passing, for where do you go to seek wisdom when you happen to be the local wise woman, yourself?

Of course, with Leo standing wet and naked in the middle of my floor while that big, ruffled cock of his secreted its magical fluid, the pursuit of wisdom should not have been first and foremost in my mind! How ironic it was that while I had been busy trying to envision the future, he could have taught me a thing or two about living in the moment! With a conscious effort to banish my depressing thoughts, I leaned back against the table to watch as he washed himself, the thick, foaming suds sliding down his body, smoothing the curls from the hair on his chest and legs before disappearing through the cracks in the floor.

"My back needs to be washed," he purred, "and the ointment applied."

"Your back looks just fine," I remarked. "It doesn't need any special treatment."

"Perhaps not," he admitted, "but it feels very good. Having your hands on me makes me forget the pain I have endured."

"And I think you're playing the sympathy bit for all it's worth," I said dryly. "You don't need me anymore, and you know it."

"But I do, my lovely witch!" he disagreed. "I need your magical touch." His lids lay heavy over his glowing eyes as he smiled seductively. "You make me beg for it each time, Tisana. Tell me why."

"Maybe because I like the way you beg," I said hoarsely. Actually, I liked everything he did, no matter how mundane it might have seemed. Continuing to stare at him, my chest tightened until my breath caught in my throat. "By the gods, Leo!" I exclaimed, the words bursting from me in a rush. "You're the most beautiful thing I've ever seen in my life! You know that, don't you?"

His smile broadened into a grin, displaying his potentially deadly fangs. As killer smiles went, his fit the description better than most.

"Perhaps," he conceded. "But, beautiful or not, still, I must plead for your touch. You know how it can be and yet you waver each time. Come, Tisana, and I—"

"Will give me joy unlike any I have ever known?" I

mimicked. "Really, Leo! Don't you think I know that by now?"

Nodding, he asked, "If you know it, then why do you resist?"

Why *did* I continue to resist, when only a fool would do such a thing? With a sudden spurt of anger at Rafe, at my situation, at Leo's predicament, as well as my own, I shouted, "Because I keep remembering that you belong to someone else!" I could feel my body shaking, my anger and frustration barely contained. "That I can only have you for a short time, when I want you forever! It's impossible for me to be with you and not think it!"

My words echoed into the silence that followed. Leo's expression was unreadable—almost blank—as if he were staring back through the mists of time. His voice, when he spoke again, sounded equally distant. "Had you ever been a slave, you would know that such pleasures are seldom to be enjoyed, and you would take them where they are offered—without hesitation and without question."

He was right, of course. Sighing deeply, I shook my head and said with a rueful smile, "And here I was wondering where to go to find wisdom! You know something, Leo? You're a very wise man."

"I have lived through much," he said with a nod, "and I have suffered pain and hardship. During that time I have learned not to shun such moments of joy, or even to question them, for they are rare and precious gifts." His lids lifted slightly, and his golden gaze focused on my own eyes. "You are also wise, Tisana, but you have known pain—of a different kind, perhaps, but you have known it—just as I have. I look into your lovely green eyes and see there the scars of loneliness and despair. Do not refuse this gift."

Smiling, I said quietly, "But if I hadn't been so reluctant, I would never have heard you say those words. They are true ones, Leo, and I thank you for them."

"Then come, and do as I ask," he said, his voice a soft, rumbling sigh. "Love me and care for me, Tisana, and let me give you joy. Do not waste a moment of this time we have together, for it is beyond price."

Which was the only thing he'd said thus far that wasn't true because the unfortunate truth was that our time together did, indeed, have a price, though I couldn't pay it. It was the price of a slave. I let it pass, though, and lifted the kettle from the fire, delighting in his soft groaning purrs of pleasure as I rinsed the soap from his skin. Yes, he was beautiful; handsome didn't even begin to cover it. He was positively stunning to the eye, and sent swirling rivers of desire cascading throughout my body, making me long to touch him, taste him, feel him...

Suddenly, my arms seemed weak, too weak even to raise the kettle to pour water from it. It made a loud clang as I felt the handle slip from my fingers and, dropping my hands to my sides, I looked up at him in despair.

"Leo," I whispered hopelessly. "What will I do when you're gone? How will I go on?"

"We go on because we must," he murmured in reply. "There is no why or how. These things just are. Some things we may choose, but most are chosen for us. We are here, together, for now. That is all that matters." Reaching down, he removed a droplet of fluid from his cock and touched it to my lips. "When I am gone, you will remember this," he promised, "as you will remember me. But you will go on."

Gasping as the first shuddering climax took me, I shook my head in denial. "But I won't want to," I protested. "Without you, how can there ever be any joy?"

"You will find it," he assured me, "for I am not the only source of joy in this life."

"Just the best," I sighed, melting into his embrace. "The very best of all."

"I am pleased that you think it," he said, as his clever fingers became engaged in deftly removing my clothes. I felt his hands, warm and damp upon my skin as he caressed me, filling me with overwhelming desire for him. "Come closer to the fire, Tisana," he murmured, his voice deep and rumbling. "Stay warm and soft in my arms and forget your pain. This gift of my love is all I have to give you. I cannot give myself to you forever, but I am yours, for a time."

Sighing as his lips gently teased my own, I opened myself to him, as I always did. And, as always, it was as though I were discovering him for the first time. The feeling never changed, never wavered. It remained just as before; that sense of belonging, of coming home to find the warmth of love waiting for me. Kissing him deeply, I lost the will to move or speak, wanting only to feel.

But Leo wanted more. "Lick me, Tisana," he urged, pushing me to my knees. "Let me drive you into a frenzy of delight. Suck me until I am empty and I have filled your mouth with the elixir of my love." He slid his big, ruffled cock over my face, rubbed my cheeks and lips and tongue with it, before seeming to change his mind and then pull me back into his arms. "No, I was wrong. It is not enough. I must have all of you, Tisana. Wrap yourself around me. Love me with your whole body, your entire being. I want all of you. Leave nothing behind."

I took him in, holding him as closely to my heart as was humanly possible, realizing then that all of the joy and the ecstasy meant nothing to me, for he was what mattered most—only him, and how much I loved him. I held him inside me—safe, warm, and loved—as his passion mounted until it reached its pinnacle, bursting forth to fill me with his love.

If I'd had any doubts before, they were certainly banished then, and it wasn't only the sensation of new life beginning inside me that made me so certain of it. And while I could already feel that life—could sense it growing and multiplying steadily, sheltered deep within my womb—there was something else, some other particle of his essence that seemed to plant itself firmly within me—something that I knew I would carry with me always, even after my child was born and Leo was taken from me. I could never truly lose him, for he had become an integral part of me—one that would be with me until the day I died. He was more than just my lover, or even the father of my child. He was the one.

I lay there after Leo had fallen into a doze, savoring the new sensations within me. Finally, finally, to have found the one—I could hardly take it in. My mother had never told me why she'd had no use for other lovers after my father had moved on, but I knew the reason now. It was because she didn't need them—or even want them. They would have been unnecessary, super-fluous. Oh, I still wanted Leo, but the mere thought of being with someone else was as much beyond my comprehension as spreading my wings and flying into the sun. It was unthinkable. She'd also never told me how changed I would feel once I'd found him. It was as if an empty space had now been filled, a long and unfinished task finally completed, or an object with a missing piece was at last made whole. I felt satisfied and complete, and Leo, as the one, was responsible for that feeling.

There seemed to be a twisted little quirk in my personal makeup that made me unwilling to tell Leo that I had conceived. It was doubtful he would guess at this stage, and since he would be gone within less than a month's time, I thought I could keep my secret from him without difficulty, though I wasn't quite sure why I felt it was necessary. I wondered if my own father had known about me, and the more I thought about it, the more I realized that he probably hadn't. I wondered what a difference it might have made if he had known I existed. He might have stayed on to assist in my upbringing, which would have undoubtedly enriched my life, but if he had insisted that my mother accompany him on his travels, the whole succession of witches might have been disrupted. Perhaps that was why the men who were capable of impregnating us usually tended to be tran-sients, rather than local people such as Rafe. I should tell Rafe that the next time I saw him. It might make him feel less…inadequate.

He'd obviously had no trouble where Carnita was concerned, though she had only produced two sons, and no more since—the youngest being roughly six years of age. My thoughts touched briefly on that. Six years. It seemed odd that there were no more. Perhaps she was no longer interested in Rafe—refused him, even—or it might have been that he felt that two sons were enough. Maybe that was why Carnita had wanted Leo.

Or perhaps it was just as Rafe had said; that she wanted him as a way of increasing their status. It made me terribly glad I was a witch! Material wealth didn't concern me, and I had no interest in my status, or that of my family. We were what we were, and there was no need to alter our social standing, let alone buy an exotic slave to increase it.

We witches were different from everyone else in our society, and not just because I could start fires with a stare. We took no part in local politics, preferring instead to study the ways of the animals and plants, to contemplate the changing of the seasons, to learn the rhythms of the wind and the wisdom of the trees, recognizing no patriarchal ruler but governed by the laws of nature. I had no surname—though exactly where along the line they'd been dropped, I had no idea—but no witch that I knew of had one, and since we seldom married in the traditional manner, it was something that we were unlikely to acquire. I smiled to myself. This was a fact that further solidified my intention to withhold the truth from Leo. After all, I didn't want my child to have to deal with a surname such as Banadänsk, and though I would always remember it myself, that information would be for my own edification, and no one else's.

As I lay there with Leo, believing that nothing more could possibly occur that would be quite as earthshaking, Rafe chose that moment to pound on my door, demanding to speak with me.

"What the devil!" I exclaimed involuntarily. I wasn't normally given to swearing—at least, not out loud—but this was an extreme case; it's not every day you find the "one," and then get interrupted by his rightful owner. "Why didn't that damned horse of his warn me he was coming?"

"He can do that?" Leo inquired.

"Absolutely," I replied, "and he's got some explaining to do!" I got up in a hurry and snatched up my skirt and tunic, pulling them on quickly, pausing briefly to pull my hair out from beneath the collar before heading for the door. I silently thanked whatever god might be responsible that Rafe hadn't simply barged in unannounced, and also that the wind was howling enough that he probably hadn't heard our voices. Oh, yes! Sinjar had better have a good story for this! "Curl up there while I answer the door," I directed Leo. "I don't know why he's here, but it can't be good. He sounds pretty agitated, doesn't he?"

Leo nodded in reply and lay back on the pallet, pulling a blanket over himself. "I will moan," he whispered.

"Good idea," I whispered back. "Delirious with fever, remember?"

Leo grinned devilishly before closing his eyes. I shook my head, for, delirious or not, he looked entirely too healthy to be convincing. My only hope was that Rafe would take my word for it and not examine him too closely. After all, he could have no reason to suspect otherwise—unless he'd received more information about Leo's species since his last visit. I was wondering who might have let the cat out of the bag when Desdemona snickered.

"Ha, ha!" she cackled. *"Very funny!"*

"Oh, be quiet!" I said, probably leaving Leo to wonder whether or not I'd been speaking to him. Rafe was shouting and pounding to make himself heard above the wind.

"I'm coming, Rafe!" I shouted. "Just hold on a minute!"

"By all the gods above and below, Tisana!" he bellowed. "Make haste!"

Upon opening the door, I noted two things. First, that he had two horses with him, and that I recognized neither of them, which let Sinjar off the hook, and second, that Rafe was genuinely distraught. Something terrible had happened, and one glance at his face was enough to make me realize that this had nothing to do with Leo.

"What is it?" I demanded.

I had never seen Rafe in such an impotent, tormented rage before. Haughty and arrogant, certainly, but this was new for him, and I could tell he was having a very hard time controlling himself.

"My sons have been taken!" he gasped, sweeping his hood from his head in a gesture of frustration as he charged into the room. "Both of them!"

"Are you sure?" I ventured hopefully. "Could they not have simply gotten lost?"

The look he shot at me would have set him on fire, had it come from me. "My sons would not simply get lost!" he said, grinding out his words. "They were taken by force and their servant killed!"

"Oh, surely not!" I protested. "Could it have been an accident, perhaps? They might have been afraid and—"

"Her throat was slit, Tisana!" he bellowed. It was at that point that I decided it might be best to shut up and listen or he might be tempted to do something similar to me. "It was no accident!"

"Any idea who might have done it?" I asked.

"No! There have been no ransom demands," he reported, "no word at all. No one was seen, and we found no clues other than Kartin's body, which was cold by the time it was discovered."

Something in his tone made me wonder if this woman had been more to him than a mere servant, but this was not the time for such remarks. I knew now why he had come.

Years before, I'd been able to locate a small child who had wandered away from her home, and while it might have been assumed that I'd had the Sight to guide me, that wasn't the case at all. No, all I'd done was to consult the local squirrels, who had seen the child in the woods and told me where to look. I have no doubt that it was an impressive demonstration to those who witnessed it, but it wasn't what Rafe thought it was. I'd never explained to anyone how I'd done it, and in this case, if no animals had witnessed the kidnapping, I wouldn't be able to help him at all.

On the other hand, Leo might be just the one we needed. Rafe had mentioned something about him being a good tracker when he'd brought him to me. Perhaps that was why he'd come. If so, I couldn't in good conscience maintain the illusion that Leo was still too sick and weak to be equal to the task. Oh, yes, the party was definitely over, and Rafe's next words proved it.

"I need you and that slave to help me search," he said.

"But, why not your own men? Surely they would—"

"I cannot trust them, Tisana," he said, cutting me off abruptly. "There was no stir, no untoward noises, nothing to raise an alarm. Therefore, it's possible that some of my own people let these criminals into my house, though they all deny it—which they would in any case."

"But why, Rafe? Why would anyone take your children?"

"To use against me in some way, or to ensure that my land would be free for the taking in the event of my death." He threw up his hands in a gesture of frustrated ignorance. "Who knows?"

"But these are surely not the only children you—"

He cut me off again, but with a gesture this time. It was a moment or two before he spoke. "There will be no more," he said tersely. "Carnita is barren. The last birth was apparently…damaging to her."

Which was something that I might have been able to remedy, if I'd been given the opportunity. "You might have sent for me, but you never did," I accused him. "Why?"

He looked toward the fire, hardly seeming to notice Leo lying there. Staring into the flames for a long moment, he said, finally, "It is…difficult for me to come to you."

"Why?" I demanded. "Because we were lovers once? Did you really think I wouldn't have helped you because of that?" Call it professional pride, if you will, but I was angry that he would have suspected me of being so petty about the whole sordid business. I'd always been of the opinion that I'd taken it rather well. I hadn't put a curse on him, though under the circumstances, it was something he should have expected. No, I'd always felt that he'd gotten off quite easily, and I doubted that he would have been as forgiving had our situations been reversed.

He shook his head. "No, I know very well that you would have, Tisana," he said with a sigh. "It was simply that I could not ask it of you."

Even saying that much cost him, I could tell. Rafe, perhaps for the first time in his life, seemed to be feeling humble, and it wasn't setting very well with him. I couldn't blame him. If I'd had to beg favors from a woman I'd scorned, I might have been feeling a trifle out of sorts, myself—which was pretty much the way I *was* feeling at the time, particularly in light of his unfortunate sense of timing. However, since he now owned something that I wanted very much—namely, Leo—I decided that I should at least be helpful, if not generous. I didn't know Rafe's sons, but they were not to blame for their parents' shortcomings. And the extent of the danger to them was not yet clear.

"But you're asking me now," I said gently, "and I will help you if I can." I didn't bother to ask why it was different this time, since the answer to that was perfectly obvious. With a barren wife, those two sons were crucial, both for the succession and for Carnita's future should Rafe happen to predecease her. I wondered which aspect of his dilemma troubled him the most. I didn't get the impression that he was even now considering Carnita's distress over the loss of her children; her future comfort would mean even less.

But perhaps I was judging him too harshly. Surely Rafe couldn't be that callous about such a thing, could he?

"And your slave is well enough to help," I said in what I hoped was a neutral tone. If Rafe knew how much I wanted Leo, he might take a perverse notion to refuse to even consider letting me keep him for another month, let alone set him free. "He's just resting right now. I would have sent word to you sooner, but the month was nearly up, anyway."

He dismissed this information with a terse nod. "I hope the fool I bought him from didn't exaggerate his abilities."

"I wouldn't know," I said with a shrug. "I haven't seen him do any tracking, but then, he hasn't been out much."

"Any problems with him attempting to escape?" he asked. "I need someone loyal, someone whom I can trust."

I regarded Rafe with considerable skepticism. "And what have you done to instill such feelings in him?"

Rafe's gaze was knowing, if not arrogant. "I bought him when he was nearly dead, and then I brought him to you, Tisana," he said evenly. "I'd say he owes me his life."

Something in his expression gave me the impression that there was more meaning attached to those words than was immediately apparent—almost as if he'd known that Leo and I were lovers, and that he also considered that fact to be a part of the debt. I wondered if I should tell him about my child—after all, I might have some interest in the fate of my child's father—but decided that if Rafe knew that Leo had succeeded where he had failed, it might make matters that much worse. I could see Rafe refusing to even consider the possibility of letting us remain together, out of sheer spite. I reminded myself that Leo didn't know about the baby yet, and if I didn't plan on telling him, I certainly couldn't tell Rafe! No, the more I considered the matter, the more convinced I became that he didn't need to know. I seriously doubted that he would ever grant Leo his freedom just because he was my child's father and I wanted him, but if, on the other hand, we were to locate his sons…

"I hope he sees it that way," I said, purposefully directing my statement toward Leo, hoping that he understood, because helping Rafe was probably the best way to help ourselves. Fortunately, he'd had sense enough not to do much moaning and groaning—possibly because he wanted to hear our conversation.

"Well, get him up and let's get going," Rafe said, his impatience to be gone resurfacing. "I can't believe he's slept through all of this anyway. Is he deaf?"

"No," I replied, barely suppressing a smile. "Just… tired. You know how soundly cats sleep."

Rafe let that one pass without speculating as to what Leo might have been doing to wear himself into such a stupor.

When I went to rouse him, Leo made a convincing show of waking up, uncurling from his pallet and stretching with a loud purr before yawning hugely to display that impressive mouthful of razor-sharp teeth. On the surface, he seemed to have no idea what had been taking place while he slept, but the significant flick of an upswept eyebrow left me with no doubt that he'd heard the entire discussion.

"We've got to help Rafe find his children," I said briskly. "Do you think you can ride?"

Leo nodded and sat up. Unfortunately, there was no hiding the fact that he was completely naked. Whether Rafe thought I had kept Leo from escaping by keeping him barefoot and nude I never knew, but left him to draw his own conclusions. As it happened, Leo's nakedness served to remind him of something else.

"I brought some clothes for him," Rafe said. "I'll get them."

"Well, I certainly hope it's something warm!" I remarked acerbically. "I had to burn the clothes he was wearing when you dumped him off here. Really, Rafe, you should have brought something with him then!"

His nonchalant shrug as he made his way to the door told the story. Before this, he hadn't cared one whit for Leo's comfort, and it was only now that he needed him that any regard was shown for him at all.

Leo stood up, leaving his blanket on the floor, his unbelievable cock standing up as stiffly as ever.

"Do you ever have trouble walking with that thing?"

Lips curling into a delightfully coy smile, he said informatively, "I do not use it to walk."

"Cute. Very cute," I remarked. "But please, at least try to keep your suggestive remarks to a minimum, or Rafe will figure out what's been going on and end up charging me for your use instead of paying me for healing you! And for goodness sake, put a blanket over that before he sees you!"

"He would be—" he paused, as though searching for the right word, "—jealous?"

I rolled my eyes. "I think anyone would be jealous of

that!" I assured him. "I've never seen one to compare, unless you want to count Sinjar's. You know, now that I think of it, there are some similarities—in shape, that is—and though he's got you beat when it comes to size, I don't think Sinjar has fluids that can do what yours do. I'll have to ask him about that."

"Who is Sinjar?"

"Rafe's stallion," I replied. "You know, the one who should have warned me he was coming? Of course, there's a good reason for that, since Rafe didn't bring him this time. I wish he had, though. He's such a sweetie and so funny—a great guy to have along on a journey of any length. He'd certainly keep you laughing."

"I cannot understand horses," Leo reminded me. "You would have to translate."

"And I couldn't very well do that with Rafe along, could I?" I said ruefully. "Oh, well. Would have been fun—at least in that respect. I—"

I had to stop there, since Rafe had returned with an armload of things for Leo, including boots and a heavy cloak, which Carnita had probably sent in order to keep her precious "trophy" slave from getting frost-bitten. I wondered if talking to her rather than Rafe would be the best tactic. Getting her sons back would make her grateful enough to consider my request, as I hoped it would with Rafe. It seemed that finding those two kids was becoming more imperative by the second.

Deciding that distracting Rafe from Leo's remarkable physical attributes would be best, I took Rafe aside for further discussion, hoping to keep him occupied at least until Leo got his pants on.

"We'll have to go back to where they were taken for us to track them," I said. "I'll get Morgana ready to ride, if you'll keep an eye on Leo."

"Leo?" Rafe echoed, as though he didn't know who I might have been referring to. Then the light seemed to dawn. "Is that his name?"

"You mean you don't know?"

"I didn't ask, Tisana," he said haughtily. "After all, he's only a slave."

I started to say something nasty, but thought better of it. As a matter of record, I must admit that I hardly ever *do* tell Rafe exactly what I'm thinking. In the end, I only said: "His real name is a bit of a mouthful. Leo was simpler, and he didn't seem to mind."

Rafe merely nodded, his interest in Leo's nomenclature waning fast. "Do you need to see their room, or just get back to the town?"

Unless the boys had a pet of some kind that I could talk to, I doubted that seeing their room would be much help, but I decided that, for a seer, returning to the scene of the crime was probably standard operating procedure, and since I wanted to be as convincing as possible, I should probably start there. Plus, Leo might be able to pick up a scent of some kind, though I had no idea what methods he would use when it came to tracking them down. "I'll need to start from where they were taken," I replied. "I have no idea what Leo might require."

Rafe nodded as though I'd merely confirmed his own plans. "I thought as much," he said, "so I brought my fastest horses to get us back. I've already set servants to work on getting provisions ready for the journey, so you won't need to bring much with you. Can your mare keep up?"

"If she can't, I'll follow as quickly as I can. Leo can go on ahead with you." I was glad Morgana hadn't been there to hear that particular exchange, since she tended to be touchy about being slower than the "guys." Sinjar had outrun her once, and while he was good-natured enough not to tease her about it, she still seemed to consider it a sore spot. I sometimes wondered if that wasn't why she was so down on males in general.

I packed up an assortment of herbs and ointments I thought might come in handy along the way, though the gods only knew what we would be up against. Frostbite was the most likely problem, but, of course, I had my own nonmedicinal ways of treating that. Still, there are always minor injuries on any adventure—and this one promised to be more dangerous than most—and it pays to be prepared.

Bundling myself up against the cold, I went out into the wind, noting that it was snowing again. I sent out a mental call to Morgana, following it up with a vocal one. Rafe's horses looked at me strangely, and I heard the voice of the big bay gelding nearest me, saying, *"So, you're the one! Sinjar thinks very highly of you."*

"It's mutual," I replied. *"How come he's not with you?"*

"Not fast enough," the chestnut said smugly. *"He might be the master's favorite, but it isn't because of his speed!"*

"Aw, now, be nice," I chided him. *"Sinjar's a helluva guy."*

"I suppose so," he grumbled. *"My name is Calla, by the way, and the bay is Goran."*

"Nice to meet you," I said politely. *"Morgana will be here in a minute—and please don't tease her about being too slow!"*

"We'll be perfect gentlemen," Goran promised.

"Which one of you is Leo going to ride?" I asked. *"If he wants to run away, don't take him, please. I'd like to keep him."*

"I thought he was our master's slave," Calla remarked.

"Yes, but I like him a lot," I said. *"So please, don't let him run away. I'm going to try to figure out a way to get Rafe to give him to me."*

Goran snorted. *"Find his sons for him, and he just might."*

"That's my plan," I said. *"You two don't know anything about the kidnapping, do you?"*

"No, but the kids have a dog," Goran replied. *"He might know."*

"Think he'll talk to me?"

"I don't see why not. He's a grouch sometimes, but he likes the boys. He'll want to help you find them."

"Maybe we should take him with us," I suggested.

"Too old," Calla said decisively. *"He'd never be able to keep up."*

It was becoming fairly obvious that Calla was a bit arrogant. He and Rafe were two of a kind, apparently. Goran was confident, but without the chip on his shoulder, reminding me more of Leo.

Morgana trotted up then, and I introduced her to Goran and Calla, and, as I might have expected, she ignored them completely. I followed her into the shed and brushed the snow off her back before heaving the saddle on. *"What's going on?"* she asked.

"Someone has kidnapped Rafe's children," I told her as I pulled the girth up snugly. *"He wants me and Leo to find them."*

"I'm sure you could do it on your own," Morgana said. *"We don't need him."*

"Oh, come on, Morgana! Give the guys a break for once! It's gonna be the two of us girls and four men! If I have to listen to you bitch about them the whole time, I'll—"

"Tisana!" Rafe bellowed, sticking his head inside the shed. "By the gods below! Aren't you ready yet? We've got to get moving!"

"Rafe," I replied evenly. "I understand the need for haste, and it should be perfectly obvious that I'm doing the best I can. I know you're upset, but please try to keep a civil tongue in your head, unless you intend to find someone else to help you."

"You must have bewitched me years ago," he declared. "Otherwise, I could never have gotten past your waspish tongue."

"I think you had something to do with the condition of my tongue," I retorted. "I was a sweet young thing when I first met you. If my tongue is waspish now, you're a large part of the reason why."

For some reason Rafe found this amusing. "You were never a sweet young thing, Tisana," he chuckled. "There was always fire in you."

If he only knew… "Oh, just go get on your horse and leave me be," I grumbled. I had to control my temper better. Make him really angry and I might never see Leo again, let alone get to free him. I picked up the bridle and offered Morgana the bit, which was something I normally didn't need, since I could always tell her what I wanted, but this time it was for show. Fortunately, she understood this.

"He's not worth the effort," Morgana assured me, taking the bit. *"Neither is that other one."*

"You've never gotten a taste of Leo, so I'll excuse your ignorance for now." I paused as a novel thought crossed my mind. *"Ever have an orgasm, Morgana?"*

"No," she said. *"And I don't want to."*

"Your loss," I said with a shrug. *"You know, you really should give it a try sometime—when you're in season, that is. I mean, that Sinjar is one sexy stud!"*

She rolled her eyes at me in reply.

"Oh, come on! He's not a bit like Rafe! He's funny, he's good-looking…he's one terrific guy!"

This time she snorted.

"Okay, then," I said. *"Let's get going. It's a long way to town."*

"I know," she said. *"Just be sure to put something for me to eat in that saddlebag. I'm kinda hungry."*

"You're always hungry," I pointed out. *"I've never known you to turn down a snack."*

"It's a horse thing," she said simply. *"We eat all the time."*

I started to make the comment that eating all the time tended to cause her to do something else all the time, but since I'd never had to clean up after her, I chose not to mention it. She may have heard the thought anyway, but she was a little more tactful than Desdemona and usually did her best to ignore my thoughts unless I directed them toward her, preferring, instead, that I actually speak to her aloud first. Sinjar had confided to me once that he enjoyed hearing the sound of human voices—provided they weren't screaming at him—but it also might be that horses are more willing than cats to accept things at face value. They were certainly more forgiving—and more trusting.

Which was more than I could say for Rafe. When I led Morgana out of the shed to mount up, I noted that Rafe had a lead rope tied to the bit on Leo's horse. Calla, the horse in question, seemed to be upset about it, too.

"Couldn't you just tell him I won't let the damned slave escape?" Calla complained. *"I told you I wouldn't, and I never lie."*

I might have been able to explain to Rafe that Leo probably wouldn't run off, but it would be very difficult to describe how I knew that the horse wouldn't. In the end, I told Calla he'd just have to learn to live with it. Calla was a bit of a prick, it seemed, and was making me wish once again that Rafe had brought Sinjar instead.

Darkness was falling as we set off, and with the horses' footfalls muffled in the snow, we moved on with no sound other than that of creaking leather and the occasional grunt of effort from one of the horses. A surreal silence enveloped us; not another sound came from the snow-laden pines through which we passed, lulling me into the illusion that we were the only living souls on that entire world. I wondered what Rafe had been thinking when he'd asked if Morgana could keep up. He was a fool if he thought we could gallop through the snow, which was nearly a foot deep by then—but perhaps he'd been too distraught to be thinking clearly.

I still didn't understand why anyone would kidnap Rafe's children. If someone wanted to eliminate his heirs, killing them would have been much simpler and far more effective. So why would anyone take children? Because they had none of their own? Or because they... oh, yes, I thought, that must be it! They wanted to lure Rafe out of his stronghold to kill him. *Then* kill his sons and take his land. I wondered if Rafe had considered this possibility. If he had, he certainly wouldn't be going with us—or shouldn't be. Of course, Rafe was the kind of man who seemed to think he was invincible. Foolish man! No one was invincible. Anyone could die...

Lost in these thoughts, I was startled when Gerald, the squirrel, threw a nut at me to get my attention.

"Where the devil do you think you're going at this time of night?" he chirped from his perch in a nearby tree. *"It's getting dark! You'll get lost!"*

"I don't think so, Gerald. Trust me, Rafe knows the way through these woods blindfolded."

"Whoo-hoo, that other one is a mean-looking cat, isn't he? Doesn't like to hunt squirrels, does he?"

"You've seen him before, Gerald," I said dryly. *"I know you must have seen him when he ran away."*

"Yeah, I did," he remarked casually. *"I would have told you where to find him, but you didn't seem to need any help."*

"Obvious trail," I agreed. *"What are you doing up, anyway?"*

"Keeping an eye out," he replied, twitching his bushy tail. *"That Rafe caused quite a stir when he came flying*

through here a while ago. What's up with him, anyway? Got a sick wife?"

"No, someone kidnapped his sons. We're going to help him find them."

"You'll need me then," he said, leaping down from his branch. *"I'm coming with you."*

"And just how will I explain that?" I demanded. *"You know very well people will comment on a squirrel riding double with me."*

"Let them wonder," he said. *"But warn that horse, will you? They're a nervous, jumpy bunch!"*

"Look who's talking!" I thought with an inward chuckle, but I did warn Morgana that Gerald had decided to hitch a ride.

"Don't suppose I could just hide inside the front of your cloak, could I?" he asked as he landed on my shoulder. *"It would be a lot warmer, and I'd be less noticeable."*

"Haven't got fleas, have you?" I teased. I might have been kidding, but I really didn't want to get fleas, either.

"No, of course not!" He seemed offended that I would even suggest such a thing. I'd never been close enough to Gerald to know whether he had fleas or not; he'd always struck me as being a bit standoffish, and it seemed odd that he'd decided to get so chummy.

I knew my self to be growing and changing with recent events. Could it be enhancing my bond with the animals? I'd always had an easy rapport with horses, and with Desdemona, of course. With the wilder creatures, being able to talk with them didn't necessarily mean they would listen—or cooperate. The rabbits I suspected of purposely misunderstanding the dire threats I directed at their quick little minds whenever I chased them out of my garden. The only thoughts I picked up from most of them were innocently focused on the pleasures of whatever tender vegetable they were chewing on. They didn't seem to understand my annoyance at their stealing my lettuce—though they might not have known that I could hear them out there laughing their little whiskers off afterwards. And look at Gerald—I mean, usually he just threw things at me and laughed whenever they hit me. I wondered what had happened to make him take such an interest in what I was doing.

"Bored," he remarked, obviously having been eavesdropping on my thoughts as he wormed his way inside the front of my cloak. *"Nothing to do, you know? Plenty of food stored up, and no more to be had with all this damned snow on the ground! I could use a little adventure. Besides, it'll give us a chance to get to know each other better."*

I pondered this for a moment, wondering exactly how a little squirrel might be helpful on our quest. I remembered who had helped me find that other lost child. Gerald could consult with others of his kind along the way—which would save me a lot of time, because I'd yet to talk with a squirrel for the first time who didn't turn a simple question into a long, drawn-out discussion of who I was and why I could talk with them. You have only to listen to them chattering in the treetops to know that they like to talk a lot. And, like most prey animals, they're good lookouts, too—they don't miss much, and it's pretty hard to sneak up on one.

"Okay, then," I said. *"When we get to Rafe's keep, would you ask around and see if anyone's seen his kids?*

I'll ask the other animals, but if you could talk to the squirrels, I'd appreciate it. Morgana can check with any horses we meet, but it might have been too dark for them to see much. Of course, any direction the kidnappers would have gone would take them through the forest, so you tree dwellers would be the most likely witnesses."

"Righto!" Gerald said, curling up inside the double-breasted front of my cloak. *"My point exactly! You let me know when we're getting close. Right now, I think I'll nap for a bit."* Yawning hugely, he settled himself for the journey. *"This is very nice, Tisana. Don't know why I never did it before."*

"Too busy picking on me, I suppose," I remarked grimly. *"You know, I don't usually give horseback rides to those who enjoy tormenting me."*

"Sorry about that, Tisana," he said, his whispering thoughts growing fainter as he drifted off to sleep. *"I'll try to restrain myself…"*

Once he was asleep I decided that if his help would enable me to find the boys and then talk Rafe out of a certain slave I was rather partial to, he could throw rocks at me for all I cared.

Chapter 4

WE WERE A TIRED AND BEDRAGGLED CREW BY THE TIME we reached the quiet, snow-shrouded town and passed through it to Rafe's home. I've referred to this as Rafe's keep, but in truth, it was a large house surrounded with a wooden palisade just inside the town. Unfortunately, those walls had been completely useless when it came to keeping the people inside safe from harm.

The boys' nurse had been killed. I couldn't remember ever hearing of such violence in our neck of the woods. We'd been spared having to deal with such things—at least during my lifetime. People had come here from Earth many generations before, in part to escape from hatred and violence, but, unfortunately, it had followed us here. Utopia wasn't truly Utopian, not as I understood the reference. I doubted, for example, that slavery had been intended as the primary mode of labor in the original model, nor would there have been a need for each lord to have a company of fighting men at his disposal. But, as with many great and noble ideas, it became bastardized when put into practice.

When I looked at Leo, it seemed abhorrent to think of him as the property of another person. It was wrong; and down in the deepest recesses of our hearts, we all knew it was wrong—even those who owned many slaves. What it would take to free them, I didn't know, and still don't. It had become too much the accepted norm in our society to change very easily. It had occurred out of necessity, perhaps, but that didn't excuse it, and the necessity could be argued as well.

Still, deplorable as it might be, it did exist, and the one I loved was caught up in it as surely as a fish in a net. Dismounting at Rafe's door, it seemed to me that Leo should have been the master there. Rafe himself was rough and uncultured, whereas Leo was refined and regal in his bearing, though a less arrogant man I'd seldom chanced to meet. It was as though, even as a slave, he was a superior being, and being superior, he had no need to bring it to your constant attention. There was an aura of greatness about him, and it didn't take fine clothes or a crown to make it visible.

Entering the great hall of Rafe's keep, I opened my mind to hear the thoughts of the animals therein. The boys had a dog, Calla had said, and if so, I should be able to call him to me. It was unfortunate that I couldn't communicate with Leo in that manner, because with Rafe around, our conversation was kept to a minimum.

We passed through the hall into a smaller, torch-lit chamber where three dogs lay in blissful slumber before the huge fireplace. I walked toward them purposefully before I realized that I should be behaving more like a seer and holding my hands out to find disturbances in the fabric of time or some such thing. I tried it, but as I reached toward the fire and stared into it, the flames leaped higher, sending a flurry of sparks up the chimney and startling the dogs with its sudden roar.

"Well, at least you're awake," I said, meeting their eyes. *"Yes, it's me talking to you. I'm here to find Rafe's sons. Which of you was their companion?"*

An old and very frail-looking black hound got slowly to his feet, gazing back at me with big, sad eyes. *"I am called Toraga,"* he said. *"Four men came and took the boys. I know nothing other than that. I was kicked out of the way when I tried to stop them and left for dead. The one they killed was…kind to me. It makes me very sad that she is gone."*

"Don't miss those boys, though, do you?" a younger hound remarked. *"They just about ran you into the ground."*

"Better to wear out than to rust out," Toraga said with wheezy dignity. He yawned, stretching his jaws until they cracked. *"Find them, my lady. They were still alive when last I saw them, and though they are boys and behave as many such beings do, their hearts were good."*

"I will do my best," I assured him. *"Is there anything you can tell me about the men? How they were dressed, their style of speech?"*

"I wouldn't know, my lady," the old dog replied. *"It happened very quickly."*

"Did any of the rest of you see them?"

The younger dog looked at me with regret. *"I was asleep,"* he said mournfully. *"I wish I had been there to sound the alarm, but I wasn't."*

"It's no fault of yours that you were not," I said reassuringly.

Nodding, I turned to Rafe. "There were four men, but who they were, I cannot say."

"You saw this in the flames?" he asked.

Since this was as good an explanation as any, I let

him think that. Leo, of course, knew exactly where my information had come from.

"Can you track them?" I asked Leo.

"Perhaps," Leo replied. "The scent is faint, and the trail is old, but I believe I can follow it. I can smell blood, but it goes in two directions."

"The body was taken out through the rear of the house," Rafe said. "Any other would be the direction the kidnappers took."

Leo nodded. "I will need to see the boys' room to get their scents, as well."

"This way," Rafe said with a gesture. "We must hurry."

"Rafe," I said slowly. "Why would someone take your children? Why not simply kill them?"

He shrugged. "I have no idea, Tisana," he replied gruffly. "This is why I came to you. I have no notion of who would want them."

"No enemies? No one who covets your land?" *Or your wife?* I left that question unasked, but with Rafe gone chasing after his sons for an unspecified period of time, anyone who wanted Carnita would have an excellent opportunity. That there might be men willing to kill to have her was evident in the flicker of interest I saw in Leo's eyes as she rushed into the room.

I might have been moderately attractive as women go, but Carnita? Well, Carnita was the stuff of which most men's dreams were made, and even after bearing two sons, she was still breathtaking. With eyes the color of a summer sky and long, thick golden tresses floating over shoulders that were just one more beautiful part of a body to die—or kill—for, she made me, and just about any other woman you'd care to name, look like a hag.

Well, okay, so that was an exaggeration, but men have been driven insane by the thought of possessing something so beautiful. Sort of made me want to stare at her long enough to set her hair on fire. I knew I shouldn't do it, but she was near enough to the fire that a random spark *might* set her gown ablaze—if I was lucky.

It was a nice thought, but I realized that it would only give the men an excuse to rip her clothes off— just to save her from the flames, you understand. I wondered who would win if Rafe and Leo were to fight over her. My money was on Leo, since I knew firsthand how quickly he could move, but you know how fierce men can be when they're fighting to maintain possession of something.

Carnita stopped short when she saw Leo. I couldn't blame her, since he *was* the most stunning creature I'd ever seen in my life. I saw her swift, assessing glance take him in, and an inappropriately carnal light flickered in her eyes. She was upset, but not so upset that she couldn't take the time to appreciate an outstanding male specimen. Leo's eyes were glittering as he turned toward her, regarding her in a way that no slave should ever look at his mistress. If Rafe had seen that look, he would have knocked Leo sprawling, but with Carnita in the room, I somehow doubted that Rafe was looking at anyone else.

"Have you found them?" she asked in an anxious, breathy voice.

I waited a moment, and, since no one else seemed willing to talk, replied, "No, Carnita. We've only just begun our search. I can tell you nothing yet but that four men took them alive. Leo thinks he can follow the scent, though. Can you take him to the boys' room, or give him something they've worn?"

She threw a questioning look at Rafe.

"Yes," he said shortly. "Go, and be quick about it!"

Drawing Leo to her with an abrupt gesture, she was gone as quickly as she'd arrived, with Leo in her wake.

I gave it a moment or two to let them get out of earshot, and commented: "Still beautiful, isn't she?"

"What?" Rafe asked, seeming distracted. "Oh—yes. Yes, I suppose she is. Sometimes I forget."

Eyeing him with skepticism, I expressed my doubts as to his sincerity.

"What, you don't believe me?" he asked.

"Not really," I said candidly. "She's far too beautiful ever to be forgotten."

"As are others I could name," he muttered. He seemed about to say something else, but appeared to think better of it, saying instead, "I didn't know you could see things in the fire, Tisana. Is this some new power of yours?"

"I couldn't say, exactly," I replied evasively. If I seem unnecessarily reticent concerning my powers, let me explain that I had heard tales of witches being burned at the stake—as well as being stoned, crushed, or drowned—and while that sort of thing hadn't happened in a very long time, I was still understandably nervous. With that gruesome chapter in history in mind, my ancestors had always done their best to keep their true powers a secret and had done their utmost to rely solely upon herbal medicine to treat their patients.

I don't know why, but I suspected that to Rafe, my being able to see things in the flames would seem less disquieting than communicating with animals.

"Yeah, you might learn how he treats his dogs," the young hound put in. *"He can be a bit testy at times. Really, though, we do the best we can! He's just very hard to please."*

I tried to hide my smile, but Rafe caught it, anyway. "What?" he demanded irritably. "What is it you aren't telling me?"

"There are a great many things I haven't told you, Rafe," I said loftily. "This is just one more. Learn to accept it, will you?"

He managed to hold his tongue; perhaps thinking that if he wanted my help, it would behoove him to keep me placated. Not that I would ever stoop so low as to deliberately mislead him in the search for his children, but as long as he didn't know that, it might help keep him in line.

"Good luck," Toraga said dryly. *"If you do keep him in line, you'll be the first."*

I really did need to get out more! Talking mostly to Desdemona and Morgana had cut me off from a whole wide world of fascinating conversations. Other people's pets were a wonderful source of insight into their characters.

"Yes, and when he's mating with his wife, he makes lots of noise," the young hound reported. *"Sounds like a pig."*

"She knows that, you idiot!" the old dog wheezed. *"They were lovers once!"*

"Oh, yeah, right!" the other said. *"Forgot!"*

Despite the gravity of our current situation, I couldn't help but burst into laughter. *"What are your names?"* I asked.

"I'm Max," said the young hound, *"and, like he said, this old guy is Toraga. That other lazy bum is called Nod. Aptly named, don't you think?"* Since Nod had yet to open his eyes, I was forced to agree.

"Well, Max," I began, *"I think you need to come with us. You can keep up with horses, can't you?"*

"In snow?" he scoffed, prancing at my feet. *"I can outrun them! No sweat!"*

"Dogs don't sweat," I reminded him, *"but I take your meaning. I have a squirrel with me, too, and he's a friend of mine, so please don't kill him."*

"I'll try not to," Max said, grinning. *"This will be fun!"*

"I doubt it," I said aloud.

"Doubt what?" Rafe asked, eyeing me curiously. "Tisana, are you, perhaps, losing your mind?"

"If I am, it's your fault," I said grumpily. It can be difficult to remember to think rather than to speak your thoughts, and carrying on a conversation both ways at the same time was something I hadn't had much opportunity to practice. Like I said, I didn't get out much.

Leo returned with Carnita then, so the conversation ended there.

"Got the scent?" I asked Leo.

He merely nodded in reply, but I saw his eyes slide over to take one last look at his mistress. I couldn't blame him for it; after all, she truly was a devastatingly beautiful woman. It was possible that Leo might decide he preferred to be Carnita's slave, but I did my best to avoid thinking about it and, instead, focused on the task ahead.

On impulse, I suggested to Rafe that he ride Sinjar and that we load Goran up with the bulk of our supplies. I knew Sinjar better than the other horses, and thought it would be nice to have another friend along—aside from the entertainment value. Goran might have been the faster of the two, but speed isn't that much of a factor when it comes to tracking someone. Besides, I knew for a fact that Sinjar was pretty handy in a fight—and something told me it might come to that before this adventure was over.

While Rafe directed his servants to gather supplies for our journey and then went to get Sinjar, Leo and I took our leave of Carnita and went out to where Calla and Morgana were waiting, with Max at our heels. Someone had already filled the horses' saddlebags with packets of dried food, and there was a canteen of water and a bedroll tied to each saddle. The servants were in the process of adding a nosebag for each horse, along with a fair-sized bag of grain and chopped hay, leaving us reasonably well provisioned.

Gerald hopped over and informed me that he had gotten a lead on which direction our search should take from one of the local squirrels. Gerald was completely unprepared for the newest member of our band, however, and let out a screech before streaking off toward the nearest tree, with the hound bounding after him baying enthusiastically. Obviously, I'd have to have a few more words with Max regarding his behavior.

"Which way do you think we should go?" I asked Leo, to verify our heading.

Leo pointed in the same direction that Gerald had indicated. "The scent goes that way," he said. "But it is very faint. I may not be able to follow it for long."

"Good thing we've got other methods at our disposal, then," I remarked with newfound optimism. "Really, Leo! Those guys don't stand a chance!"

He nodded and remained silent. And since the silence was a long one, I just *had* to ask: "So, what did you think of Carnita?"

Leo met my eyes with a steady gaze. "She is very beautiful," he replied. "But her heart is not...steadfast."

"What makes you say that?" I prompted him. "Did she make a pass at you?"

"A pass at me?" he asked, puzzled.

"Well, you know," I began, groping for an example to use. "Did she tell you you're really sexy, or that she likes your hair, or pinch your ass, or something like that?"

"No," he said firmly. "But there is something she holds back. She is afraid, and it is not only fear for the safety of her children."

"What makes you so sure about that?" I demanded. "Are you a seer, too?"

"Some things I can see in my mind," he replied. "They are...visions. They come rarely, but when they do, I know they are true."

I considered this for a moment. I really knew nothing about Leo or his species as a whole, so I had no way of proving or disproving his claim, but there are some things that must simply be taken on faith, and this was one of them. "Guess I'll have to take your word for that," I said. "So, Carnita is hiding something, then. Hmm... Wonder what?"

"That, I cannot see," he said. "But there is something about her."

"Well, if you happen to 'see' anything else, let me know," I said. "In the meantime, we need to get going. Gerald said—"

"Who is Gerald?" Leo asked, cutting me off.

"The squirrel," I replied, as Gerald reappeared and leaped up onto my shoulder. I could feel his little heart pounding, but he appeared to be unharmed.

"What'd you do with Max?" I asked. *"Leave him barking at the base of an empty tree?"*

"Nah," Gerald said with a cackle. *"Lost him in the forest, but he'll be back soon—unfortunately. What d'you need a dog for, anyway? They're such noisy beasts!"*

"I know," I told him soothingly, *"but we need all the help we can get. Leo might need help with tracking, and we can't afford to waste time."*

"Big, dumb Leo!" Gerald chattered. *"Needs a hound dog to help him track! Ha! Maybe I should throw something at him."*

"No, please don't," I said. *"I happen to like Leo, and it isn't a good time for teasing right now."*

Leo nodded wisely. "This is the one who throws nuts at you, is he not?"

"Yes," I concurred. "But he's not so bad, really. He's going to help us find the boys."

Leo didn't seem very sure about that. "If he has been hateful to you in the past, why do you trust him now, and why does he offer his help?"

I hesitated for a moment before answering. I still suspected that finding the one had changed me in ways I had yet to understand, but it was hard to put it into words.

"I don't know," I said a little lamely, "but he really does want to help. Besides, he says he's bored this winter and could use a nice, rousing adventure to liven things up."

If Leo's expression was anything to go by, I doubted that he would trust Gerald any farther than he could throw him—which would probably be a long way. Gerald muttered a few squirrel curses, having picked up on at least the gist of what Leo thought of him.

At that point Max came trotting toward us, panting. *"Sorry about that,"* he said. *"Just couldn't help myself."*

Gerald squeaked and tried to climb onto the top of my head. I could see it was going to take some diplomacy to get this bunch to work together as a team.

"Be nice, Gerald!" I admonished him, wincing as his sharp little claws clutched at my scalp. *"Actually, I can see Leo's point. After all, you've never been particularly friendly before, you know."*

"Never needed to be," Gerald stated firmly. *"But not being friendly doesn't necessarily mean I'm not trustworthy. And, besides, there's something different about you now, Tisana."*

"That's very interesting, Gerald," I replied, detaching him from my head and moving him firmly back to his perch on my shoulder. *"But would you please try to be nice to Max and Leo, at least for the duration of this little adventure?"*

"I'll try," Gerald grumbled.

"And Max, you stop chasing Gerald!" I scolded him. *"He's here to help—not to provide you with sport."*

Max just grinned and thumped his tail in the snow. *"But, Tisana!"* he protested. *"I love chasing squirrels! I mean, I'm a hound. It's what we do."*

"Well, that's something you're just going to have to learn to rise above," I said firmly. *"Understand?"*

Max dropped his head sulkily and looked up at me with his dark, hound dog eyes, his tail no longer wagging. *"Okay, I'll try harder."*

"What about you, Leo?" I asked. "Think you can get along with Gerald?"

"I will be nice if he does not torment me," Leo said equably. "I am not hateful."

Which was certainly true. There are some people who exude hatred and animosity, and don't have any qualms about spreading it around. Leo, on the other hand, must have had plenty of reasons for feeling hatred toward those who had abused him in the past, but I didn't feel it when I was around him. In fact, most of the time he reminded me of an old poem about the "fat cat on the mat, kept as a pet." He gave off the same aura of contentment, but like the cat in the rhyme, who "does not forget" his deeper instincts, I had no doubt that Leo could turn into a spitting, clawing wildcat when the need arose. I just hoped the need would not arise anytime soon.

"Hey, Tisana!" Sinjar called out to me as he and Rafe approached. *"Thanks a whole, big bunch! Taking me out of my nice, warm stall on a day like this. I don't get any respect around here at all!"*

"Nice to see you, too," I returned sweetly.

Cocking an eye toward Leo, he went on to comment: *"Well, he's certainly looking better! What'd you do? Love him back to health?"*

"Something like that," I replied. *"Hey, guess what, Sinjar? He's the one! I'm pregnant!"*

The big stallion let out a loud snort. *"Well, I'll be damned! Congratulations! Just wish I could rub you-know-who's nose in it! Or should I say his dick?"*

I did my best to stifle a laugh, but Rafe, unfortunately, wasn't one to miss much. "What's so damned funny?" he demanded.

"Sorry!" I blurted out before dissolving into giggles. I always found it difficult to be serious with the irreverent Sinjar around.

"Tisana," he warned. "You're going to be locked up as a lunatic if you don't watch it. Mount up."

I would, of course, set fire to anyone who ever tried to lock me up, but, unfortunately, I had to let that one pass, saying merely, "I'll try to remember that."

It occurred to me belatedly that it might have been a mistake to bring Sinjar along on this trip because he would undoubtedly keep me laughing the whole way—especially if he started hitting on Morgana, who was ignoring him, as usual.

"You know, if I didn't know better," Sinjar remarked, *"I'd say he was a gelding after all the carousing the two of you did back then and never managed to get you in child."*

"That's 'with child'," I corrected him. *"You're only 'in foal' if you're a mare."* Of course, I simply *had* to ask this next question. *"Seen his balls, have you?"*

"Oh, yeah," Sinjar replied. *"See them all the time—big, hairy human balls. Not as big as mine, of course, but he's got 'em, all right."*

"His dick's not as big as yours, either," I said as I climbed aboard Morgana.

"True." No brag, just fact. *"What about the cat?"*

"Nice big dick," I replied. *"Just tasting the fluids from it gives me orgasms."*

"Whoa!"

We started off then, with Gerald on my shoulder and Max at Morgana's heels. What Rafe might have thought about the menagerie I was accumulating, he didn't say, and I chose not to bring it to his attention since he already seemed to consider me to be a bit touched in the upper works. I ignored him and kept up my conversation with Sinjar.

"You know, Morgana says she's never had an orgasm. Do mares generally climax?"

"Well, all the ones I've covered have," he said— again, no brag, just fact. *"Of course,"* he added reflectively, *"I suppose they might have faked it. Couldn't say for sure."*

"So, it's normal for a mare to have one?"

"Yeah, I think so."

"Hear that, Morgana?" I said, giving her a nudge on the withers. *"Told you Sinjar could help you out!"*

Morgana's reply was the most disgusted snort I believe I've ever heard from a horse in my life.

"Lost cause there, Sinjar," Calla said. *"She really doesn't like studs—or geldings, either, for that matter. I mean, she won't even talk to me!"*

"Now, guys," I said soothingly, *"you know very well that the fact that it's wintertime has a lot to do with her attitude. Wait until she comes into heat this spring and I'm sure she'll change her mind."*

While this might have been true, Morgana didn't seem to appreciate being talked about and gave a little buck. I decided I'd better take the hint and shut up.

"Okay, guys," I said with a sigh. *"Let's talk about something else. She's getting miffed."*

We'd gone a fair distance in apparent silence before Rafe said—rather nastily, I thought, "I know there aren't any flames around here to see in, Tisana, but do you have any idea where we're going?"

I didn't, of course, since I was only following the directions Gerald had given us and hadn't seen any other squirrels. Fortunately, Leo had a reply ready.

"We are following the scent," he said simply. "We do not need flames to see if the scent is strong."

Rafe glanced up at the sky. "It's getting dark," he went on. "Can you follow the trail at night?"

I thought this was a pretty stupid question, myself. I mean, you only had to look at Leo's eyes to know he could see quite as well in the dark as any other cat—and this was aside from the fact that he was following a *scent*—but perhaps Rafe wasn't thinking very clearly. I could understand why, of course, but *still…*

I doubted that I could have responded to that without at least being a little bit sarcastic, but Leo had been a slave for a long time, and there was no malice in his voice when he replied with a simple affirmative. Obviously, he wasn't going to waste either the time or the energy to get angry or defend himself unnecessarily. Of course, he didn't know Rafe very well, and was possibly being cautious since it wouldn't do to start off on the wrong foot with a new owner. This new master/slave relationship would be a strange one, and though it was interesting to watch, the implications still troubled me. It wasn't as though they were recent acquaintances, nor was it like starting a new job. Leo *belonged* to Rafe—in body, if not in soul—and I found that idea disturbing. No doubt the horses would have had some pithy comments to make if I'd consulted their own thoughts on the subject, but I held off doing so because, as I said before, it was disturbing.

We rode on in silence for a time, but then Gerald began chattering away at something I couldn't see in the rapidly growing darkness.

"Find out anything?" I asked when he was quiet again.

"No, they say they didn't see anyone pass this way," he chirped. *"Think the big cat knows what he's doing?"*

"I have no idea," I said truthfully, *"but I certainly hope so! I mean, if he leads us on a wild-goose chase, Rafe will probably beat him to death."*

"Looks like someone already tried that—several times, in fact," Gerald commented. *"He must be pretty hard to kill."*

"Maybe," I conceded, *"but I'd still like to see to it that no one ever abused him again. Looking at the scars on him, it's nothing short of amazing that he's managed to survive this long. I wonder what he does to make people so angry with him?"*

"Well, I can tell you this much," Gerald said roundly. *"If what you said about him a while ago is true, I certainly wouldn't let him near one of my women!"*

I took his meaning instantly. *"You think jealous men did that to him? Really?"* I'd had similar thoughts, myself, of course, but for real? I didn't think so.

"Do you want any other man now that you've been with him?" Gerald asked. *"Could anyone else ever measure up? If you were to ask me, which you didn't, I'd say it's a wonder no one's ever castrated him."*

He'd even had scars there, I'd noticed. As I've mentioned before, what I didn't know about Leo would fill volumes.

"He's old, too," Gerald went on. *"He may not look it, and it may not be in actual years, but there's something about him...I can feel it. His soul seems ancient. Like an otterell's."*

Unlike many other wild creatures on Utopia, otterells were one of the few indigenous species for which there seemed to be no Earth equivalent, and for which early settlers had had to come up with an original name. They were strange beings, somewhat reminiscent of owls—especially in their reputation for wisdom, which was due, in part, to their remarkable longevity—but in appearance they were more reptilian, having scales instead of feathers. Their eyes, however, were very much like an owl's: large and deeply set in an almost flat, oval face, giving you the feeling that they could see past any sham and knew the deepest secrets of your soul. I had spoken with one once, and while he did *look* like an old sage, I reached the conclusion that he was either wise in the extreme, or he was completely crazy, like a reclusive holy man driven insane from the sheer lack of human contact. He spoke in parables and riddles, and, while I might have understood his words, his meaning was obscure. In the end, I decided that I simply wasn't enough of a philosopher to figure him out and left it at that.

But Gerald was at least partly right, for I had also noted that Leo *seemed* older than he appeared. I found it interesting that Gerald could sense it without having spent much time with him. Animals will often surprise you with their insights into humans and their behavior. Well, they surprised *me* often enough, anyway. I really couldn't vouch for anyone else, since the only other person I knew of who could talk to animals was my grandmother, and she'd been dead for many years, so I had no idea how directly she had been able to communicate with them.

"Must be awful to have been a slave for so long," I thought, *"though I've got to admit that I, for one, am very glad no one has ever castrated him."* Then it occurred to me that there were at least two castrated males in our company. *"Gee, I hope Goran and Calla aren't listening in on this conversation! Well, my half of it, anyway! That might be a sore subject for them."*

"Water under the bridge," Goran, who obviously *was* listening, put in. *"It happened so long ago, I hardly remember."*

"Ever resent it?" I inquired curiously. His casual dismissal of what most men considered to be an integral part of themselves and something to be protected at all costs surprised me. I think I would have been sorely tempted to kill anyone responsible for yanking out my ovaries, so I wouldn't have blamed any gelding I knew for not doing his level best to kick the nuts off of any human male he happened to meet, just on general principles.

"Not really," Goran said. *"I mean, I see a mare and I know that she's attractive, but that's about it. Some geldings are different that way, but really, I just don't give a shit."*

"There you go, Morgana!" Sinjar said heartily. *"A guy who isn't hot after your pretty little tail! Hey,*

maybe you'll talk to him, seeing as how you won't ever talk to me."

If Morgana had anything to say in reply to this, I must've missed it. In the conversational lull that followed, I realized that I'd much rather have been talking to Leo, which made me wish very much that Rafe had stayed home.

"Wish I could talk to Leo the way I can with you guys," I lamented. *"I could be having a terribly erotic conversation right now."*

"It's just as well," Sinjar said morosely. *"We'd have to listen in and then I, for one, would get all hot and bothered and Little Miss Frigid there would still ignore me—or kick me in the teeth if I tried anything."*

"You could try Leo's line on her," I suggested.

Sinjar's ears pricked up at this, even turning his head to eye me with significant interest. *"Oh, yeah? Might be worth a try. What is it?"*

"'I will give you joy unlike any you have ever known'," I quoted. *"It's true, too."*

"You know, it's impolite to talk to another species while I'm around," Gerald complained. *"I can't understand the horses at all. I'm only getting half of this."*

"Well, I'm afraid you'll just have to get over it!" I shot back at him. "Because I refuse to translate!"

Unfortunately, I said that last bit aloud, and while Leo might have guessed that I was addressing the squirrel that was perched on my shoulder, Rafe didn't.

"Have you gone completely mad living in that house all alone?" Rafe demanded. "First you laugh at nothing, and now you're talking either to yourself or to some imaginary person."

"All witches are insane," I replied. "Didn't you know? We'd have to be to do what we do."

Rafe's response to that was a growl of sorts. Leo remained silent, and while I would have given anything to be able to read his thoughts, it was probably best that he couldn't read mine since I *was* carrying his child! I wasn't ready to divulge that secret yet.

According to my mother, humans were pretty hard to read, anyway. She thought it was because people had too many thoughts going on at one time and had never been able to carry on telepathic conversations the way I could with the animals. Animals are more straightforward in their thinking, and, being somewhat telepathic themselves, they can communicate in ways humans could normally only guess at. Unfortunately, the fact that they can't do it across species is readily apparent, even to the most casual observer. I hoped the local animals wouldn't hit on the idea of using me as an interpreter to settle disputes, because then I'd be in the middle of even more fights than I was now. Of course, if they pissed me off too much, I could always end the conflict by killing and eating them.

"You should be a vegetarian," Gerald commented, obviously having read that thought. *"We'd be more trusting."*

"Didn't anyone ever tell you it was impolite to eavesdrop?"

"I never claimed to be polite," Gerald countered. *"I'm a squirrel, remember?"*

I'd never been around so many chatty, nosy animals before in my life! "You guys are starting to get on my nerves," I said, growling about as much as Rafe had. "Why don't all of you be quiet?"

"I haven't said a word for miles," Rafe said defensively. "You're the only one who's said anything."

"Forgive me, O exalted one!" I grumbled. Probably shouldn't have said that, since pissing Rafe off might be a bad idea with respect to Leo. Then I decided, what the hell, and finally asked the question which had been nagging at me since we began this quest. "So, Rafe. If we do manage to find your kids, how will you repay us?"

Rafe didn't reply for a moment—for once in his life, perhaps choosing his words carefully. "He is my slave, so I owe him nothing," he said at last. "You are simply helping out an old friend." He put an ironic emphasis on that last word, making me wonder why he didn't say "lover." It could have been that he didn't want Leo to know we'd been lovers once, but the reason for that escaped me.

I could have pointed out that chasing his boys through a snowy forest went above and beyond the call of duty, even for an old "friend," but knowing that Rafe could be downright bullheaded when it suited him, any argument I might have made was probably futile, anyway. *Well, so much for getting Leo in payment for services rendered,* I thought irritably. *"Crap!"*

Gerald chuckled. *"Want me to bite him?"*

"Nah, don't bother," I replied. *"It'd just piss him off even more, and he's annoying enough as it is. Any ideas as to what I ever saw in him?"*

"Not really," Gerald remarked. *"But then, I'm not a human female."*

"True," I agreed. *"I don't know if it's because of Leo and my being pregnant and all, but Rafe doesn't do a*

thing for me anymore, and, quite honestly, if he made a move on me now, I think I'd set him on fire."

Gerald seemed to think this was terribly funny, but commented, *"Must be nice to have that ability, but tell me, Tisana, have you ever actually done that to anyone?"*

"No," I admitted, *"but that doesn't mean I haven't been tempted."*

After pausing for a moment to consider this, he went on to say, *"You could roast me alive while I was sitting in a tree, couldn't you?"*

"Possibly."

Gerald didn't say anything more, but I had an idea he might be regretting all those nuts he'd thrown at me.

Chapter 5

Leo might have been able to follow a scent in the dark, and Rafe might have wanted to keep going all night, but after a few hours, the horses began to complain. Not verbally, of course, but with the occasional grunt or stumble in the way that horses often will. Max was more vocal: he sat down and began howling as though he'd stepped on a hornet's nest and was now suffering the consequences. Rafe responded by shouting at him, but I, for one, agreed that it was long past time for a break.

"I don't know about you guys," I said wearily. "But I've had just about enough for one day. It's time we stopped for the night."

I heard the swift intake of air through Rafe's teeth and waited for the inevitable acerbic comment, but he seemed to think better of it and said simply, "Very well."

We found a place beneath some thick pines where the snow wasn't quite so deep and decided to make camp there. Gerald scouted the area, trying to get some information from the local squirrels, but reported that there weren't any around. I hoped we found those boys soon, because if we were to run out of food and Rafe began firing arrows at the small animals along the way, I might have some difficulty in convincing them to share their information with me. We all had provisions in our saddlebags, and Goran was pretty well loaded down with supplies, but they wouldn't last indefinitely, and there wasn't any grazing available for the horses. Then there was the matter of having enough water to drink—and if you've ever tried melting snow for drinking water, you know that it can be a laborious task. I'd never been this way through the forest before, and had no idea what rivers or streams we might encounter along the way.

"Rafe," I ventured. "What about water? Have you ever been this way before? Are there any creeks in the direction we're headed?"

I thought he hesitated before replying. "Yes," he said curtly, "there should be water along the way. And I believe there is a stream nearby."

Of course, it was probably *frozen* water (which, for me, presented no problem, but I didn't want Rafe to know that), though a moving stream won't freeze over the way a lake will unless it's very cold, which it had been for the past few weeks.

And I was cold, too. I don't care who you are— witch, cat, or man—a ride through a wintry forest after dark will put a chill in your bones, especially your feet. Dismounting stiffly, I decided that I was going to have a campfire and some hot food, and I didn't give a damn if all the kidnappers in the world descended upon us as a result. While it most likely posed no danger because Max had scouted the surrounding area and reported that we were essentially alone in the forest, I could hardly tell Rafe that, at least not without having a few flames to "see" it in first—which was another good reason to build a fire. I'd have to remember that one.

I decided another thing, too. Along with hot food and a fire, I was going to share a tent and a bedroll with Leo, and it didn't matter what Rafe had to say about that, either. The men unsaddled the horses and put up a picket line. The others didn't seem to mind it, but Morgana flatly refused to be tied anywhere near Sinjar, so I left her loose, knowing she'd never leave me, anyway.

While the men were busy with their chores, I gathered up some branches and kindling for the fire, and then set off to locate the stream. I found it at the foot of a gentle slope, but, as I expected, it was completely frozen over. Staring at a spot near the bank, I was able to melt through to the running water underneath, but it looked too deliberate, so I melted the snow down to the water's edge to make it appear more natural.

I tried to be as unobtrusive as possible, but Max, who had just returned from squirrel-chasing duty, saw me and was duly impressed. Cocking his head to one side, he said, *"You can melt ice?"*

"Yes," I replied. *"I can melt ice."* Giving him a sidelong glance, I added, *"And I can also set things on fire."* Giving that a moment to sink in, I went on, *"Thought I told you to leave Gerald alone."*

"I'm sorry," Max said with a whine. *"But you know how it is...don't you?"*

"Not really," I said. *"Look at it this way: how would you like it if I beat up on one of your friends?"*

Max appeared thoughtful, but said: *"They'd probably deserve it. Just like I deserve it for chasing Gerald,"* he added mournfully. *"But there are some things that dogs can't help doing. I try, but I just can't!"*

"Try harder."

Eyeing me warily, Max stepped carefully down to the water's edge and began lapping up the water I'd melted for him. I'd never set him on fire, of course, but what he didn't know wouldn't hurt him. I had to keep the boys in line somehow.

Meanwhile, Morgana, knowing exactly what I was doing, had followed me down to the creek, and after drinking her fill, did her best to trample the area even further to make it appear to be a much-used watering hole. After swallowing a few sips of the icy water, I filled my canteen and then went back to tell the men where to water the other horses.

Having sent Leo and Rafe out of sight, I started the fire. I knew the animals wouldn't rat on me, and Leo probably wouldn't either, but I wasn't so sure about Rafe. This was one of those cases where what he didn't know wouldn't hurt him.

By the time the men returned, I had gotten a lively blaze started, filled a pot with meat and vegetables and snow, and then given it a good, long, hot look to hasten the cooking process, after which I set about making my bed for the night. Leo had already laid his own out on a leather pad near the fire, and I put mine right next to his, pitching the tent over both of them. Leo's reaction to the proposed sleeping arrangements was an unobtrusive, though satisfied purr. Rafe's response was yet another growl.

"You're sleeping with my slave?" he demanded, scowling at me with blatant disapproval.

"Unless you'd rather sleep with him, yourself," I retorted. "In case you've forgotten, he's been extremely ill and needs to be kept warm. And he might need me during the night."

This inspired explanation occurred to me very much on the spur of the moment, though it left out any reason why Leo hadn't needed to be kept warm while we were traveling during the day. And the way it came out, it was open to interpretation. However, since what Rafe didn't know about Leo's species would have filled volumes, I knew I could invent all sorts of peculiarities, and he'd never know the difference. If asked, I might have said something about his basal metabolic rate taking a significant drop at night, which holds true for humans, as well, but Rafe had never been an avid student of physiology.

But studious or not, he was still suspicious. "Been sleeping with him while he was in your house, as well? I wouldn't think it would be necessary," he said shortly. "Seemed warm enough in there to me."

"Yes, it is," I agreed, and went no further with my reply. It was a lie of omission, and though I knew I would be guilty of more of them before this adventure reached its end, I hoped the gods would be merciful and understanding.

The gods may have understood, but Rafe didn't seem to think my reply was adequate and pressed me for details. "So, you're saying you've never slept with him before?"

"No," I replied. "I didn't say anything about that."

He didn't seem to care for that reply, either. "You've never slept together, but now that we're out here in the snow, you're planning to bed down with him?"

"Yes," I replied irritably. I'd had just about enough interrogation for one evening, and the truth was, I was so cold and tired and hungry that I wanted nothing more than to curl up with Leo and let him send me into oblivion with that magical cock of his. Leveling a stern look at Rafe, I said sharply, "Tell me something, Rafe. Do you want us to find your boys or not?"

He seemed taken aback by this. "Of—of course," he sputtered. "That's why—"

"Then shut up and let us find them," I snapped, cutting him off in midsentence. "Who I sleep with is no business of yours, anyway."

"Well, it is if it's my slave!" he exclaimed. "Really, Tisana!"

It was the last thing I wanted to hear. Now that I'd finally found the one, he belonged to my former lover, who obviously wasn't intending to let me have him. How's that for irony? Actually, as long as I didn't hurt Leo, I couldn't see why it mattered to Rafe whether I slept with him or not. It wasn't as though he would end up maimed or anything, and the gods knew he hadn't been a virgin when I met up with him!

No, I thought as my temper heated up, the very least he could do would be to let me enjoy Leo for as long as I possibly could before he hauled him off to play exotic slave boy for Carnita. As long as Rafe refused to see this little adventure as a favor that might earn me Leo as a reward, I saw no need to sugarcoat it anymore. At the moment, I didn't give a damn how angry he got—as long as he didn't take it out on Leo.

"Listen," I said hotly, "I didn't ask to come on this rescue mission; you're the one who came begging for help, not me! The way I see it, we're all you've got right now, so if I were you, I'd keep my mouth shut. In fact, if you had any sense at all, you'd be promising me the moon and stars to help you find your boys, but, instead, here you are fussing at me for sleeping with Leo! So what if I sleep with him? It's no skin off your nose. It's not like you're my husband."

There was the slightest chance that it might have been "the woman scorned" talking there, but it wasn't just that. Had I actually married Rafe, I had no doubt whatsoever that I would have set fire to him at some point. In fact, it was a wonder he wasn't smoldering now.

As I stormed away from the cheery warmth of the campfire, it occurred to me that perhaps I should throw my weight around a little. If I played my cards right, I could come out of this deal in possession of Leo. I was pretty sure that Rafe and Leo wouldn't be able to find the boys without the aid of my animal spies and me, but the unfortunate irony was that I couldn't explain to Rafe why it was that I would be so much better at finding the kids than Leo would be alone.

Leo didn't have to worry, because he had already admitted that the scent was faint, and as the days went by, it might become even more difficult for him to follow. No one would think anything of his losing the trail, since following a scent was a relatively nonmagical way of tracking someone, and I seriously doubted that he would be burned at the stake if he failed. I knew deep down that I probably wouldn't, either, but I couldn't forget that it wasn't for failing in their duties that witches had been so persecuted in the past—it was for being witches at all; for being different, foreign, strange. Rafe's assumption that I could see things in the fire was no less magical than the ability to communicate with animals, but I had no desire to add anything more to my list of crimes.

I had walked a little apart from the men and horses, with Max following closely at my heels. I leaned against the rough bark of an alowa tree, wanting to scream, or cry, or do *something*—anything to rid myself of the impotent anger I felt! Truthfully, at that point, I'm not sure whom I was angrier with: Rafe, or the gods who had put Leo in his power.

I began to form a thought intended for Max, just to ventilate my feelings, but a light touch on my shoulder informed me that Max wasn't the only one who'd followed me.

"Tisana," Rafe began, "I—"

"Please, Rafe," I said wearily. "Just go away and leave me be."

Surprisingly, he did as I asked, leaving me alone with my thoughts.

My mother never told me how hurt she had been when my father left her behind to continue on his journey. Had she had the time to truly begin to care for him as I had with Leo, or had it been such a brief encounter that she barely remembered his face? I didn't know the answer to that, but I did know beyond a shadow of a doubt that even if Leo left right then and I never saw him again, I would remember every nuance of his behavior, every word he'd spoken in my presence, and every sensation he'd evoked within me. I loved him so deeply, it hurt.

My heart might have been aching like the devil, but, in the end, it was my stomach that got the better of me. A broken heart won't kill you, but I had a child to consider, and it wouldn't do to starve her to death.

Rafe looked up as the smell of hot food lured me back to the campfire. "Forget it, Rafe," I said bluntly. "I don't want to hear anything you have to say."

Ignoring that remark, he announced: "You may sleep with my slave, Tisana." With a glance at Leo, he added more quietly, "I believe you were right about him."

Looking up in surprise, I noted that Leo was, in fact, huddled in a blanket by the fire, trembling visibly, his teeth chattering against the rim of his cup as he attempted to drink some hot broth.

I ladled some soup out of the pot into a cup of my own and sat down on the end of my bedroll next to Leo, who leaned into me for warmth. Putting an arm around him to pull him closer, I knew it didn't matter whether he was cold or was merely pretending, because I was with him, holding him the way I wanted. Tears slid down my cheeks, and I let them fall.

Leo had been right about taking pleasure where it was offered without question, though he had failed to mention how bad it would feel when you knew it was gone for good.

Max curled up with his head in Leo's lap and let out a deep sigh. *"Is he really that cold?"* he asked.

"I don't know," I replied truthfully. *"It doesn't matter, though. We'll keep him warm anyway."*

"He's been pretty quiet for a long time," Max commented. *"Maybe he really is sick."*

"Maybe," I conceded. *"We'll see."*

Max looked up at me with dark, expressive eyes, no doubt seeing my tears. *"You love him, don't you?"*

"Yes, I do." I replied. *"Very much."*

"Love hurts, doesn't it?" Max observed, seeming unusually somber for a young dog.

"Yes, it does," I agreed. *"More than I would ever*

have imagined. Funny how you don't think about that when you're wishing for it."

"*I guess I love the boys more than I knew,*" Max said, "*because it hurts now that they're gone. I don't think I want to love anybody else.*"

"*Sometimes it comes to you, whether you wish for it or not.*" I told him. "*And when you least expect it, too.*"

"*Think we'll find them?*" Max asked.

"*I'm sure we will, Max,*" I said reassuringly. "*With your help—and Gerald's.*"

Max didn't reply, but his eyes flicked toward me as though he understood what I was getting at. Sighing again, he closed his eyes and settled down to sleep.

Sighing myself, I said quietly to Leo, "Do you think you'll be warm enough? Or are you going to have to hibernate through the night?"

"Your body will provide all the warmth I require," he replied. "I am already much warmer from having eaten the soup."

"I could use a little of that myself," I commented, giving my stew a quick stir. I took a bite, noting that while it was fully cooked, it hadn't simmered nearly as long as I would have liked. I stared into my bowl for a few moments until it began to bubble, after which I gave Leo's bowl a quick glance to warm it up. I wondered if he would notice.

Not wanting him to scald his tongue, I murmured casually, "The soup *is* pretty hot, Leo. Better be careful."

If he deemed it odd that I should warn him after he had already swallowed most of it, he said nothing, but his next sip was slightly more cautious than the previous one had been. Registering the fact that it was, indeed, much hotter, he gave me a sidelong glance with his golden eyes, and a sly smile touched his lips, curling the corner of his mouth to reveal one of his fangs.

"Witch," he whispered softly.

Nodding in reply, I took another sip from my own cup, though I believe I could have spoken aloud and Rafe wouldn't have heard me, for he had taken a seat across the campfire from us and seemed to be deep in thought, absently eating his food as though its taste, texture, and temperature meant nothing to him. It hit me belatedly that he must be thinking about his children, and I chastised myself for not having remembered that sooner. I shouldn't have been so sharp with him, should have been more understanding, and I tried to imagine how I would feel if someone had absconded with my own child.

The quick spasm of murderous rage I felt was enough to give me some idea of what Rafe was feeling, and I knew I owed him an apology.

"Rafe," I began. "I'm sorry for being so…testy. I know you must be worried about your boys."

His reply was a short nod, but I knew he understood, and perhaps even forgave me. Rafe had never been one to make speeches about how he felt; most of the time, his feelings were expressed as anger. I should have remembered that, too.

Leo finished his dinner and crawled under his blanket, leaving me to follow. I set a bowl of stew out in the snow for Max and told him to be sure to lie next to Rafe to keep him warm. The horses were dozing, and when I pulled back my own blanket, I found Gerald curled up there, already fast asleep. Nudging him aside, I lay with my back to Leo, leaving him to spoon up against me for warmth. Much as I wanted to make love with him, I didn't have much hope of that with Rafe so close by. I wondered sadly if we'd ever have the chance again, and was beginning to doubt that we would.

Not long after that, Rafe got up to put more wood on the fire, and I sent the flames leaping higher with a quick glance before snuggling down to sleep. When I heard Rafe begin snoring a short time later, I was fairly certain that Leo was asleep as well.

Until, that is, I felt him move closer and push my clothing aside. The contrast between sitting on a bedroll in the snow and then having the heat of his body pressing against my bare skin was shocking, and when he thrust his cock between my thighs, it felt quite hot, indeed. My body responded with an immediate gush of fluid that probably drenched him, though he was already dripping with that slick, intoxicating moisture of his own. I wanted nothing more than to have him inside me, warming me from within.

I could feel as well as hear him purring when he grasped my hips and pulled me back onto his stiff cock.

"You don't feel the least bit cold to me," I whispered. "In fact, you feel hot as fire."

"I was…convincing?" he inquired, nipping my earlobe gently with his fangs before teasing it enticingly with the tip of his tongue.

"Very," I replied. "In fact, you had me a little worried there for a while—and Max was, too."

"I am sorry to have caused you any distress," he said gently. "I will apologize now."

I started to assure him that he didn't need to be making any apologies, but wound up gasping, instead, as the first of many orgasms shook me, rendering me speechless.

Then he began to move, bouncing me quietly against his groin, sending shock waves running throughout my body. My mouth dropped open, panting in amazed joy as he took me higher and higher, washing away all the tiredness and pain from my body and my soul.

After a bit, Leo stopped bouncing and pulled me tightly against himself, burying his cock deep inside while he swept my inner walls with the ruffled head of his penis. I put a hand over my mouth, trying desperately not to moan, or scream, or make any sound that might give us away. Of course, his purring was probably doing just that—no matter what I did. It was a loud, persistent roar as he continued to lick my ear before moving on to my neck while caressing my nipples with his fingertips.

Reaching between my thighs, he teased me mercilessly, all the while moving his cock inside me, setting off wave after wave of mind-numbing pleasure, prolonging the effect, stimulating, delving, until I was sure I could take no more. When at last I heard the swift intake of breath that signaled his own climax, I relaxed into him, just waiting for it. He exhaled slowly as he came, spurting deep inside me, loading me up with a dose of orgasmic thunder that hit me like a bolt of lightning. I must admit, I didn't even feel the after-effects, going out like a light until the sun came up.

Chapter 6

MORNING BROUGHT WITH IT ANOTHER DAY FOR OUR quest, but as luck would have it, one that was destined to be fraught with frustration and indecision. The forest seemed ominously silent—I didn't even hear any birds chirping when I awoke—and to make matters worse, Leo had lost the scent.

It wasn't merely faint anymore, he said, it simply wasn't there. The wind had changed during the night, and what traces he had been able to catch before had all been blown away. We had never been following an actual trail, for the snow would have obscured any tracks our quarry might have made, and that scent had been our only guide. Gerald reported that he hadn't found any squirrels that knew anything at all, which did nothing to help me decide which direction to take.

While Leo cast about for the scent, I fixed breakfast and waited for the inevitable display of anger from Rafe—which never came. It was possible that Rafe wasn't worried, because he assumed that where Leo's ability might leave off, my own would kick in—which it might have done if I'd actually seen any animals to talk with. Still, the fact that he wasn't displaying any anxiety made me think that, despite his apparent need for our help, he could have made a good guess as to which direction to take on his own. He'd already admitted to having been this way before and had known what lay ahead, and I began to suspect that perhaps he knew more than he was saying, not only about who had taken the boys, but why. However, he said nothing to confirm my suspicions, so it was obviously going to be left to me to find some other means of tracking the boys.

As I packed up my gear after breakfast, I decided that, with no other animals about, what we needed was a bird—a big, high-flying bird that could see for miles and could tell us what direction to take. I had tried in the past to talk with the birds near my home, but they were a wary lot, and I had yet to make what I would call a friend of one of them. They had no problem eating the food I threw out for them, but whenever I stepped outside, they would flutter off just as if I'd screamed at them.

I'd never been sure whether they simply didn't trust me enough to listen, or were unable to grasp the idea that the thoughts I was sending to them were actually coming from me. I might have envied their ability to fly, but I certainly didn't envy their brainpower, and I've already mentioned what a waste of time it was to talk with an otterell.

But I knew I should try again, or we might never find the boys. My mother had never mentioned any enhancement of her powers after she found my father, but finding the one had changed my grandmother—or so I'd been told. Her greatest gift had been reading the thoughts of humans. She was better at reading my mother than anyone else—not surprisingly, since her power was apparently unleashed with my mother's concep-tion. There was the slightest chance that, having found Leo, I might become better at...something. Gerald's attitude toward me was certainly different, and while bird communication had always eluded me in the past, it would be extremely useful now. If I could only find a cooperative bird....

Once mounted and ready to travel once again, Rafe simply looked at me and asked, "Which way?"

To which I replied candidly, "I have absolutely no idea. Other than the fact that we've seemed to be headed in a fairly straight line to the east, I couldn't say."

"Couldn't, or wouldn't?"

This surprised me, even coming from Rafe. "I would tell you if I knew," I said evenly, doing my best to contain my anger. "I simply do not know."

"But you found that other child," he said accusingly, his own anger now coming quickly to the surface. "Why can you not look into the fire and see where my sons have gone?"

"I didn't see it in the fire," I began, exasperated with him for continuing to harp on that subject. "I just—"

"Tell him to shut up, and I'll take you in the direction we need to go," Morgana said suddenly.

"You know?"

"Yes, I know," she said.

"How?"

"I can smell their horses," she replied.

"Why didn't you say anything before?"

"You seemed to be doing fine without me until now," she remarked. *"But the big tomcat doesn't have as good a nose as I do."*

"Well, that's good enough for me," I said gratefully. *"Lead on."*

Morgana moved off through the snow at a slow, heavy trot, leaving Leo and Rafe behind with the packhorse.

Sinjar began to make a move to follow us, but Rafe curbed him sharply. I heard the stallion's grumbling protest and turned in the saddle.

"Follow me," I said over my shoulder. "I can see it now." I wasn't sure exactly how a real seer would have put that, and thought I ought to work on my dramatic presentation, but they followed me without much hesitation, anyway.

"No fire this time?" Rafe inquired with a smirk as he rode up beside me.

"No fire," I said firmly, though I'll admit I was sorely tempted to start one—on the seat of his pants, perhaps—but Sinjar wouldn't have been pleased. It occurred to me that Leo had, perhaps, imprinted the wrong scent before we started, though, in truth, the boys had been the only choice we had.

"When you were following the scent, could you smell their horses?" I asked him.

"No," Leo replied. "The horses we are riding would interfere."

"Hmm," I remarked. "Interesting…" By that, I could only assume that Morgana had been right about having a better nose—or perhaps I should say, a better nose for following horses.

We had been following Morgana's lead for some time, when, with a loud flap of its wings and the resultant shower of snow, an enormous bird took flight just ahead of us. I didn't see that we had much to lose, so I sent a call out to it.

Now, I will say this, if you've never seen a bird do a double take in midflight, let me tell you, it looks pretty funny. If I hadn't known better, I'd have said the thing was drunk.

"Who spoke?" the bird said, circling back around to make a pass above us.

"I did," I replied, waving at the bird. What Rafe thought about that was anyone's guess, though perhaps he thought I was warding off falling feathers or bird droppings.

As the creature settled in the branches of a tall hemlock tree ahead of us, I could see what it was. We had always called them vultures, since they were carrion eaters like those on Earth and were comparable in size, but the resemblance ended there. While the true vultures had been rather ugly birds with scrawny, naked necks, these were actually quite beautiful.

The females are normally a dull, grayish blue, but the males wear deep purple plumage during the winter months, and, in spring, turn a lovely shade of lavender. Added to that, their feathers have a metallic sheen that reflects the sun so brightly it almost hurts your eyes to look at them. Their delicately streamlined heads are equipped with large, keen eyes and are set upon graceful, slender necks even more aristocratic than Carnita's. They had always been very rare in my corner of the forest, so I'd never spoken to one before and had only been able to catch fleeting glimpses of them.

I hoped this one would be smarter than the average bird—the fact that he heard me call and had responded immediately spoke of a more intelligent nature than most—either that or my "bird voice" really *had* improved. I reined in Morgana and stared up at the beautiful creature.

"Ah, one of the interlopers," he said. *"Go warily through this forest, for dangers abound."*

"I can believe that," I remarked. *"Have you seen others of our kind pass through here in the past few days?"*

"Yes," the bird replied. *"I have seen others."*

"With young ones?"

"Yes. There were two young ones." The bird paused, making an odd cackling sound. *"They would have been good to eat."*

"I'm sure they would have," I said, trying to sound gracious, but it took all I had to suppress a shudder of revulsion. Then I remembered that carrion eaters don't kill. *"They weren't dead, were they?"* I asked anxiously.

"No, they were living." The vulture ruffled its feathers and settled on its perch. *"Pity."*

"Yes, well, we would much prefer them to still be alive," I said briskly. *"Can you tell us where they are now?"*

"I could, I suppose," the vulture replied. *"It might be to my advantage."*

"And how is that?"

"They were in a company of well-armed fighting men. In battle, you would be no match for them, therefore, they might kill some of you."

"And?" I prompted.

"I would eat well for many days on your carcass—as would my mate and her young."

"Well, now, that's not very nice!" I chastised him.

"I must think of my clan," he said. *"They must survive."*

"Of course," I said. Thinking quickly, I added, *"If we were to ambush and kill them, I would have no problem leaving those fighting men there for you to feast upon."*

The vulture turned aside in a disdainful gesture. *"Too tough. You and the young ones would be far more tender."*

I was tempted to set fire to the branch he was sitting on for voicing that opinion, but tried to see it as a compliment, instead. *"But they are much larger and would last longer,"* I pointed out.

"True," he said, though he sounded reluctant to admit it. *"One in my position cannot always be selective."*

"Well, I suppose I can't blame you for trying."

"It's all I can do," he said. *"We learn patience very young, but there are times when I feel compelled to simply kill something, instead."*

"Never thought of arranging battles to come out to your advantage, then?"

"There are seldom battles amongst you humans. Pity," he said again. *"Wish you were more warlike. Your men train for war, but you are still much too peaceful for our purposes—and the fact that you tend to bury your dead is a most annoying waste of food."*

"I can see where it would be," I agreed. *"But forgive me if I find the idea of being eaten rather unsettling."*

"But you would be dead," the bird said reasonably. *"What would it matter?"*

"Oh, I suppose it wouldn't, but it still gives me the creeps."

"The creeps?"

"Yes," I replied. *"You know, something that makes your skin crawl to think of?"*

"Like having one's feathers plucked?" the vulture suggested.

"Yes," I replied. *"Exactly like that. Would you like to be eaten?"*

"No, I do not believe I would," he replied after reflecting on this for a moment. *"But one day, I am certain I will be."*

I took a peek at Rafe, who was carefully pulling an arrow from his quiver. *"Then might I suggest that you take off now,"* I said calmly, *"or we may be having you for lunch."*

I could feel the wind as his wings beat the air when he departed.

Not surprisingly, Rafe was irate. "Couldn't you have kept that thing bewitched for a moment or two longer?" he demanded. "Carnita has wanted some of those purple feathers for a long time."

"She'll have to wait a bit longer, then," I replied. "Besides, I have no control over birds, Rafe. I didn't do a thing to it."

"I don't believe that for a moment," Rafe snorted. "I've seen you bewitch animals before."

"I do not 'bewitch' anything," I said loftily. "I merely look at them. If they don't fly away, it is because I don't shoot at them."

I stole a quick glance at Leo and caught a glimpse of his smile as he turned to hide it. At that moment, the only thought in my head was that it would have been nice to ride double with him so I could have had my arms around him throughout this long, cold journey. It occurred to me to ask Morgana to pretend to be lame, but it would have slowed us down too much. *Pity,* I thought, echoing the vulture.

Rafe growled as he let his arrow slide back into the quiver.

"Or growl," I added. "You know, you'd be a much better hunter if you didn't do that."

"I hunt very well, thank you," he shot back. "When I don't have you here to warn the animals that I'm about to shoot at them."

The look I gave him would have withered an oak. "Did you see me do anything at all?"

"No," he replied, "but you are a witch, Tisana. You are capable of many things. I've seen too much to not know that about you—and the rest of your kind."

He had an odd expression on his face, which prompted me to say, "I didn't bewitch you, Rafe. Whatever you may think of me, believe me, I wouldn't do that, even if I could."

"Yes, well, just don't bewitch my slave," he cautioned. "Nor do I want you giving him any of your radical ideas about abolishing slavery."

"Abolishing slavery?" I echoed. "Radical? Really, Rafe, you haven't been keeping up with your history lessons! I wouldn't be the first to want slavery abolished, nor will I be the last!" I also thought he should have considered that possibility before he brought Leo to me for healing. Given my "radical ideas," I might have sent Leo on his way with renewed health and the promise of freedom. "On the other hand," I remarked casually, "Leo would be a great help to me. Maybe I should buy him from you."

Rafe waved aside this possibility as being remote. "You have no money and nothing of any value," he reminded me. "And Carnita would not wish to sell him, in any case."

"No, but you might," I muttered.

"What was that?" Rafe demanded.

"I merely said that you might consider it at some point," I said carefully. "You may decide you don't want Carnita to have such a slave."

"Oh, and why not?"

"He has a certain…appeal to females."

Rafe regarded Leo with scorn. "He just looks like a big cat."

"True, but you know how women love their cats."

"Carnita would never stoop to loving a slave," he scoffed. "She knows her own value too well."

"Well, don't say I didn't warn you," I said. "You may think he just looks like a big cat, but, trust me, he is much more than that."

"You've simply become attached to him, as you would any pet," Rafe said knowingly.

I was looking right at Leo and wondering what he might make of being referred to as a pet, so I saw the sudden curious intake of breath through his nostrils at the precise moment it occurred. He smelled something.

"Have you got the scent again?" I asked him.

Nodding, he said, "It is not the children, but it is familiar." He pointed into the depths of the forest to the south. "It is there," he went on. "Faint, but growing stronger." As the wind blowing from that direction had been responsible for scattering the original trail, it now seemed to be making up for it by bringing us a new one to follow. "Are you sure it's the same people we've been after?" I asked.

"I believe it is," Leo replied. "Their trail must have turned here, and the wind is now blowing the scent back to us."

"Either that, or they've circled around to ambush us," I remarked, remembering what the vulture had said. He'd been hinting that we might be in for some trouble, but his need for food had kept him from coming right out and saying it. "This forest is perilous, Rafe," I said earnestly. "If we're attacked, we'll all be in danger."

"So?" As Rafe was sitting there with a knife at his belt, a bow and quiver on his back, a sword in his scabbard, and a shield on his arm, he obviously felt perfectly capable of defending himself. I had my own means of defense, but Leo didn't have anything but his fists.

"Leo needs a sword," I said plainly. "Or at least a knife."

Rafe's expression was thunderous. "I will not give my slave a weapon to use against me," he said. Aiming a warning eye at me, he added, "And you will not either, Tisana."

"You always were an idiot," I remarked. "Too narrow-minded to see the entire picture."

"Which is?" he prompted.

"That there were at least four men who took your boys, Rafe," I said patiently. "What's to say that they haven't gotten wind of our pursuit and that their leader hasn't sent two or three of them back to take us out—or at the very least, try to slow us down? And remember this, while they're on horseback in the forest, they're vulnerable to attack themselves, but once inside a stronghold, we may never be able to take the boys back.

We need to be able to do more than just track them. We may have to fight." He seemed to be wavering ever so slightly, so I added, "Rafe, if you had done such a thing and assumed you'd be followed, what would you do?"

He sighed grudgingly. "That very thing," he admitted. "You are right, Tisana. The concern for my children has clouded my judgment in this matter."

"So, give Leo a weapon," I prompted, "and while you're at it, you might also think about untying his horse from your saddle. He will not attempt to escape."

"How can you be so sure?" Rafe demanded suspiciously. "With a horse and sword? I'd be long gone, myself."

"With very little food and nowhere to go?" I scoffed. "He isn't stupid, Rafe! He knows he's better off staying with us. But in the event that we are attacked, he must be free."

"May I remind you that he is a slave, Tisana," Rafe said. "He may not have been trained in the use of weapons."

"You told me he was a good hunter and fighter when you brought him to me, Rafe," I reminded him. "Didn't you ask for more details when you bought him?"

Seeming to ignore this remark, Rafe turned to Leo. "Which weapon would you choose?"

"I would take the sword," Leo replied. "Though I am proficient with a bow and knife, as well."

What Rafe thought of that, he didn't say, but with no more than the raising of an eyebrow, he unbuckled the scabbard. "What about you, Tisana?" he asked with a trace of amusement. "Going to rely on your wits, or would you like the knife?"

"My wits will do just fine, Rafe," I replied. "Besides, you might need the knife if they get too close for you to use your bow."

Leveling a stern glare at Leo, Rafe said, "Have I your word that you will not attempt to escape or to use that sword against us?"

"You do," Leo said simply.

Rafe handed him the sword in a manner which seemed almost ceremonial, though it was perhaps more significant in other ways. Words like honor, faith, and trust flitted through my mind, and I knew that Leo would prove to be worthy of all of those things, though Rafe had no way of knowing it at the time. He was simply trusting my own judgment of Leo, rather than his own, and I had to admire him for that. Of course, Leo might have had something to do with it himself. Certainly, he could pretend to be more cold or sick than he truly was, but an inherent honesty seemed to shine out from his golden eyes when he spoke solemnly. He should have been a leader of men, not a slave, and that quality in him was apparent even to the most casual observer. Leo had not been a slave by birth, and he had a certain integrity about him that seemed to envelop him like a cloak. Rafe had not spent a great deal of time with his new slave, but perhaps he could still see it, for, sitting there on his horse with a sword in his hand, Leo looked almost kingly. It was something in the set of his shoulders or the tilt of his chin—I couldn't have said, exactly, but it was there, nonetheless. Carnita might see him as a toy, and I might see him as a lover, but Rafe could look him in the eye, one fighting man to another, and know him for the warrior he was.

Rafe held his gaze for a moment, then untied the rein from his saddle and tossed it to Leo. I thought he might remind Leo not to run off, but he didn't, obviously having taken Leo at his word. How Rafe could continue to regard him as property after that, I couldn't begin to guess. Perhaps he didn't. Calla heaved a sigh of relief, for being tied like an untrustworthy colt had irked him considerably.

"So, forward into the fray, then?" Rafe said amiably.

"Forward into the fray," I agreed.

Leo nodded. "They are not far and cannot know that we are coming this way. If we wait for them, they may ride right to us."

"So, you think we should plan an ambush ourselves?" I asked. "That sounds good, but I wouldn't like the idea of doing such a thing, only to discover that we had ambushed some innocent people."

"True," Rafe agreed. "We must be certain."

"But how can we be?" I asked.

Rafe rubbed his chin thoughtfully. "Too bad we haven't got a scout of some kind," he mused. "It would be very useful to have one who could identify the men."

It occurred to me then that we did have someone who could spy for us; it just so happened that he was a dog.

"What do you think, Max?" I asked. *"Could you go on ahead and get a look at them?"*

"Oh, you bet I could!" Max replied, dancing with excitement.

"Well, be careful, and try not to let them see you," I advised.

"I will!" he said firmly and shot off into the woods, kicking up a spray of snow behind him as he went.

Rafe's head swung around suddenly as he watched him go. "What's gotten into him, I wonder?"

"Probably saw a dmisk," I said casually. "You know how dogs are."

"He might give us away," Rafe said ruefully. "We shouldn't have brought him with us."

"Oh, I think he'll be fine," I said.

"Saw that in the fire, did you?" Rafe suggested.

"Really, Rafe!" I said disgustedly. "I've never seen things in the fire! Will you please forget it?"

Rafe looked at me pointedly. "I know full well you have powers which you don't advertise, Tisana, which is one thing that has always irritated me about you. You never trusted me enough to tell me."

I couldn't argue with that, because it happened to be true. I'd told Leo some things, of course, but even he didn't know everything. The truth was, I didn't trust much of anyone, which may have been the result of the tenuous acceptance accorded to witches—as though we were nothing more than a necessary evil. And we weren't evil at all; it's just that we might be perceived that way. After all, my mother and grandmother could read people's minds. How might that talent be subverted and used for evil purposes? No, it was best to keep quiet. Animals knew too many things that humans would prefer no one else knew—and their loyalty to their owners might not be enough to prevent them from telling tales. They seldom lied, but still…

"No, Rafe," I said evenly. "I didn't tell you everything. Had you been the one, I might have."

"Touché," he said, acknowledging my hit. "Perhaps neither of us has much cause to trust the other."

"Perhaps not."

No one said anything for a moment or two; we merely sat there on our horses, as though waiting for Max to return with a report. Of course, I knew that was what I was doing and was why I wasn't making any moves, but it did make me wonder about Rafe and Leo. On the other hand, given Rafe's position of authority, I suppose we might have been waiting for his orders. Or Rafe might have come to the conclusion that Leo should have been leading us and was waiting for him to say something. Either way, it seemed odd. Then I realized that they were both staring at me as though I'd suddenly grown horns.

A soft peck on my shoulder made me turn around, and I found myself looking right into the dark, round eyes of the purple vulture, who was now perched on the back of my saddle. How he had managed to land there without spooking Morgana, I have no idea, but there he was. Poor Gerald had seen him, however, and after a frozen moment of terror, with a loud squeak, took a dive into my cloak.

"I thank you for the warning," the bird said. *"I am called Royillis. I am now in your debt and will help you as well as I am able."*

"Don't shoot at it, Rafe," I cautioned him immediately.

"I wasn't planning to," he assured me. "You've bewitched that bird, haven't you?"

I began to protest that I could do no such thing when it occurred to me that it was easier than admitting that I'd talked with him. "I—yes," I said suddenly. "Sure, I bewitched him. I do it all the time. Maybe I can talk him out of a feather or two for Carnita. Just don't kill him."

Then another thought occurred to me. "Think Carnita would trade some of those purple feathers for Leo?"

"Why do you want my slave?" Rafe asked pointedly.

"Oh, I don't want him," I lied. "I just want him to have his freedom."

"Planning to free all the slaves one at a time, then, are you?" he said dryly.

"Maybe."

"I'll ask Carnita," he said. "In the meantime, what are you planning to do with that bird?"

"Nothing in particular," I said. "Animals just take to me, that's all. Hadn't you ever noticed it before?"

"I suppose so," he said, glancing about me. "You do seem to have accumulated quite a following."

"It is because she is kind to them," Leo said quietly. "I have seen it."

Rafe shot a surprised and surly look at Leo, the way any slave owner would who did not expect that his slave would speak unless spoken to. But Leo had done just that.

"She is kind to all living things," he went on, "and she does not treat them the way that most humans do. She treats them as equals."

Leo was looking right at Rafe when he said that, meeting his eye with a steadfast gaze. The "not as slaves," was left unsaid, but was easily understood— even by someone as bullheaded as Rafe.

I waited breathlessly for Rafe's explosion of anger at Leo for forgetting his own, lowly status. But this time, Rafe surprised me.

"She does at that," he said equably. "Now if we could only teach her to treat humans that way."

Of course, I knew which human he was referring to. "Meaning yourself, I suppose?"

"Myself and others," Rafe replied. "You tend to act as though you were above us, Tisana. All witches do, or so I'm told, which is why we sometimes resent you."

"I don't know that I feel that way precisely," I said, choosing my words with care. "I simply see things differently, is all."

"More enlightened, perhaps?" he ventured, though the slight sneer on his lips made it seem less of a compliment and more of a slur.

"Perhaps," I conceded. "But you're the one who said that, I didn't."

"Still, that may be why you are better able to get along with slaves and animals," he suggested. "We mere humans don't warrant such treatment."

Royillis interrupted our argument by nudging me with his beak. *"They are coming."*

"Rafe," I said trying to keep my voice steady. "We can argue later, but right now, we're about to be ambushed. Don't you think we should, you know, hide?"

"And how would you know that?" he scoffed.

"A big purple bird told me!" I shouted in reply, wheeling Morgana around to head for cover. "And if you don't believe that, ask Max!" Max was on his way back, leaping through the snow into the clearing in which we stood.

"There are three of them!" he reported. *"And all of them big and mean!"*

"Swords or bows?"

"Both," he replied. *"And shields, too! We're in big trouble, aren't we?"*

"Maybe so," I replied. *"Keep yourself safe!"*

I'd never fought in a skirmish of any kind, and I wasn't looking forward to it. Leo, however, appeared to be delighted at the prospect. Drawing his sword with a flourish, he put a surprised Calla into a spin just as the three horsemen burst through the pines at the edge of the clearing. Calla leaped forward under Leo's spur, surging through the snow to meet our attackers with a clash of steel that sent sparks flying from their blades.

Only one of the men stayed behind to engage Leo, while the other two rode hard for Rafe. Apparently they knew exactly who they were up against, and also which one of us was Rafe. Of course that wouldn't have taken much brainpower to figure out, since Leo was obviously not human and I was just as obviously not male. Royillis launched himself from his perch on my saddle and soared after them, driving his sharp beak into the sword arm of the nearest rider, a big, burly, dark-bearded man on a huge bay, momentarily distracting him from his murderous charge, but, unfortunately, not causing him to drop his weapon.

Sinjar turned and planted his hooves firmly in the snow, awaiting the impact of sword on sword—except Rafe didn't have a sword, since he'd given it to Leo. He'd drawn his bow, however, and though the first and only arrow he managed to get off was a good shot, his opponent was able to deflect it with his shield. Not having time to draw his bow again, Rafe was now left to challenge two swordsmen with only his knife. Rafe was a good fighter, and he might have done well against them anyway, but I decided to even the odds, staring at the bearded man's blade until it turned red-hot. With a loud oath, he flung it from his hand. It sizzled when it hit the snow, sending up a cloud of steam where it fell.

Meanwhile, Leo was engaged in battle with his own opponent, and I'll admit that the temptation to simply sit back and watch him was strong, for in battle he was breathtaking. He had no shield but didn't seem to need one; his sword was a flashing blur as it moved with a speed that I wouldn't have believed possible if I hadn't seen it with my own eyes. I'd never seen a more skillfully wielded blade, and Calla was in his element, leaning into the other horse and pushing him back toward the trees.

Unfortunately, our opponents must have been wearing some sort of armor under their tunics, for I noted that several of Leo's thrusts were being deflected. Royillis followed up his attack on the dark-haired man, but the other rider, a longhaired blond on a rangy chestnut, drove in on Rafe with a killing thrust.

I thought Rafe was done for, but I had reckoned without Sinjar—who was proving once again that he was so much more than an amusing companion. Rearing up to his full height, he struck at the chestnut horse, driving him back, cancelling the blond's advantage. When Sinjar landed, however, the blond's sword engaged Rafe's knife hand once more, leaving it red with blood, and, again, the situation appeared to be pretty grim. In desperation, Rafe began fighting more with his shield than the knife, though he couldn't possibly hope to defeat his opponent in that manner. I tried to heat up the sword, but it was moving so fast, I couldn't seem to focus on it well enough to do it. Rafe needed a sword, and badly.

Royillis was keeping the other rider well occupied for the moment, so I decided it was safe to make a run for the fallen sword. Remembering where it had landed, and knowing that the snow would have cooled it enough to handle by then, I urged Morgana in that direction. She was reluctant at first, but went on anyway, kicking up clouds of snow as she ran. Gerald took one look out of the front of my cloak and bailed out with another loud squeak, scampering off through the snow to the relative safety of the trees.

Pulling Morgana to a sliding stop as we reached the place where the sword lay, I leaped from her back and began frantically digging through the snow to find it. Rafe and Leo were both pretty busy at the time and probably didn't see what I was doing, but Sinjar did.

"No!" Sinjar screamed at me. *"We can do this, Tisana! Stay back!"*

Ignoring his warning, I kept on digging and, suddenly, the blade was in my hand. It felt warm through my gloves, but I knew I could handle it without any danger—at least not from the heat. Unfortunately, despite Royillis's best efforts at distraction, the blade's rightful owner saw me with his sword and spurred his horse in my direction, obviously intending to ride me down to retrieve it. Max was between the oncoming foe and me, and I screamed at him to move out of the way.

But Max was a tough, courageous little hound and, standing his ground, he made a leap for the big bay's throat at the last second. It might not have been enough to cause any damage, but it was enough to turn the horse and rider away from me slightly, and when they passed by, Morgana went after them with teeth bared. She caught them, too, biting the bay horse hard by the tail as

WARRIOR 143

I made a run for it, my legs churning through the snow as I headed for Rafe.

Sinjar apparently saw me coming, for he backed away from the other horse and rider so quickly that Rafe was nearly unseated. Rafe's opponent lost his balance and nearly fell as well, having been carried along by the momentum of a violent swing at a target that was no longer within his reach. Leaping through the snow, Sinjar ran to me, and I held up the sword by the blade without fear, knowing that he would not miss. Rafe reached out to grasp the hilt as they swept past me and then rounded on the two riders. Sinjar's blow hadn't done much more than make the chestnut angry, and I could hear him cursing as he ran, threatening Sinjar with every dire fate known to horsedom—not the least of which was having his balls ripped off. The big bay had shaken off Max, who had kept the horse occupied, but had by no means incapacitated him. Royillis was still harassing the rider, and Morgana was snapping at the bay's hindquarters, but then, suddenly, with a fist clenched tightly around the hilt of his knife, the man struck the bird with a stunning blow, sending purple feathers flying through the air to land scattered about on the snow. That done, he came after me.

Standing there as he rode down on me again, time seemed to slow to a crawl. Morgana was behind them with no hope of catching up before they reached me. I was no longer in possession of a conventional weapon of any kind and couldn't even seem to remember how to shoot fire from my eyes. Instead, I merely gazed past them and watched as Leo's sword at last found the chink in the breastplate of his opponent's armor and slid through it effortlessly to pierce his heart. On the other side of the clearing, the blond's sword engaged Rafe's, and there now seemed to be nothing between me and death at the hands of the oncoming rider but a few yards of snow-covered ground. Out of the corner of my eye I saw Calla spin away, withdrawing Leo's blade from his victim's body as it fell.

Leo saw me then and didn't hesitate for a moment. Drawing back his arm, he launched his sword, and I watched as it flew, hilt over blade, flashing in the sunlight until it hit my attacker in the back with enough force to burst right through the middle of his chest. Then, seemingly out of nowhere, Max charged in again to seize the galloping horse by the nose, turning him sharply to keep him from running me down. Having followed the flight of the blade, Leo and Calla were upon them in seconds, and the big cat snatched his sword from yet another slain opponent's body that stained the pure white of the snow with a spray of crimson as it fell.

But the fight was far from over and, with a roar, Leo wheeled Calla around and together they rode to Rafe's aid. The blond rider heard the roar and, seeing their charge, was momentarily distracted—which was all the advantage Rafe needed to slip under his guard. Leo was right behind him in moments, and the man fell, pierced by both blades at once. The impact of Leo's thrust at a dead run drove his sword right through the chain mail and sent the man flying from the saddle, only to be slammed against the trunk of a large pine. That impact alone probably would have been enough to kill him, but I was pretty sure he was already dead.

I glanced around the clearing, taking in the sight of the three dead men, their riderless horses, and one large, stunned purple bird that was attempting to right himself in the deep snow. Max was grinning hugely and wagging his tail in victory. Gerald was nowhere to be seen, and Morgana, having bitten the bay on the butt again, trotted up to me seeming terribly pleased with herself. Rafe was taking a moment to bind up his bleeding wrist, and Leo—oh, my God, Leo!—was cantering toward me with his blood-stained sword held high, his hair flung out behind him in the wind, and joy shining out from his eyes—the very essence of a triumphant hero. Flinging his sword into the air once again with a shout of laughter, he caught it easily as it returned to earth before swinging it unerringly into its scabbard with a movement that spoke of years of practice. No, this man was no slave, he was a warrior, and I gazed up at him with every ounce of my love for him written plainly on my face.

Rafe rode up a moment later, but I didn't even look in his direction, for I was still staring at Leo, speechless with admiration.

"Are you all right, Tisana?" Rafe called out as he approached.

"Just fine," I said absently, my eyes never once leaving Leo's face. By the gods, he was magnificent!

"Well, then, mount up and let's get going," Rafe said curtly. "Though we probably should gather up their weapons first, since we may need them before this is over." When I didn't move, he said again, "Are you sure you're all right, Tisana?"

"Yes," I replied. I glanced over at Royillis, who was

now standing upright, but still seemed a bit woozy. That he was also rather tattered was a given.

"Well, come on then!" Rafe urged. "We still have to catch the rest of them!"

"Rafe," I said suddenly, and rather breathlessly, "do you think Carnita would let me have Leo if I gave her the whole bird?"

Chapter 7

ROYILLIS HAD PROBABLY SAVED ALL OF OUR SKINS AND deserved nothing less than our undying gratitude, but, given the circumstances, I think I could be forgiven for blurting out such nonsense.

"I doubt it," Rafe replied grimly. "Especially now that she's gotten a look at him."

"Now wait a minute, Rafe! I distinctly remember you saying that he just looked like a big cat," I reminded him. "What's the matter? Change your mind about that?"

Rafe's response was more of a grumble than actual words.

"I wouldn't let her have him if I were you, Rafe," I said, wagging my head. "He's too—"

"Save it for later," Rafe said, cutting me off. "We've got to get moving."

"Okay then," I said. "But I promise you, you'll be sorry!" Starting toward Royillis, I added, "You guys can go get their weapons, but I'm going to gather up those loose feathers! I've never had anything of any value in my life, and I'm not passing up the opportunity."

"I'm not really sure they're worth all that much," Rafe began. "I only—"

"I don't care!" I declared. "I'm taking them anyway! You go get all the swords and knives you think you'll need—Leo and I could both use shields, too—and we might as well take their horses while we're at it. Spoils of war and all that, you know! And remember, we might have killed these three, but there may have been more than the four in their party that Toraga saw. We probably haven't seen the worst of it yet. And, Rafe, you'd better let me see your hand—let's not have any macho 'it's only a scratch' stuff—you're bleeding."

Rafe, unfortunately, zeroed in on the one part of my little tirade that I wished he hadn't heard. "Toraga?" he echoed, dismounting. "Do you mean to say that the boy's *dog* told you?" He was staring at me as though I'd lost my mind, which was wearing thin, so I assumed a similar expression and aimed it right back at him.

"Were there any other witnesses that you know of?" I snapped, pulling out my medicine pouch.

"Well, no," he conceded, backing off, "but do you mean to say that instead of seeing it in the fire, you were talking to the dogs?"

Rolling my eyes, I nodded glumly. "That's my claim to fame, Rafe," I admitted. "I can communicate telepathically with animals."

I could almost see the wheels turning in his head as I tended to his injured wrist; fortunately, it really was only a scratch. "That explains a lot," he said at length. "You don't bewitch the animals, you actually talk with them." He paused to think a moment longer before adding, "But the flames rose when you were staring into the fire. How do you explain that?"

"Do I have to tell you that one, too?" I moaned. "Really, Rafe, I'd much rather—"

"Just tell me, Tisana."

At that point my blossoming entrepreneurial spirit

kicked in and, cocking a speculative eye at him, I said archly, "What's it worth to you?"

"Nothing more than the knowledge," he replied. If he wasn't being honest with me, his expression certainly didn't give him away. Nope, couldn't get Leo from him that way.

"Well, there go all of my secrets, then," I said ruefully. "But, please, Rafe, could you at least promise me you'll keep quiet about all of this?"

Obviously I shouldn't have said that, since he replied, "If you make it worth my while." He was smiling, but somehow, I knew he meant it.

Peering at him disdainfully, I said, "Well, you can just forget it then. It's something you don't need to know." I looked up to see Gerald bounding across the snow toward us. *"Hey, Gerald!"* I said. *"I see you made it through the battle all right and tight! I don't suppose you'd give me a hand picking up these feathers, would you?"*

"Sure thing, Tisana!" he said brightly. *"The big cat put on quite a show, didn't he? Made ol' what's-his-name look like a regular bejeteil."*

I gave a shout of laughter, since bejeteils were a species of small, furry creatures that were well-known for their ineptitude when it came to defending their territory. When confronted, they usually gave up and played dead—after that, they simply moved on to live somewhere else. They might not have been particularly brave, but there certainly were a lot of them around. Of course, Gerald hadn't actually made a stand of any kind himself—and had lived to tell about it, so I suppose there was some logic in making a run for it in times of trouble.

From the look in his eye, it was fairly obvious that Leo had some idea of the nature of the exchange that had just occurred between Gerald and me, but he had sense enough to keep quiet about it when Rafe, again, demanded to know what was so damned funny.

"You don't need to know that, either," I said haughtily and began to trudge through the snow to where Royillis was sitting. He appeared to be feeling much better and seemed especially pleased when I informed him that we'd killed all three of the men and also that we had no intention of stopping to bury them.

"Then you may take as many of my feathers as you like," he said graciously. *"I shall be molting soon, anyway."*

"I wish I'd thought of that before," I said candidly. *"You had me worried there for a minute! Still, you lost an awful lot of feathers! Are you sure you can fly?"*

"Yes," he assured me. *"My wings are undamaged. He hit me in the head, actually."*

"Hard-headed, then?" I inquired.

"Quite so," he replied.

I reached out and lifted his head with a finger beneath his beak. Scrutinizing him carefully, I was able to report that while his head didn't appear to be damaged significantly, he did, indeed, have a small area of swelling beneath his left eye.

"It will pass," Royillis said dismissively. *"I have recovered from far more serious injuries."*

"Well, you might consider leaning your head against an icicle for a while," I advised. "It might keep it from getting any worse."

"I thank you," he said politely with a slow blink of his large eyes. *"But now I must take my leave."*

"Hey, why don't you come with us?" I asked. *"You're pretty handy in a fight. We could use you. We're trying to find his children,"* I added, with a gesture in Rafe's direction. *"These men we killed were some of the ones who kidnapped them."*

Royillis was sympathetic to our cause, but reminded me that he had his own family to consider.

"But we've left them well provided for," I pointed out. *"We carry food with us, too, so you'd be well fed."*

"True," he conceded. *"Very well, then. I will consult with my mate and possibly join up with you again. If I do not return, I wish you good fortune."*

Waving at him as he flapped his huge wings and flew away, I commented to no one in particular, "Beautiful, isn't he?"

"Really, Tisana!" Rafe exclaimed. "We could have used that bird! Why didn't you ask him to help us?" While his words didn't convey his sarcasm, his tone of voice certainly did, which made it obvious that he still wasn't convinced. Perhaps telling him my secrets wouldn't have had too many repercussions after all.

"I did," I replied. "He's gone to ask his wife's permission."

Leo made a heroic effort to control his reaction but couldn't quite manage it and roared with helpless laughter. Rafe began scowling at him and probably would have made some curt remark except that Gerald, in the meantime, had gathered up all of Royillis's stray feathers and chose that moment to hop over to hand them to me. Well, he didn't actually hand them to me because, instead of his paws, he had used his cheek pouches to carry them in, so when he jumped up onto my shoulder, he looked as if he had a pair of shiny purple feather dusters sticking out of his mouth.

Rafe took one look at Gerald and gave up even trying to appear stern. Quickly mounting and turning Sinjar, he rode off to catch one of the other horses, but I could see his shoulders shaking as he went. Sinjar—whom I *could* hear—was chuckling to the point of succumbing to a coughing fit, while Max sat there and grinned.

"Thanks, Gerald," I said, retrieving the feathers from his pouches. *"I think we needed that."* He gave a pleased twitch of his tail in response and scampered over to the edge of the trees to nibble on a nut, and, for once, Max didn't chase him. I took a handkerchief from my pocket and folded the feathers up in it carefully before stowing them in my saddlebag. Then I looked up at Leo, who was still sitting there on Calla, smiling broadly. "You really were something out there, Leo," I remarked. "I'm glad you were on our side."

"I will always be on your side, my lovely witch," he said softly, "it is for you that I fight, and no other. You are very brave, as well, though you should be more careful." He paused for a moment, as his smile grew even wider. "Especially now that you carry my child."

My jaw dropped in surprise. "And just how would you know that?" I demanded when I found my voice again. Considering what we'd been up to for the past month, he might have guessed, but the funny thing was that he didn't seem to be guessing; he seemed to know.

"I cannot explain it anymore than you can explain this gift you have of communicating with animals," he said. "I simply saw you standing there in the snow as that outlaw galloped toward you, and I knew." As I watched, I saw a fleeting glimpse of the horror he must have felt pass over him at the mere thought of what might have happened to me—and to our child. "That knowledge gave me increased strength in my arm and a greater keenness in my eyes. I knew I would not miss, for you are my mate, Tisana, and it is my purpose to protect you."

Gazing up at him while my eyes filled with tears, I said, hopelessly, "I may be your mate, Leo, but that doesn't mean we'll ever be together. I don't believe that Rafe has any intention of setting you free." In fact, I thought he might actually take a perverse pleasure in keeping us apart, though I hoped he wouldn't be so cruel. Actually, Rafe was already beginning to seem more human than he had in a long time; perhaps there was a chance, if only a slim one, that he might swallow that stubborn pride of his long enough to let Leo and me have our own chance for happiness.

"We shall see," he said. "There may yet come a time when it will be so, but for now, we must do our best to find Rafe's children while we protect our own."

I nodded, though my tears continued to fall as I mounted Morgana. The adrenalin rush of the battle was wearing off, and I was suddenly overwhelmed with sadness at the sight of the men lying dead on the ground. I could have used some more of that comic relief, I decided. Where was Gerald when I needed him?

"I'm right here, Tisana," Gerald said quietly as he jumped up behind me. *"Don't feel much like being funny, though."*

"Me, either," I agreed. *"Don't feel much like it at all. Really, there was no need for such bloodshed! I know that men train for combat, but I've always considered it to be more of a sport than a necessity—or possibly a deterrent to actual violence. As far as I can see, it was a waste of three perfectly good men who had no reason to hate us; they were simply following orders."*

As so many soldiers had done in so many wars. Earth's history had been a turbulent one, whereas ours had been relatively peaceful overall, and it saddened me to think that it might be taking a turn for the worse. I smiled at Leo as bravely as I could, but I wasn't feeling particularly brave at the time. No, actually, now that it was all over, I was beginning to feel the aftereffects, realizing how close we had all come to meeting our deaths. There had been heroism, bravery, and valor, to be sure—all those words we use when we have to fight to stay alive, and often in the face of insurmountable odds—but the truth was, we shouldn't have been there to begin with. This whole rescue mission shouldn't have been necessary, and Rafe's children should have been at home, safe in their beds. It was all so *wrong,* just as it was wrong for Leo to belong to Rafe.

"Tisana, I love you very much," Leo said gently. "Whether we are together or not will not change the way I feel." He edged Calla closer and leaned from his saddle to kiss me. Our lips met urgently, desperately, as though it might have been for the last time. I prayed to the gods that it was not, but as we all know, there are no guarantees in this life. I looked away from him, not wanting to let him see how much despair I felt. He meant more to me all the time, and I simply couldn't lose him! He was everything! And Rafe held the key to my happiness in his pocket.

"We shouldn't let Rafe see you kiss me, Leo."

"He can see," Leo said. "He knows."

"How?" I demanded. "I know we slept together last night, but there was a good reason for that—well, maybe not all *that* good, but at least it was plausible."

Leo raised a skeptical brow. "If you could see your eyes when you look at me, Tisana, you would not need to ask that. He must know. He has seen that look before, has he not?"

"I seriously doubt that," I said scathingly. "I've never felt about him the way I feel about you, and most of the time I'm scowling at him."

"But you loved him once."

I began to form a reply, but my words died unspoken. He was right, of course, because Rafe *did* know. It had been foolish of me to think I could hide it from him, for he not only knew the look, but also knew precisely what it meant. It might be stronger when I looked at Leo, but it was still the same. The charade was pointless. Rafe might have let me think I had him convinced that I only wanted Leo in order to set him free, but it wasn't true at all, and he knew it. Love was the reason I wanted Leo—perhaps not the only reason, but certainly the most important one.

The question remained as to whose happiness Rafe would see as the most important: mine, or Carnita's. I think he was beginning to understand that there was something about Leo which women found irresistible—and it wasn't only the way he looked or his sexual nature; no, it was the man himself. Leo was a genuinely good man, a highly desirable man, and he had all the makings of a hero on top of that. There was little more to be said.

Rafe wordlessly handed me a sword, a shield, and a knife when I caught up with him. As I took the reins of the chestnut, I tried not to look at the bodies of the three men where they lay, but whispered a prayer for the destination of their souls. I felt badly for them. This violence was pointless; they should still be alive and well and pursuing their own lives—lives I could only wonder about. Did they leave behind wives, children, lovers—those who would mourn them, even knowing that mourning would not bring them back?

No one ever came back from the dead—I might have been a witch, but it was beyond my powers—or anyone else's—to bring about such a thing. Death is the end, and whether you believe in an afterlife or not, with respect to this life, it is final, and killing is one of the few acts which can't be undone. The finality of death is such that no one can deny it, nor can anyone deny the utter futility of praying that it was not so. The gods know it, too, and if they ever pay any attention to such prayers, there is never the slightest evidence. Those who suffer such losses are left to seek the silver lining to the cloud of death all by themselves.

These depressing thoughts clung to me as we left the battlefield and re-entered the depths of the forest. My menagerie stayed close by, but I didn't want to talk about what had occurred—any of it—and I believe they must have known it, for my thoughts went undisturbed by anyone for the next several miles. Morgana took the lead once again, as if she still knew where she was headed, and by that I had to assume that she could still smell the other horses. I couldn't have cared less which direction we took; I only wanted to get away from that place where the bodies of the men we had killed lay stiffening in the snow, waiting for the carrion eaters to pick their bones.

Rafe rode on without speaking, leaving me to wonder what he was thinking. Was his mind occupied with the fate of his children or with the fate of the men who lay dead behind us? Did he spare a thought for my happiness, or Leo's, or Carnita's? Or was he focused on the possibilities of what lay ahead? When I looked back at him from time to time, his face was unreadable, but the more I thought about it, the more convinced I became that he was trying to figure out how to turn all of these events to his own advantage.

I knew this to be unkind of me, no matter how much in character it might have been for Rafe, and I rode on, seeing nothing ahead of me but the way through the dense forest. I could barely make out a faint, snow-covered trail ahead, but it was getting colder, and as Morgana picked her path carefully, it began to snow again, shrouding us in silence once more.

It was so quiet that when Gerald gave a little chirp, it startled me, my sudden movements nearly sending Morgana into headlong flight and almost landing me in the snow.

"What is it?" Rafe whispered fiercely. "Do you see anything?"

"I can't *see* anything at all," I said irritably as I regained my seat. This was true, for the snow was now falling thick and fast, and anything beyond a few yards was completely obscured. Royillis should get his family to the clearing soon, I thought idly, because before long, they were going to have a very hard time finding the bodies of those men.

It was difficult to see much of anything and had we been following that trail of footprints I'd glimpsed earlier, we'd have had to give up the search long before this. I wasn't so sure I could have been found myself, had anyone been searching for me, dusted with snow as I was and sitting astride a grey mare. From time to time, I shook the snow from my cloak and hood, but they soon became thickly shrouded once again. It wouldn't have been stretching disbelief to say that I could have passed unseen within ten feet of an enemy. You could barely even hear the horses' footfalls unless they stumbled.

Of course, Rafe hadn't been referring to "sight" in the usual sense. "You know what I mean!" he hissed.

"Yes, I do," I replied. "Gerald just chirped and startled me was all. It was nothing."

"Nothing, hell!" Gerald disagreed, fairly quivering with excitement. *"I think we're on to something!"*

"Onto what?"

"The bad guys! They're right ahead of us!"

"Oh, that's impossible, Gerald!" I protested. *"We stopped to fight and everything! We were behind them by a good day or so at the very least."*

"I don't care," he declared. *"Maybe these are waiting for the others to catch up."*

"Well, that certainly wouldn't be very smart," I said tartly. *"Whoever it is should have kept on going, no matter what. They couldn't have been so sure that at least one of us wouldn't have escaped their little trap."*

"Whoever said they were smart?" Gerald inquired reasonably. *"Besides, the ones ahead of us might be waiting to learn the outcome of the fight."*

"I'd be curious, myself," I conceded. *"But it's still stupid. They should have kept on going, no matter what..."* I stopped and gazed ahead into the swirling wall of snowflakes, suddenly feeling...something, just on the edge of my awareness. I'd never thought of myself as clairvoyant, but as I quieted the logical arguments in my mind, I knew all at once that Gerald was right. They were out there, and not very far away.

"There's another squirrel up in the tree there," he said, in answer to my unconscious question. *"She told me someone passed this way not long ago."*

"Not waiting for us, then?"

"No, but not far ahead and moving slowly."

"Well, we aren't exactly moving very fast ourselves." Actually, our progress had been hampered considerably by the horses we'd acquired. I couldn't prove it, but I think they might have been deliberately dragging their feet to slow us down.

"Rafe," I said aloud. "They're just ahead of us."

"How many?" Rafe asked, not questioning my sudden assurance. "Are the boys with them?"

I posed the question to Gerald, whose information, unfortunately, hadn't included such pertinent details, and I reported this to Rafe.

"Well, they're as blind as we are in this storm," Rafe remarked. "I don't suppose we can still follow them, can we?"

As Morgana was still continuing on without hesitation—at least, with regard to direction—it was safe to assume that there had been no change in the scent trail she had been following. "My 'sight' is as good as ever," I said cheerfully. "We can keep going until the snow gets too deep for the horses to move, though I'm beginning to believe this snow is falling on purpose to slow us down."

"Do you mean to say that the gods don't want me to find my sons?" Rafe said sharply. "For what reason would they do such a thing?"

I personally didn't think the gods cared one way or the other, but I didn't say that, merely shrugging.

Rafe didn't see fit to leave it at that, however, and demanded a reply.

"I said the *snow* was trying to slow us down, not the gods," I said by way of clarification. "Didn't say anything about the gods."

Perhaps Rafe knew why the divines might be holding a grudge against him and simply wanted to discover whether I knew it or not. I didn't, of course.

"Snowfall is directed by the gods," Rafe reminded me. He was one who tended to believe that everything— and I do mean *everything*—has something to do with the intervention of some higher power. Perhaps he was right, and the gods truly had nothing better to do than to wreak havoc on those of us unfortunate enough to be mortal, but I thought not.

"That's a matter of opinion," I said neutrally. Then I decided to probe more deeply. "So, Rafe, *have* you done something to offend the gods?"

His reply was inaudible over the howling of the wind, but his gesture was distinctly surly, leading me to believe that he had committed some sort of misdemeanor—or at least he thought he had—which was all the evidence needed to convict him. Of course, that was assuming that the gods truly gave a damn, and I didn't think that Rafe had ever done anything remarkable enough to bring down the wrath of the gods upon himself and his family. I doubted that he'd ever killed anyone before now, and if being attacked and fighting for your life didn't absolve you of that particular offense, what did?

"It's only snow, Rafe," I said soothingly, regretting that I'd ever brought up the subject. "Just snow—and I'm sure it's slowing them down, too." I looked back at Leo, noting that he was as covered in snow as I was and also that the horses were struggling. None of them were complaining as yet, but it was fairly obvious that they were having difficulty. I thought of the boys in the group ahead and wondered how they were faring. No one had mentioned that any of their own clothing was missing. Would a kidnapper be concerned enough for their welfare to provide them with warm cloaks? I had no idea and didn't care to raise the question. Rafe already felt bad enough.

"It could be that the kidnappers had some way of knowing that this storm was coming and made their plans accordingly," I pointed out. "Under normal circumstances, this sort of weather would have made tracking them impossible." I couldn't see Rafe's face at the time, but he grunted in what I assumed was agreement. "And even Leo's nose isn't *that* good," I muttered. "Though we should probably be thanking the gods for Morgana's."

"What did you say?" Leo asked, attempting to ride closer to me.

"Morgana," I replied. "We're following her lead—or hadn't you guys figured that out yet?"

This time when I turned around to speak, I could see Rafe's face, and he rolled his eyes in apparent disdain. "Do you mean to say that your *mare* is leading us?"

"Well, yeah, Rafe," I grumbled. "She is, actually—and has been for some time now." Noting that Rafe's expression was a mixture of disbelief and annoyance, I felt the need to remind him about a few innate equine abilities. "Honestly, Rafe! Haven't you ever been lost and just dropped the reins and let your horse find his own way home?"

"Home, yes," he conceded. "They always seem to know where their stable is. But tracking someone? I've never heard of a horse doing that."

"That's because you never knew how to ask your horse to do it," I pointed out. "They can understand human speech better than most animals, but only up to a point. I can be more clear about what I'm trying to say through my thoughts." I had never tried to explain the process before—it just came naturally to me—and it sounded peculiar when put into words.

Leo smiled. "And how do they feel about being ridden?" he asked.

One slave to another, I thought, favoring him with a rueful glance. "I don't think you really want to know that, Leo," I said evasively. "And if it's all the same to you, I'd just as soon not get them started. They're having enough trouble with the snow as it is." As if to illustrate this fact, the chestnut gelding I was leading nearly fell, almost wrenching the reins from my grasp. "We may want to think about turning these others loose."

Leo nodded, and Rafe appeared to consider this. "If we did that, then they would return to their home, and we could follow them. They might clear a path for our own horses." Rafe's next question seemed to cost him something to ask. "Have you...spoken with them?"

"No," I replied. "I thought it best not to." I know it sounds odd, but I still saw them as the enemy, though I doubted that they truly held a grudge against us just because their masters did. Horses are generally pretty neutral when it comes to taking sides in the disputes between men—well, after the battle, anyway. During a skirmish, they can fight like another comrade on your behalf, though this is usually more a matter of training than loyalty.

"What's the matter, Tisana?" Rafe said scathingly. "Afraid they'll give us away?"

"That idea had occurred to me," I replied. Rafe might have been being sarcastic, but he was right, because that was exactly why I hadn't. Knowing that these horses couldn't talk to any other humans should have been a given, but the fact remained that we were traveling outside my domain now, and for all I knew, there might have been another witch nearby who possessed similar abilities—though I doubted it. Any animal I'd ever spoken with thus far seemed to consider me to be unique in that respect, and since the borders of a witch's domain meant nothing to them, they were bound to encounter others of my kind.

"Those horses might be able to give us some useful information, you know," Rafe said reasonably. Obviously he wasn't having much trouble grasping the valuable nature of direct communication with animals. Still, there were nuances there that he might not understand.

"If they'll talk at all," I reminded him. "They might not trust me."

For some reason, Leo found this remark terribly amusing.

"And what's so funny about that?" I demanded.

"You," he chuckled. "Why would anyone—or any animal—not trust you?"

I stared back at him blankly.

"He's got a point," Rafe conceded. I suppose having someone come to your aid in battle will put you on a more even footing with them, even if you do claim to own them, because Rafe didn't seem to notice Leo speaking up anymore than he would have with any other man. I hoped this change in attitude continued.

"What are you talking about?" I snapped back. "They have no reason to trust me at all!"

Leo rolled his eyes. "Just look at you!"

"What?" The best I could tell, I looked like a snowman, and I'd never heard that snowmen were particularly adept at instilling trust in animals, or anyone else.

He went on patiently. "You have a squirrel that comes down out of the trees to ride with you, a dog that does your bidding whether you speak or not, and a horse that does not truly require a bridle. Huge purple birds perch on your saddle and will even let you approach them when they are injured. By that alone, a horse should be able to feel that he could trust you."

"Maybe," I conceded. "But horses are different— having been prey animals and all. They generally

run first and ask questions later. We have more in
common with other predators—you know, like dogs
and, um...cats."

Leo didn't miss the reference to himself, and I got a
sly, suggestive smile in response. "Yes," he said evenly.
"Cats do seem to like you very well."

"But not always right at first," I cautioned. "Sometimes
they take a while to warm up to me."

He didn't miss that, either—and neither did Rafe.

"Speaking of warming up, are the two of you planning to keep warm together again tonight?" he asked
conversationally, brushing the snow from his sleeves.

No, we hadn't fooled him, and it made me wonder if
he hadn't heard us the night before and drawn his own
conclusions. I mean, I'd *tried* to keep quiet, but I suppose
the occasional moan or gasp might have slipped out
inadvertently. Leo could do that to me more easily than
any other man, and there was always the offside chance
that Rafe remembered a few things about the time we
were together. However, on this evening I thought I'd
be the one who was nearly frozen and in need of the heat
of another body to make it through the night. I'd had to
glance at my hands and feet every so often to keep them
from freezing, and I do not recommend a heavy dusting
of the white stuff on anyone—the possible insulation
factor notwithstanding—because you're still covered in
what is, essentially, ice. Oh, yes, I had every intention of
spending the night in Leo's arms, and I said as much.

"He might not need to be kept warm tonight, but I
certainly do," I declared, shrugging my shoulders to
dislodge the crusts of snow from my back. "And I am
not, and I repeat, *not*, sleeping with you!"

"So, we're right back where we started last night," Rafe said equably. How he wasn't getting angry about it, I couldn't begin to fathom, though perhaps it was a "brothers in arms" thing. Of course, I'd always heard that soldiers before or after a battle were all pretty randy—the "I might die tomorrow" mentality was a powerful sexual stimulant prior to battle, followed by the "I didn't die!" relief the night after—which Rafe and Leo could both be reasonably expected to feel, despite the foul weather. And this time, unlike the night before, I couldn't very well say that Leo was sick, since he'd already demonstrated just how healthy he was.

"Yes, we are," I said firmly. "Unless Max will sleep with me. Dogs have a remarkably high body temperature, you know."

"I hope I am more than body heat to you," Leo said, sounding slightly indignant.

"And I hope that I would be a more desirable partner than a dog—or a cat," Rafe remarked with a disdainful glance at his feline slave.

"Not really," I said with a nonchalant shrug.

This remark was met with silence, since neither of them was sure which of them I'd been responding to. I thought I'd let them stew for a while—I really didn't care to discuss it. I was cold, tired, and hungry, and the thought of spending a night curled up in a sleeping bag in the snow all by myself held no appeal for me whatsoever, whether I had a tent or not. I still hadn't shaken off the effects of the battle, and even though I knew the animals could probably warn us in time if there were to be another attack, I was still a little nervous. I just hoped we didn't get our throats slit while we slept.

Finally, Sinjar spoke up—though I was the only one who heard him—and it was apparent that he had either been reading some of my thoughts or that he understood human speech better than I'd have believed any horse could.

"You could sleep with me, Tisana," he said kindly. *"I've got more body heat than any of them."*

"Yes, but you usually sleep standing up," I reminded him.

"Oh, I can go either way," he said. *"No problem."*

"For you, maybe, but I have no desire to curl up with anyone who has hooves."

"Afraid you'll take one in the belly?"

"Actually, I'm more worried about taking one in the head, but you get my point, don't you?"

"Yes. Pity, that." Sinjar shook his head and snorted. *"Might be the only female companionship I get on this venture."*

"Aw, give her a break, Sinjar," I suggested. *"Morgana's not in season—though much more time spent in your company should do the trick. Be patient."* Glancing over my shoulder at him, I smiled secretively and turned away.

"You were talking to him, weren't you?" Rafe said accusingly.

"Talking to who?"

"Sinjar," he snapped. "Did he by any chance mention what the other horses might have told him about my sons?"

"No," I replied, still smiling to myself. "That wasn't what we were talking about."

"Well, could you ask him, then?" he prompted.

"I suppose I should," I said, sounding as weary as I felt. "It might save us some trouble after all. Besides, the animals are easier to talk with than you two."

"What do you mean?" Leo inquired.

"I mean I don't have to watch what I say quite so carefully."

"You don't have to do that with us," Rafe disagreed.

"Oh, don't I?" I said dryly. "Pardon me, but I believe I do! These animals and I exchange thoughts, so it's pretty hard to be anything other than completely honest with them, but with other people, I hardly ever say exactly what I'm thinking—not so I can be heard, anyway."

Rafe's reply was as dry as my own. "Funny, I've rarely known you to mince words."

"No?" I inquired coolly. "You might be surprised."

We rode on. Leo said very little, which was probably wise of him. I'd probably be sorry if Rafe had any idea what I'd said about him to Leo. Or had I said anything? Honestly, I was getting so tired and brain-fogged that I couldn't think straight, and I couldn't remember. Perhaps it was the fact that I could barely see ten feet ahead of me that was messing with my mind. The snow seemed to be blowing at me as fast as Morgana was moving, making it seem as though we were standing still in a surreal sort of way.

As the horses struggled through the deep snow, my mind began to drift like the snowflakes swirling around my head. Rafe kept rattling on about talking to the horses but he seemed to be getting farther and farther away. My hearing and vision were so muffled; reality was difficult to interpret. It felt as though I was dissolving into the storm itself, and the cold no longer bothered me. I picked up random thoughts from the animal's minds, and if I hadn't known I was capable of actually doing such a thing, I would have assumed that I was asleep and dreaming.

Somewhere along the way I must have fallen asleep or frozen solid or something, because I forgot to work at keeping myself warm and, reportedly, keeled over suddenly, slipping from my saddle to plunge headlong into the snow.

Chapter 8

IT PROBABLY WASN'T VERY WISE TO TAKE A PREGNANT witch on a rescue mission during a snowstorm. Of course, the fact that I hadn't volunteered the information that I was expecting hadn't been terribly brainy of me. No doubt I should have protested against such an undertaking, but there were children to rescue, and I wasn't ready to tell anybody about my baby at that point. Leo, however, had no such qualms, and I could hear him bickering with Rafe as I regained my senses.

It was still snowing. I could feel the flakes touching my face as they fell, first cold, then wet upon my skin. That was about all I could feel—I was pretty numb. I was being carried—in Leo's arms, I thought hazily. I knew this only because when I heard his voice, it was louder than Rafe's, and, therefore, closer.

"I didn't know she was pregnant!" Rafe hissed. "How was I to know that?"

"You never asked her how she felt, did you?" Leo said accusingly. "Never gave her the opportunity to refuse to go on this quest."

If Rafe thought his slave was being too uppity, he apparently managed to overlook it, for they were talking man to man, not slave to owner. Rafe sounded defensive, but Leo was angry; I could hear it in his voice, though he wasn't bothering to waste his energy by shouting.

"You didn't know then, either, did you?" Rafe said in an effort to exonerate himself. "And how could she know? For that matter, how could anyone know so soon? You've only been together for less than a month!"

"She is a witch," Leo reminded him. "When I told her that I knew, she did not seem surprised."

"And exactly how did *you* figure it out?" Rafe said scathingly. "Was she glowing or what?"

"I knew it only when I saw that she was in danger," Leo replied. "My kind are gifted with sudden insights at times. They are rare, but certain. I had only to look at her, and I knew."

"Well, my kind isn't that gifted," Rafe said irritably. "We have to be told these things—which is what she should have done."

Leo took several moments to form his reply. "She chose not to tell you, and I do not believe she intended to tell me."

"And why not?" Rafe said indignantly. "If you are the father, then you should be told."

"I am a slave," Leo reminded his rightful owner. "Perhaps she felt it would be best that I remain ignorant."

I didn't catch Rafe's reply—though I believe it was more of a grunt than actual words. Rafe knew very well that he was the only one who could change that slave status of Leo's, and I wanted to say so, but I found that I couldn't get my mouth to move well enough to form the words. After a while, I gave up trying.

I could hear Rafe talking again. Leo was standing still, continuing to hold me in his arms, which under other circumstances would have felt very nice, indeed, but I was *so* cold. Rafe's speech was short and rather breathless, making me wonder what he was doing.

"A man's children are all he has to carry on when he is gone," Rafe was saying. "Keeping them from their father is a terrible thing."

"On this world, perhaps," Leo said. "Not on others."

"On any world!" Rafe snorted. "How else can a man know that his life has been worthwhile? Who can he leave his property to when he dies if he has no children?"

It was so like Rafe to focus on that aspect of it, rather than how much he cared for them. Not having children to love and be loved by, I thought of my own mother, who had loved me very much. She was firm with me—had needed to be in order to train me to replace her—but I had always known that I was loved—never had the slightest cause to doubt it. I wondered about Rafe's boys; would they be able to say as much about their relationship with their own parents when they were grown? That Carnita was very self-centered, I knew, and my experience of Rafe was that he wasn't much better than she was at putting other people's needs before his own.

"This society of yours is very backward in that respect," Leo said reasonably. "Children were very important to us on my world, but not so much so that someone would steal them."

"It rarely happens here, either," Rafe said. "It's peaceful here, as a rule, though the possibility of disorder is always present—which is why we stay ready for battle." I heard a soft thud as something heavy landed in the snow. He was unsaddling the horses, I thought—or perhaps pulling off Goran's pack. "There," he said. "Put her down and then we'll pitch a tent over her and build a fire nearby—though the gods only know how we'll ever get one going in all this mess! I'd like to know how she did it last night! Must have been witchcraft, because I can't imagine we'll find anything that isn't too cold and wet to burn."

Leo didn't reply to that, but I felt my body being shifted before settling into something soft. Not particularly warm, perhaps, but soft and dry. A hot tongue swiped across my cheek—which wasn't something I thought Leo would do, so it must have been Max. Yes, it was Max. His feet were cold and wet, but his body was warm as he snuggled up against me.

"Are you awake?" he asked.

"Yes, just can't seem to find the strength to talk out loud or open my eyes yet," I said. *"What happened?"*

"Dunno," he replied. *"You got too sleepy, I guess, and fell off the horse. Are you okay now?"*

"I think so." I replied. *"Just cold, and very, very tired."*

"Well, I'll keep you as warm as I can," Max said, licking my ear. *"I have to, because I don't think they'll ever get a fire started."*

Gerald crawled in with us. *"Tell that dog not to eat me!"* he said. *"I made a leap for it when you fell, Tisana, and he chased me again, but I'm back! Br-r-r, it's cold! We're crazy to keep going in this weather!"*

"I thought you were tougher than that, Gerald," I said critically.

"Well, I am," he said staunchly, *"but you obviously aren't!"*

"Couldn't help it," I said. *"I must have drifted off or something."*

"Hypothermia," Gerald said, sounding firm in his convictions. *"You need a fire and a hot stone to put at your feet."*

The fact that this was exactly what I'd done with Leo after I'd pulled him out of that snowdrift led me to suspect that Gerald had been lurking nearby at the time and had been listening in on my thoughts—the little eavesdropper! That episode seemed so long ago now, and my mind had been much clearer then. Good thing he was around to remind me.

"You sound very knowledgeable," I remarked. *"You should be a healer. Too bad you can't actually do any of that."*

Gerald's only comment was a loud chirp as he crawled back inside my cloak. I suppose it didn't pay to remind a squirrel of his shortcomings

"Ack! You're all wet!" I exclaimed, rising up slightly.

"Hey, Tisana," Max said, giving me a nudge. *"I think you're going to have to get the fire going yourself. The men aren't having much luck."*

Rafe and Leo had a fair amount of wood stacked up, but the usual methods for starting a fire were useless given the current weather conditions. Of my three most carefully kept secrets, there was only one left, and keeping it hidden now seemed pointless—if not suicidal. With a substantial effort, I managed to rise up on one elbow. I was feeling light-headed and dizzy when I moved, but was at least able to open my eyes.

Clearing my throat, I said weakly, "Stand back, guys."

The men both seemed startled to see me awake, but were able to grasp my meaning and drew away from the site of the campfire. I knew I might only have one shot at it, so I focused my bleary eyes on the wood as well as I could through the curtain of swirling snowflakes that threatened to obscure it, and fired a blast of heat right into the heart of the pile. With a loud, sizzling pop, the branches ignited, sending a shower of sparks leaping into the air, only to be extinguished when they fell into the snow. I felt the welcome warmth immediately and sank back into my bedroll. Max grinned happily, thumping his tail, obviously pleased with the result of my efforts.

"Way to go, Tisana!" Gerald said, adding a few chirps of approval.

"Ha!" Rafe exclaimed. "I *knew* it was witchcraft!"

Leo smiled at me as though he'd known I could do it all along. He must have been more alert than I'd supposed during some of the previous instances in which I'd used that trick. He'd known I could warm up soup, of course, but starting a fire was different.

"Gerald says I'm hypothermic and that you need to heat up a stone to put down by my feet," I murmured from my pallet. "Couldn't have put it better myself."

"Gerald?" Rafe echoed. "You mean the squirrel knew that?"

"Yep," I replied with an almost drunken giggle. "The squirrel knew that. Smart guy, huh?"

"That would have been my suggestion, as well," Leo said equably. "But does he have any idea where a stone might be found?"

Following Leo's gesture, I realized that stones of any kind would be hard to come by, seeing as how everything was buried under about two feet of snow.

"He didn't say," I replied. "Don't suppose we have any on the pack horse, either." Sighing deeply, I added,

"Guess it'll have to be you then, Leo. Get warmed up by the fire and then come in here and warm me up, too."

"Hot soup will help, as well," he said, but from the curl of his lips, I knew he took my meaning.

"Yeah. I *am* hungry," I muttered. "Get it together, and I'll cook it real quick."

"So you *did* do that!" Rafe exclaimed. "I thought it was ready awfully fast last night!"

"Yet another of my claims to fame," I said, as I began to drift back off to sleep. "Instant soup."

Gerald nipped me on the neck with his sharp teeth.

"Ouch!" I gasped, sitting up abruptly. *"What was that for?"*

"You have to stay awake, or you'll freeze!" he warned.

"Well, there's certainly no danger of that now!" I declared. "Falling asleep, I mean."

Rafe looked at me questioningly. I think he was finally beginning to get used to the idea of having to listen to those little bits of one-sided conversations that I had with the animals when I forgot myself and spoke aloud. Gerald, on the other hand, probably didn't understand my spoken words, though I think he got the gist of what I said, based on the fact that I'd smacked him—a purely reflexive response, of course.

"Gerald says I have to stay awake, or I'll freeze to death," I explained, rubbing the side of my neck. "And he bit me just to make sure I would."

"Nice guy," Rafe remarked.

"Yes, he is," I said. "Well…sometimes. He used to throw nuts at me, but, now that I've gotten to know him a little better, I think that's just a squirrel's way of having fun."

Max tried to do his part to keep me alert by licking me in the face again, but I told him not to bother, that Gerald's bite had been quite enough. I liked Max very much, but I've never particularly liked being licked in the face by a dog. Long ago, I had asked another dog why they often felt the need to do that, and he told me it was because they have claws on their feet and attempting to paw at someone would hurt too much—which seemed reasonable enough to me. When I explained to that particular dog that people didn't always like getting licked in the face, he said it didn't matter, because they felt compelled to do it; said it was one of those canine social behaviors, like people hugging someone they haven't seen for a while. He also told me that dogs jump up on people because they're trying to reach their faces. I told him I didn't particularly enjoy being jumped on, either, and he said he could understand that, but if I would just kneel down, he wouldn't have to jump, which also made sense. I chuckled to myself, thinking how odd were the things that come to mind at such times....

Leo remarked that he'd never trusted Gerald because of his habit of throwing things at me, but I didn't hold it against him—or the bite, either, really. He was just trying to keep me alive the only way he knew how. I hoped I didn't have to stay awake for the rest of the night, because I truly didn't think I could do it for much longer. I had about reached the limits of my energy.

Leo filled up the stew pot with food and snow—the meat and vegetables were all frozen, as well as dried, now—and brought it over to me. Without my visual heating ability, we'd have had to wait a long time before anything was edible—possibly half the night—and without a fire, it would have been impossible to even gnaw off much of anything and eat it the way it was, either. My reserves being low at the time, it seemed to take more concentration than usual, but soon I had everything thawed out and bubbling enough that hanging it over the fire could finish it up.

"Why did you never tell me you could do that?" Rafe marveled.

"Because I didn't want to risk getting burned at the stake," I said, as I flopped back down on my bedroll. "That sort of magic tends to make people nervous, you know."

"Yes, but no one would ever bother you if they knew you could start fires like that."

Honestly, he could be so naïve sometimes! "No, they'd merely sneak up behind me, hit me over the head, and *then* burn me at the stake! Thank you, but no, Rafe—and I'd prefer that you not let that become common knowledge. I might be able to take out anyone who faced me head-on, but I'd just as soon not have to. It would be a pretty terrible death—and anyone who saw me do it might at least *try* to burn me at the stake."

"Well, yes," he conceded, though reluctantly, "but you could look at an animal in a tree, or running through the forest, and have it cooked and ready to eat in no time. That would be very useful—especially in a situation such as this."

"I happen to prefer more humane ways of preparing my food," I remarked acidly. "Do you think you'd like being roasted alive?"

"Well, no," he replied with a grim look that seemed to become even darker the more he thought about it. "But there are some people in this world who might deserve such a fate—and I would be glad to watch it happen."

"Meaning the ones who took your sons, I suppose."

He nodded. "They deserve the most horrible death you can imagine," he said. "To steal someone's children…it is a terrible crime."

Now that I'd regained my senses, I took a moment to give my hands and feet another quick glance to warm them up—and Max's feet, as well, since his were pretty chilly and we *were* sharing a bed at the moment. He seemed to appreciate the gesture and thumped his tail gratefully. It occurred to me then that dogs don't really have to be able to talk, since their emotions are fairly transparent most of the time, anyway. I dried out Gerald as well, and though he looked a little less like a drowned rat, he had to work on his tail for a while to fluff it up.

Having done that, I looked up at Rafe. "You still haven't told me everything," I said evenly. "You know who took your boys, don't you?"

"Is mind reading another talent of yours, perhaps?" he ventured, a little nervously. Dipping some of the broth out of the pot, he took a careful sip, obviously not intending to say anything more on the subject.

"No more so than anyone else with two eyes in their head who can see what's right there in front of them!" I responded. "You know where we're headed, too, don't you?" I gave it a moment or two before adding, "Mind telling me why that's such a deep, dark secret?"

When he still didn't reply, I stared at his cup until it got too hot for him to hold onto anymore and laughed mirthlessly as he cast it aside into the snow, cursing me for an evil witch. I glanced over to watch the steam rise from where it fell and then looked back at Rafe.

"Oh, so now I'm evil, am I?" I remarked dryly. "You see what people truly think of witches, don't you, Rafe? And you also see why."

He didn't answer me, but he was obviously considering the matter. I could have had a *very* evil reputation, if I'd done any of the things he'd suggested—which was why I'd taken such care to safeguard against the possibility of being coerced into doing them. He, on the other hand, already knew what I could do, so I figured it didn't hurt to threaten him with it.

"Listen, I can make things very uncomfortable for you, Rafe, so you'd better tell me. After all, I think Leo and I deserve to know what we're up against."

His silence dragged on, goading me to anger.

"By the gods, Rafe!" I exclaimed. "We had to kill those men back there! Tell me why that was necessary—who would want your sons badly enough to kill for them?" When he still didn't answer, I added reflectively, "Or is it that someone wants to kill you?"

Rafe took a deep, ragged breath and said evenly, "You don't need to know, Tisana—and neither does he. No one does. Just understand that this is a very serious matter."

"Oh, is that right?" I snapped back at him. "As if I couldn't have guessed that! Let's see now, so far four people have died—I believe I'd call that serious!—and you know the reason why!" I took a deep breath and regarded him scathingly, but my voice was somewhat softer when I continued. "Look, I'm here to help you if I can, Rafe, but I'm not moving another inch until you tell me the truth! I have no intention of being the next fatality in this grand adventure—and I'd just as soon that we not lose anyone else, either!" I took a moment to steady my voice again, thinking that a good measure of anger worked very well to keep a person from drifting off into the long, cold sleep of death. I'd have to remember that if the need ever arose again—which I would do my utmost to avoid in the future. My demands weren't swaying Rafe in the slightest, however, so I decided to take a different tack.

"Fine. Don't tell me what I want to know, and I'll just take all my little animal friends and go home! I'd like to see you try to track them without us—and don't forget, Leo lost the scent a long time ago, so he can't help you, either! Of course, if what I suspect is true, you really don't need us to find them, though you may need me for some other reason," I suggested. Rafe continued to stare stubbornly—and mutely—at the snow just beyond his feet. "Look, Leo *has* to go with you, he's your slave and is bound to follow your orders, but I'm not!"

A few paces away, Leo was busy stirring the soup; I could smell it cooking from where I sat and, judging by the aroma, it was nearly ready. Leo seemed to be keeping very quiet at that point—perhaps to follow the conversation, or perhaps because he was as tired as I was. Rafe followed my gaze, as if to assure himself that Leo was still there.

Picking up the one thread of my tirade that he could safely follow and not reveal any of his own secrets, Rafe commented quietly, "I'm not sure he was ever my slave. I believe I gave up ownership of him the day I dropped him on the floor of your cottage."

"That may be true," I conceded, my heart leaping at the thought that he might finally be seeing at least *some* things my way, "but you're changing the subject." I added sharply, "Answer me, Rafe!"

Rafe's eyes were as cold and bleak as the rapidly darkening sky. "If I let you have him, will you not insist that I tell you anything more?"

I stared back at Rafe for a long moment before replying. What could possibly be so important that he would give up as fine a slave as Leo, just so he wouldn't have to tell me the truth? Under ordinary circumstances, I would have jumped at the trade-off, but I still stood an excellent chance of losing Leo—as well as my own life—if things kept on as they had been.

"I didn't realize you had as many secrets as I did, Rafe," I said dryly, ignoring his offer for the moment. "I've told you mine—out of necessity, perhaps, but still, I've told you. We've been through a lot together—you should be able to trust me more than that, don't you think?"

"No, Tisana, I cannot." His voice was weary, but firm, and he added ruefully, "There seems to be no one I can trust." He seemed certain about that, and subsequently drew himself up straighter, as though having come to a difficult decision. "I will give you my slave in payment for your help if I must, but I will not tell you anything more."

I thought perhaps I should have gotten that in writing—or at the very least, a sworn oath or a handshake—but instead, I chided him, "You might buy my silence that way, too, you know."

He shook his head. "No." It was absolute and final. He simply wasn't going to tell me.

"For heaven's sake, Rafe! What could possibly be so bad?"

I waited for his reply, but he remained silent.

"You know very well that I'll probably find out before this is all over," I grumbled, "but you always were a stubborn man."

Leo brought me a bowl of soup and as I sat sipping it, huddled in my blankets against the cold, I decided I'd better press my advantage before Rafe had the chance to conveniently forget he'd said anything of the kind.

"Very well, then, Rafe," I said briskly. "I'm taking you up on that offer. Leo is mine now, and I won't insist that you tell me the whole story—though it would help to have some idea of what we're up against."

"Someone has taken my sons," he said slowly, as though he'd never spoken those words before. "And I intend to get them back."

"No joke," I muttered into my soup. "You're a regular master of the obvious, aren't you?" I looked up at him from where I sat beneath my little tent. He looked so solitary, standing there silhouetted against the fire with the snow falling all around him, and for the first time, I almost pitied him. Whatever this dilemma of his was, it was weighing heavily on him—but if he wouldn't share it, it remained his problem, not mine. "I have your word, then. This slave belongs to me now."

"Yes," Rafe replied. "It means little enough to me now whether I own him or not, Tisana, but I do need your help. I cannot do this alone."

"Good," I said shortly. "Then if you want our help, you can stop treating him like a slave, because from this moment on, Leo is a free man." Just saying those words aloud filled me with a happiness that even now, I find difficult to describe. I turned to Leo, who had gone over to retrieve Rafe's cup from the snow and was now returning to refill it, and though the wind had begun to howl, I had no doubt that he had taken in every word of my conversation with Rafe. "Did you hear that, Leo?" I shouted joyously into the wind. "He doesn't own you anymore, and neither do I! You are free to do as you wish—and to say what you feel. I'd like to hear what you have to say about all of this. You've been much too quiet on this journey."

If I'd expected him to do a little dance or jump for joy, I would have been disappointed, for Leo merely filled Rafe's cup with the steaming stew and gave it to him.

"We need to plan our attack," he said. "And to do that, we must know what is ahead of us." He fixed his tawny eyes on me, adding, "We need a bird—one would do, but several of them would be best."

If only he'd asked for anything else—you know, like my undying love and devotion, a child, a new shirt, or something reasonable—I would have given it to him readily, but birds? "I don't do well with birds," I said ruefully. "Royillis was one of the few I've ever dealt with successfully. Birds are, well, a bit flighty."

"Now who's master of the obvious?" Rafe remarked snidely.

"Oh, shut up, Rafe," I snapped grumpily. "I'm too cold and tired and—"

"Happy? Pregnant?" he suggested.

"Well, all of those things, actually," I admitted. "It's just that I can't promise anything when it comes to birds."

"Well then, what about an otterell?" he suggested helpfully. "They can fly, but they aren't truly birds."

"Oh, no!" I groaned. "Not otterells! They're even worse! They're…well, they're…just plain weird! They talk in riddles and getting them to report on anything would be a waste of time because it might take *days* to decipher whatever they tell you—if I could talk one into doing it at all."

"Okay, then," said Rafe. "No otterells. But what about the smaller birds? There are plenty of them around."

"You don't understand, Rafe!" I said desperately. "When someone calls you a birdbrain, it isn't exactly a compliment! I might be able to hear their thoughts, but they don't even know that I'm the one trying to talk to them, and they don't seem to care, either. No, to tell us what's up ahead, we're going to have to rely on Max and Gerald—unless Royillis ever does come back, and like I said, he's about the only bird I've ever tried to talk to that had any sense at all. He seemed to think he might be able to help, but, you know how birds are."

"Yes," Leo said with a grin. "They are…flighty." He hesitated a long moment before saying anything more, as though he were thinking something over very carefully before saying it aloud. "I thank you for setting me free, but I do not wish to have my freedom, if it means that I will be parted from you. Forgive me for not saying this before, but I do love you, Tisana," he said, his voice gentle and sincere. "Very much." Giving me a one-armed hug, he added, "You are…" I waited as he paused once more to consider his words. "You are mine," he said finally. "And I am yours."

It sounded like a vow to me, so I kissed him to seal that vow—right there in full view of his most recent master.

"Oh, please!" Rafe begged. "No more of that!"

I couldn't help but smile. "What's the matter, Rafe?" I taunted him. "Can't stand a little romance? Or is it that you miss your wife and wish she were with us?"

"No."

He said it so quickly and abruptly that it seemed best not to say anything more on the subject—so I ignored him, focusing my attention on Leo, instead. "I love you, too, Leo," I said firmly. "You're the one."

Rafe groaned and stalked several paces away from our tent. If he didn't miss Carnita, it was probably because he was angry with her for some reason and that he wasn't in the mood for anyone else's brand of wedded bliss was equally apparent. It did occur to me that Rafe might have been feeling irked by the knowledge that his so-called slave wound up being the one to father my child, something at which he himself had failed, but it was still odd that Rafe would be angry with Carnita—and at such a time, too. After all, she was the boys' mother! What could he possibly have to hold against her for their disappearance? Or was it something else? Trust Rafe not to elucidate, I thought. He was about as forthcoming as the otterells he'd spoken of.

"Hey, Rafe," I called after him. "We'll stop kissing if you'll answer one little question. Are your sons truly in danger? Could we possibly wait until spring to go and get them?"

"I cannot promise to stop kissing you," Leo put in. "Whether he answers your question or not."

"Well, me either, actually," I admitted. "But I'd still like to know." Actually, the more I thought about it, the more I realized that I couldn't have even begun to keep my promise, for Leo's lips were begging to be kissed. "Never mind, Rafe," I murmured, leaning toward those beckoning lips. "Forget I asked."

Leo met me halfway, and our lips melted together. The warmth emanating from that point of our fusion grew and spread, clear down to my toes. He was the one, all right. There could be no doubt about it, and I should have known it from the very beginning. It was so obvious to me now. My mind drifted, my senses becoming as fogged with love as they had with the cold—but it was a much nicer feeling…

I was rudely interrupted by Rafe, who was still snarling as he slammed the lid on the stew pot with a loud clang.

"Look, why don't you pitch your tent and go to sleep?" I suggested, breaking off the kiss. "With any luck, the snow will stop sometime tonight, and we'll have better traveling conditions tomorrow."

"If we aren't buried under two more feet of snow by morning," Rafe muttered, looking up at the sky. "You don't know anything about making weather predictions, do you?"

"Are you asking me, or Leo?" I inquired. My brain warned me that Leo would probably have to be the one to answer that, since most of my mind was rapidly turning to mush.

"Doesn't matter," he said absently. "Leo?"

"The snow will stop," Leo said firmly, still gazing into my eyes, the fire within them seeming to burn even brighter than the one I'd started with my own. "And it will be much warmer tomorrow."

Rafe stood there gaping at him for a long moment before he spoke. It was apparent that he hadn't really been expecting an answer. "Is that wishful thinking, or do you know?"

"I know," Leo replied, his gaze never wavering.

"Just like that?" Rafe said skeptically. "No visions or hocus-pocus?"

"Just like that," said Leo. "And Rafe?"

It was the first time Leo had ever called Rafe by name. He was obviously getting the hang of this being a free man pretty quickly.

"Yes?"

"You should go to bed," Leo urged him. "We will need to rest well, for tomorrow may be…tiring."

"Yes, and we need to be alone for a while, too," I added hastily. "Wedding night and all that, you know."

"That was a wedding?" Rafe exclaimed incredulously.

"Well, what else would you call it?" I argued. "I believe we exchanged some vows there, in case you missed them."

"What?" he demanded. "No expensive gown? No long-winded ceremony? No feast?" Judging from Rafe's dry tone, he was obviously skeptical that it could happen so quickly and easily. I'd heard about his wedding to Carnita, though I hadn't been in attendance—wasn't invited, in fact—and it was an impressive event if the reports were accurate. As I recall, the celebration that followed the ceremony went on for at least a week and must have cost him a small fortune.

"Rafe, no woman in my family has ever been married in the traditional manner," I reminded him. "Why should I be the one to change that?"

"I don't know," Rafe muttered. "I guess I don't know anything at all. Maybe I should go to bed." I think Rafe was still slightly dumbfounded by the recent turn of events. Things were moving too fast for him.

"Yes, get some sleep," Leo said firmly. "We will try not to disturb you."

"Speak for yourself," I said. "I might be making a little noise myself."

Leo began purring then—a sound I hadn't heard much of since we left my cottage. Hearing it then reminded me just how much I enjoyed it.

"I love the way you purr," I sighed. "Don't stop."

Rafe growled. "Oh, don't tell me he purrs?"

"Yeah," I said, my frank admiration evident. "Ain't he cool?"

Rafe growled again, reminding me of some other animals I should consider.

"Gerald?" I said silently. *"You'd better move out of the way. The big cat is about to squash you."*

"Yikes!" he chirped. *"Dogs, cats! Where's a poor little squirrel going to sleep on a night like this?"*

"You could curl up with Rafe," I suggested. *"He might be in need of some company."*

"He'll probably squash me, too," Gerald grumbled, climbing out of my cloak. *"But don't worry, I'm moving!"*

"Max," I added. *"You should go sleep with Rafe, too."*

"I know," Max answered reluctantly. *"I'm going."*

"Rafe," I called out. "Gerald and Max are going

to sleep with you, okay? And remember, they're our scouting party, so be nice to them. No growling."

Rafe muttered something in reply while Leo continued to purr seductively in my ear. Gerald was chattering on about how cold it was, and Max let out a whine when his nice, warm feet sank into the snow. I believe I moaned a bit when Leo finally found his way past all the blankets I was bundled up in and slid his hot, dripping cock into me. As my orgasms began, my moans became sighs of pleasure and contentment.

Leo was mine now…I could keep him forever. It was still so hard to believe it was true, but he was there, rocking gently, filling me with his heat while I floated on a cloud of ecstasy, just waiting for the loud, satisfied purr that would signal his own climax. When it came, I felt it again; that euphoric sense of complete oneness with him—a joining of the mind and spirit, as well as the body. I knew I could face anything now, as long as he was there beside me.

Gerald later reported that he'd slept tucked up underneath Rafe's beard while Max had burrowed under the blankets to sleep curled up on his feet. I was sure they kept him nice and warm, just as Leo had done for me—though I was clearly the luckier of the two. After all, Rafe had lost a slave, and I had acquired one, only to become his wife.

All in all, it was quite a night.

Chapter 9

I DON'T KNOW IF IT WAS ONE OF THOSE SUDDEN FLASHES of insight, or just a good guess, but Leo was right about the weather, for it did change—overnight, in fact.

Darkness had given way to daylight when I awoke, snug and warm in Leo's arms, to the sound of melting snow dripping onto the roof of our tent from the snow-laden boughs above us. Not remembering much about where we'd camped for the night, it occurred to me that we might want to—*"Move!"*

Giving Leo a shove to wake him before scrambling out of our tent, I jumped backwards and fell, sprawling, in the snow, only to watch helplessly as a deluge of melting snow slid from the branches of an enormous pine to bury our supplies, our tent—and Leo, as well—under an avalanche of heavy, wet, mounded snow.

I believe I screamed, which would account for Rafe's sudden leap from his own bedroll—either that, or Gerald bit him, which was by no means out of the question. As the moments passed and there was no sign of life under the silent snow bank, I tried to fight down sheer panic, reasoning that Leo would survive the cold if he went into hibernation—after all, I'd pulled him out of a snowdrift once before—but it had taken him a while to recover, which would undoubtedly slow us down even further, as my own collapse had done on the previous evening. Rafe was obviously thinking along the same lines, for I could hear him swearing as he trudged through the snow toward me.

"By the gods, this is an ill-fated journey!" he declared. "It seems you might lose your new husband after one night."

"Not if I can help it," I said firmly. "Stand back."

Max was already frantically digging in the snow where Leo was buried, and I shot balls of fire into the mass of white to melt it. I'd seldom had occasion to do that before, but when you're trying to save the one you love, anything is possible. It occurred to me that hypothermia might be the least of our worries where Leo was concerned, for he might very well have been crushed beneath the weight of all that snow. I kept on, and finally, the snow was melted enough that the top of the tent was visible, and Rafe waded into the slushy mass and pulled the tent away to reveal Leo's crumpled, inert body. My heart dropped like a stone as I realized that he might truly be dead this time.

"Rafe!" I gasped. "Is he—?"

"Dead?" Rafe finished for me. "Well, if he isn't, he ought to be."

I couldn't believe it. The gods couldn't be so cruel—could they?

My heart was in my throat, and my feet seemed to have acquired lead weights on them. I couldn't seem to move fast enough. Falling to my knees in the slush, I rolled Leo onto his back and began frantically searching for a pulse, but my numb, icy fingers couldn't feel a thing. Too distraught to do anything useful, I couldn't even remember how to warm him, or my fingers, or do anything helpful whatsoever. I'd never been in such a state of panic before—perhaps because I'd never had so much to lose.

"If he's alive, Rafe, we're going home!" I said desperately. "This whole fiasco is pointless to me if he dies." I paused, trying to compose myself. My hands were still numb, and my voice was shaking. "Do you understand me? I don't give a *damn* about you or your boys! This is the only person in this whole, wide world that I care anything about—have *ever* cared anything about—and if he's gone—"

"Tisana!" Rafe said sharply. "This is no time for you to be having hysterics! I've always known you to be a perfectly rational female. Don't ruin my opinion of you now."

I hadn't thought that Rafe held anything remotely approaching a good opinion of me, but his stern tone cleared my head, and, suddenly, I remembered what I had to do. Thrusting Leo's jaw forward with my thumbs, I pinched off his nostrils, sealed my lips over his, and gave him a breath, and another, and another. I stopped to check for a pulse again, this time, having enough of my wits about me to warm my fingers first so I could feel it. His heartbeat was there, but was very slow. He'd gone into hibernation, or shock, or something, but not full cardiac arrest. However, if his chest was moving on its own, I certainly couldn't tell it.

"Still not breathing!" I swore angrily and began again.

Rafe sat back on his heels in the snow, watching me. Having brought me to my senses, he no longer seemed to know what to do, and he'd probably never witnessed this form of resuscitation before.

"Get some wood on the fire!" I gasped between breaths. "I'll start it, but we need more wood!" I gave two more breaths and shouted after him, "And put your bedroll by the fire!"

I checked Leo's pulse again. I thought it seemed a hair faster now. "Breathe, goddammit!" I screamed at him. "Don't you *dare* die on me!"

I have no idea how much longer I went on that way, but finally, Rafe called out for me to start the fire. I gave Leo another breath and glanced over my shoulder and shot a huge ball of flame into the woodpile.

"Careful, Tisana!" Rafe bellowed, leaping back from the flames. "You'll burn down the forest!"

"Shut up!" I snapped back at him. "And start digging out the supplies!"

I heard him grumble something about overwrought females, but I didn't give a damn. At that point, Rafe could go hang for all I cared. All I wanted was for Leo to start breathing again, and as soon as he could ride, we were heading back to my cottage! I was never letting him out of my sight, never letting him do anything remotely unsafe, never letting anyone come near him for fear that they might pass on a contagious disease. He was mine, and I wasn't about to let anything like this happen again—if he lived...

He was still cold. I stopped for a moment and focused on the snow next to his head. When it began to melt, I swept his entire body with a quick glance, as I had when I'd found him in a snowdrift before. It was funny, I thought between breaths, because I hadn't been nearly as frantic that time. I'd been calm, even making a little joke with Morgana. What a difference falling in love with someone can make! Before, he'd only been a guy I was trying to heal who just so happened to be able to produce orgasmic fluid from his cock. Now, he was my Leo—my love, my husband, and the father of my child—and if he died, I'd probably die, too. Wouldn't want to go on living, anyway.

Checking his pulse again, I found that his heart was beating at almost a normal rate.

"Tisana," Rafe said gently. "Perhaps it is time to—"

"Give up?" I shouted. "Not until I haven't got a breath left in my body."

"You don't mean that," he said. "Think of the child."

"I *am* thinking about the child!" I shouted. "And I want that child to have a living, breathing father! Not merely the memory of one planted in her mind by her mother when she's old enough to understand."

I gave Leo another breath and realized it was getting easier. He must have been pulling air in on his own. I stopped and turned my head, placing my ear near his mouth. Then I sat back on my heels, watching him intently.

Leo was breathing.

"At last you're beginning to see reason," Rafe said, sounding somewhat relieved. "I'm sorry, Tisana."

"Sorry, hell!" I said grinning and pointing a finger at Leo's chest. "Look."

"By the gods!" Rafe whispered hoarsely as he leaned closer. "You truly *are* a witch!"

"It has nothing to do with being a witch," I said firmly. "I'm a healer, Rafe. It was part of my training as a child." He still seemed doubtful, so I added, "I guess I know a few things you don't."

"But bringing someone back from the dead?" he said. "That is witchcraft."

"Sorry to disillusion you, Rafe, but it's not," I said flatly. "Of course, if you don't want to believe me, you can simply forget about what you just saw."

He nodded slowly. "It never happened."

Shaking my head in amazement, I wondered how he was able to accept my ability to communicate with animals and start fires—both of which *did* have something to do with magical powers—but not this simple, basic technique that had been passed down through generations of my family and even had its origins on Earth. There had been a great many things that we had left behind to come here and live the way we chose, but some of those things were damned useful to know! It was a pity our society had forgotten so much of its own ancient lore.

"Okay, then," I said briskly, the horror of Leo's demise beginning to fade, "let's get these wet clothes off of him and get him dry and into your bedroll."

After a quick check to make certain there were no broken bones to contend with, I began removing Leo's clothing. I dried him off with a relatively dry blanket and then we placed him carefully on the bedroll by the fire— after I'd warmed up the bedding with a quick stare.

"I see what you mean now about not letting Carnita have him," Rafe said grudgingly. "That's some tool he's got there."

"You don't know the half of it!" I exclaimed enthusiastically. "See those little scallops on the head? They secrete a fluid that chemically induces orgasms, so, no," I added firmly, "you really do *not* want Carnita anywhere near him."

This might have been more information than he needed to hear at the time, but at least Rafe was now in complete agreement with me on the subject of Carnita and her slave. "I think it might be best to tell her he's dead," Rafe mused. Then he muttered something I wasn't able to catch.

"What did you say?" I demanded suspiciously. If he thought Leo was going to die anyway, I had news for him.

"Nothing," he said shortly. "Let's get him covered up and see what we can salvage from this mess."

Max and Gerald, who had been wisely keeping out of the way until then, came over and cautiously approached Leo. No longer at odds with one another and actually working as a team, Gerald took up a position next to Leo's head and patted his face in what I'm sure he thought was a helpful fashion, while Max curled up at his feet.

"Now, don't you worry, Tisana!" Gerald offered cheerfully. *"The big cat is pretty tough. He'll be okay."*

"Yes," I said grimly, *"but to get him awake, I'm going to have to do some rather intimate things to him. Think you could look the other way for awhile?"*

"Righto!" he said, sounding equally chipper. *"Want me and the dog to help dig for the supplies?"*

"That's a great idea, Gerald! Max," I said, directing my thoughts toward him, *"why don't you go help Rafe? You're good at digging."*

Max wasn't too happy about leaving the warm, dry spot he'd gotten comfy on, but he went anyway. Once they were gone, I sat down beside Leo, warmed up my hands and reached under the blanket. To my surprise and dismay, I didn't get the response I'd come to expect.

Could Leo have internal injuries I couldn't detect? If so, it made sense that he would shut down in order to hasten the healing process. Once again, I cursed my limited knowledge of his species.

Leo was alive, he was breathing and had a good, strong pulse, and the best I could tell, no broken bones. That was the good news. The bad news was that he was totally unresponsive, and I had no way of knowing how long this condition would last. I thought back to that snowy night, not so long ago, when I had first encountered this alien whose life force seemed to be on the wane. He had survived a severe beating, sickness, and a rough trip through a cold night to be deposited unceremoniously on the floor of my cottage. I had to believe that it was only a matter of time before his recuperative powers would bring him back to me. I was tucking the blankets firmly around him when Rafe called out, "Is he alive?"

"Oh, yes," I replied. "He's still *very* much alive! But he's going to need some time to recover."

Rafe grunted noncommittally. "I've got almost everything out of here, but I'll need you to help me dry out a few things. I must say, Tisana, that heated sight of yours is very useful."

"I've always thought so," I agreed, dragging myself away from Leo's side to consult with Rafe.

"When do you think we'll be able to get going again?" he went on.

"We'll see," I replied, reluctant to admit, even to myself, that I wasn't sure when Leo would be in shape to travel. "I know you're anxious, Rafe, but it might be best to rest for the morning at least. The trail is probably cold, anyway—I doubt that even Morgana can follow it now, and until Leo recovers, I don't see how we can continue." Looking around distractedly, I added, "I need to boil some water, too—if I can just remember what herbs to use." I ran a hand through my hair. Normally I was completely unflappable in times of crisis. Where was that clearheaded inner calm when I needed it? "I don't suppose there's any of that stew left from last night, is there?"

"A little," he replied. "I'll add some more to it. Should be enough."

"Well, let me know when it's ready to cook, and I'll take a look at it."

Rafe actually laughed out loud. It was good to hear, and it was surprising how much it served to raise my spirits—not as much as Leo waking up would, but still, it was…nice.

"Remind me to be careful about what I have you look at in the future," Rafe said, still sounding amused. "It could be dangerous."

"Rafe," I said witheringly, "have I ever scorched you before?"

"Well, no," he admitted, "but now that I think of it, it's a wonder you never have."

"True," I agreed, "but I'm usually pretty careful—though now that you know I can do it, I might not be so cautious."

"You wouldn't—would you?"

"I don't know, Rafe," I said darkly. "Better watch your step, or I might singe the hair off your head."

"As long as it's the head on my shoulders, that might not be so bad," he said after a moment's consideration. "Would save me from having to cut it so often."

"What's the matter, Rafe?" I taunted. "Afraid of what I might do to your cock?"

"Actually, I was more concerned about my balls," he replied. "Not sure I could live without them."

I hoped Goran and Calla and the other geldings in our party hadn't heard that. If they had, they might have pointed out that testicles were not required for a male to live, though Sinjar might have disagreed. Perhaps Rafe only felt that way because of Carnita, though he'd said she was barren after the second child. If he didn't get his sons back and Carnita had no more, that would be a big blow to Rafe—and ultimately to Carnita, as well. "Carnita isn't still trying to have more children, is she?" I inquired.

"No," he replied grudgingly. "I just don't think I'd like not having balls."

This was more personal information than I'd heard out of Rafe in some time. He'd given me Leo to keep me from asking too many questions, and it seemed odd that he should be so forthcoming now. Maybe he was just trying to be nice, because he knew how concerned I was about Leo. This slowdown was frustrating, and I wouldn't have put it past him to suggest rigging up a travois and pushing on, but so far, he hadn't.

If Rafe wanted to talk, I wouldn't try to stop him, but I wasn't going to ask any more questions, because a nap after breakfast was sounding better all the time. Must have been the baby making me sleepy…or a reaction to the terror of thinking I might lose Leo. Either way, after brewing a restorative and bathing Leo's face and chest with it, I felt as though I could have slept the day away. Rafe probably wouldn't let me, though, and while I couldn't really blame him for that, I was beginning to develop a definite grudge against the kidnappers.

After breakfast, Rafe busied himself with looking after the horses and cutting some branches and setting up a rack of sorts to dry out some things by the fire. Some of the things he had me look at, but after a while I got so sleepy that he quit asking. I was thankful that at least he had something to occupy himself while I snuggled up with Leo and dozed.

I was beginning to get hungry again, so it must have been nearly noon when Rafe called out to me. "Tisana," he said urgently. "Your bird is back—and he brought a friend."

I rolled over and looked up into Royillis's bright eyes. *"I have returned,"* he said, bowing his head slightly. *"But I may not stay to help you just now, so I have brought someone else to aid in your search."*

Looking past him, the worst of my fears was realized. Of all the birds to choose from on Utopia, he'd brought along an otterell!

"Oh, great!," I grumbled. *"You just* had *to bring one of them, didn't you?"*

"Craynolt has agreed to help you," Royillis said. *"There was no one else."*

I wondered why, but thanked him anyway. Maybe my luck with birds hadn't improved as much as I thought. *"I don't want to seem ungrateful,"* I went on, *"but otterells are…well, they're different from other birds."*

"They are not birds at all," Royillis said a bit haughtily. *"They are reptiles. And yes, they are strange, but they can fly."*

"How is it that you can talk to him?" I asked. *"I wouldn't have thought you'd understand one another."*

Royillis gave me a look, as if to say he didn't really understand the otterell very well, either, but I suppose they had their own ways of communicating.

"Well, I guess weird help is better than no help at all," I said in what I hoped was a reasonably grateful tone. *"And thank you, Royillis. I do appreciate your efforts."*

"You are very welcome," he said. *"I wish you good fortune."*

I looked over at Craynolt, hoping he hadn't picked up on what I'd said to Royillis, because if that were the case, he might have been less anxious to help.

"It's very nice to meet you, Craynolt," I said carefully. *"Thank you for coming."*

Craynolt stared back at me, cocking his owl-like head to one side. *"You are the witch,"* he said gravely. *"We have spoken before."*

Obviously I hadn't gotten his name that last time we'd met, though I might have guessed he was the same one, since he did seem familiar, but it goes without saying that all otterells look pretty much alike—if you've seen one reptilian owl, you've seen them all. I was momentarily cheered, because this was easily the most coherent thing he'd ever said to me. Unfortunately, just when I was beginning to think he might have been sick or delirious that last time, he spoke again, and I knew we were in for an interesting time, to say the least.

"I am the wind and the desert," Craynolt said, his large eyes seeming to gaze off into the distance. *"The wind will bring you light, and the desert will not fail."*

"Oh, great," I muttered. "I can see he hasn't changed a bit."

Rafe had wandered over by this time. "What does he say?" he asked anxiously. "Has he seen them?"

"I have absolutely no idea," I said roundly. "You talk to him, Rafe."

"I can't talk with animals!" he said indignantly. "You're the witch—you talk to him!"

"I'll go stark, raving mad if I do!" I declared. "He's...I don't know...but he's..." I broke off there, throwing my hands up in frustration, not even able to come up with an apt description of him.

"Royillis," I said desperately, *"Please, please help us! I can't understand him!"*

"I cannot stay," Royillis replied. *"You will learn his manner of speech, and he will help you."*

"Maybe," I conceded, *"—by the time I've gone as crazy as he is! And what good will that do?"*

"He is not mad," Royillis assured me. *"Look for the meaning behind his words and you will understand."*

"But we don't have time to sit around and solve riddles!"

Craynolt flapped his leathery wings, as though growing impatient with me. *"I am the wind and the desert,"* he said again. *"The wind will bring you light, and the desert will not fail."*

I gave up. "Okay, Rafe, and anybody else within hearing," I said aloud. "What the devil does it mean when he says: 'I am the wind and the desert. The wind will bring you light, and the desert will not fail'?"

Rafe looked at me as though his suspicions about

my sanity had at last been laid to rest, and I truly *had* gone mad.

"It's not me that's crazy!" I exclaimed. "Honestly, that's the way he talks!"

I sent a repeat of that out to all the animals present, and not one of them had any ideas whatsoever, though Sinjar thought it might mean something about how fast he could fly.

I looked up at Royillis, thanking again him for bringing help, and then did my best to seem sincere as I welcomed Craynolt into our increasingly motley band of adventurers. Royillis took his leave of us and flew away in a flash of iridescent purple. I gazed longingly after him until Craynolt stepped forward and peered at me with his huge, mystical eyes.

"The soul is no longer alone," he said. *"Where there was one, there are more."*

Rolling my eyes, I asked, *"How many more?"*

"Not two or four," he replied. *"But more."*

"You know, this could get old real fast," I grumbled, but perhaps I was going about it all wrong. I tried for something more direct. *"Do you know where Rafe's boys are?"*

"The light is dark until dawn."

So much for the direct approach. *"I'd never have guessed that,"* I said dryly. *"And by that, I suppose you mean we'll find them in the morning?"*

"The light comes when darkness departs," he said.

That was when I decided that by the time the light got there, the darkness wouldn't have the slightest idea of what to do with it.

Chapter 10

I FELT MUCH BETTER AFTER LUNCH, BUT IT WAS TAKING so long to salvage everything, dry it out, and then pack it up again, that I was pretty much giving up on the idea of being able to strike camp, whether Leo woke up or not. The snow was melting, too, which would have made the footing pretty tricky, even if it didn't freeze up again during the night. Our next day of travel would probably be as difficult as the rest had been—perhaps even more so if it was icy—and though none of us came right out and said it, we were all just plain tired.

We spent the rest of the day there, and, although Rafe had done well enough when he had something to occupy his time, he was clearly chafing with the delay. Fortunately, he did a good job of not taking it out on me. So the time wasn't totally wasted, I sent Craynolt out on a reconnaissance mission. It pains me to admit it, but I was hoping he'd take a really long time to do it, because I was dreading having to decipher his report when he returned. In the meantime, I brewed a different potion for Leo using alowa bark—which is a good, all-around tonic—but was afraid I'd drown him if I dribbled too much of it in his mouth at a time. I had to resort to laying a cloth soaked with it on his chest to be absorbed through his skin, as I had done before, which wasn't nearly as effective. I still felt reasonably confident that he was going to be okay, but the fact that he remained unresponsive to my touch had me worried. Aside from that, while I did try to enjoy our day of rest, any enjoyment I might have had was overshadowed by the fact that the kidnappers probably weren't stopping, and our supplies were already dwindling, especially the sacks of grain and chopped hay we'd brought along for the horses—which wasn't too surprising, given that we'd acquired three more of them.

Being late winter, even if the snow all melted, there wouldn't have been much in the way of forage, and there was also the return trip to be considered, which, if we were successful, would mean that there would be two more (human) mouths to feed. Speed would be essential, as well, because we'd undoubtedly be pursued.

The grim truth that we might have to kill more men to retrieve the boys—and possibly more on the journey home—disturbed me. I didn't want to be involved with any more killing—the three lives we had taken already weighed heavily on my mind. It was all so *wrong*...

The day grew warm—almost to the point that I didn't need my cloak anymore—and we had to stake the horses out in the open to keep them from being buried under another avalanche from the trees. I took advantage of the time to see what I could learn from the horses we'd taken from the kidnappers. I tended to them, giving all of them a good rubdown while I checked them for saddle sores and such.

The big bay seemed to be growing fond of me, gently nuzzling me after I'd given him some grain. He seemed surprised that I could communicate with him—apparently our horses hadn't passed on that little tidbit—and after he apologized for nearly killing me, we chatted a bit, and I was able to glean some important information from him.

According to Darley, which was the bay's name, we were headed toward his home in the next village, and since he knew the way, this would at least spare us the need to pick up the kidnappers' trail again. When I asked him about the possibility of getting more supplies, he replied that it was a small but prosperous settlement and we should have no difficulty buying anything we needed. Unfortunately, given the circumstances, we would probably be stealing rather than buying, which would still take more time than we would have at our disposal. It was beginning to look as though our return trip was going to be a fast but hungry journey.

When I asked Darley why he thought the boys had been kidnapped, he didn't seem to have any good ideas, other than the fact that the local lord, who was apparently the one responsible for the kidnapping, had no wife and, therefore, no children. He did have a formidable stronghold, however. Darley reported that this was a very large building, surrounded by a high, palisaded wall in which were set two heavily barred doors, and it was defended by a good-sized force of fighting men.

The news that the lord had no children of his own was the only possible explanation for the kidnapping, for he would need someone to succeed him, though if that were the case, I wondered why he couldn't father some of his own. Surely, being the lord, he could find *someone* to marry him! It seemed stupid to take someone else's kids just to do that. Downright weird, actually—unless he was truly incapable of siring any of his own.

Darley didn't know for sure, and though he didn't

seem to think that the lord was necessarily a bad man, he put forth the notion that he might, perhaps, be a gelding.

I had to smile at his reasoning and assured him that humans were seldom castrated—though some of them probably should have been.

"But why would he want to take Rafe's children, specifically?" I wondered. *"Why not adopt some orphan or other?"* It was possible to do that, though the custom was seldom put to the test when it came to inheriting property. A man could name his heir, but in such cases, the succession was usually contested, and a struggle for possession was inevitable. *"He'd have to know that Rafe would come after them."*

"I don't know," Darley said. *"But, then, I've never been able to understand human behavior. Most of the time, I have no idea what they want me to do, and just when I think I've got it figured out, they do something that completely contradicts what they did before."* He snorted in frustration. *"If you were to ask me, I'd say that most humans are totally irrational."*

I found it hard to disagree with that assessment, because we *do* ask some strange things of horses—like embarking on a wild-goose chase during a snowstorm. Even Morgana didn't always think I was behaving rationally, and I had the good fortune to be able to explain things to her—but that didn't necessarily mean we shared the same priorities.

It was late in the afternoon when, to my immense relief, Leo finally began to stir. This time, when I slid beneath the blankets, his purring began almost immediately, and as I leaned closer to kiss him, I felt a delightful thrill as his cock began to stiffen in my hand.

"You know," I said ominously, "if you were faking your imminent death, you'd better never admit it, because, if so, I might have to knock a few knots on your head."

"I may already have one or two," he murmured, reaching up to rub his temple. "What happened?"

"You got buried under several feet of snow," I replied. "Given your weather prediction, we obviously should have camped out in the open. I didn't realize we were under a tree until I heard water dripping on the tent. We were almost *both* buried in a snowdrift, and I'm not sure Rafe could have gotten us out of there quickly enough if I hadn't been there to melt the snow. Good thing you can hibernate like that. Feeling okay now?"

Nodding, he squinted at the sun, which was hanging low in the sky. "Have I been asleep long?"

"Almost all day," I replied. "And believe me, I *tried* to wake you up! You had me worried there for a while."

"My kind sleep for long periods to recover from injury," he said. "One time I slept for three days."

Three days. Rafe probably would have gone on without us in that case—and I wouldn't have blamed him if he had. In fact, as testy as he normally was, it was a wonder he'd stayed put for one day. I was anxious to get a move on, myself, especially in light of what Darley had told me. Retrieving those boys from the stronghold he described would be difficult, if not impossible.

I might have kept on with this train of thought, but Leo's hard, hot cock in my hand was distracting me. The fact that a little while before it was beginning to seem as though I'd never get to touch it again made me appreciate it that much more—if such a thing was possible.

"Well, I'm very glad you're better now, and Rafe will be, too," I said, giving him a hug. "Oh, and you don't have to worry about Rafe taking you away from me just so Carnita won't be deprived of her exotic slave boy—he's seen this thing," I said, giving his cock a tug, "and I told him what it could do."

"He is envious?" Leo purred.

"Well, I'm not sure about that," I said, though I suppose he might have been—after all, it was quite a tool! "But while there are lots of things you could say about Rafe, being a foolish idiot isn't one of them, and he's not stupid enough to let you get anywhere *near* Carnita now!" I eyed him curiously. "Tell me something, Leo, is *everyone* envious, and did you really get beaten half to death by a jealous husband the way Gerald suspects, or are you just a really rotten slave?"

"I have been beaten many times," Leo replied. "But my last owner was more…energetic about it than the others."

"Energetic?" I echoed. "Well, that's one way of putting it. You really are irresistible, aren't you?"

Leo shrugged. "Our men had to be," he said simply.

"And why is that?"

"Our women were…uninterested."

I couldn't imagine anyone not being interested in sex with my Leo, but it did explain a lot. "I'll bet you were very popular in the slave quarters," I commented.

"Popularity can be dangerous," he remarked, leaving me to wonder if his owners had been the only ones to abuse him.

"Well, I don't suppose your last owner mentioned

anything about how much trouble you were, or Rafe would never have let Carnita talk him into buying you."

"I do not know," Leo replied with another shrug. "I was unconscious."

"Tell me something else, then," I said, as visions of women coming from all over to get a taste of the witch's big cat danced through my head. "Am I going to have trouble with you, too?"

Leo looked at me gravely. "I have never shared vows with anyone before this, Tisana, and I have never loved anyone as I have loved you. You say that I am 'the one' for you, but you are also 'the one' for me. No, you will not have trouble with me."

I smiled at him warmly, but when I spoke, it was with a sigh of relief. "Well, that's good to hear, because I have no desire to wind up looking like a foolish idiot myself."

Which I might have done, if anyone ever got wind of Leo's special attractions. I had an idea that singeing the hair off of a few heads might deter the more persistent, but knowing what Leo was capable of, that might not be enough. Rafe's own dogged determination to find his sons was a good example of what I might face, and, to be honest, I now had a little better handle on why he was so upset. He really did love his sons, even though he didn't say much about it. I could understand him not wanting to waste any time going after those boys— though waiting until the weather improved might have been advisable—because the mere thought of losing Leo nearly had me unhinged. Before Leo came along, I'd simply never had anyone I'd ever cared this much about.

Oh, sure, I'd probably cared about Rafe once upon a time, but I got over that pretty quickly when he ditched me for Carnita.

"So, on the whole, how do you feel?" I asked solicitously. "Think you can ride?"

"Perhaps," he replied, still purring softly. "That feels very good."

I glanced over my shoulder at Rafe, who was going through our dwindling supplies for the makings of a meal. I shrugged, "Might as well keep doing this for a bit, then. It looks like it's going to be a while before we get any dinner—which is unfortunate, because I'm starving!"

Leo's smile was sinfully seductive. "You may have some snard to help allay your hunger until the food is ready."

The sinuous pelvic thrust that accompanied that statement gave me some idea of what he was referring to. "By which I suppose you mean semen," I said dryly. "I'll have to say, I've heard it called a lot of things before, but snard? Never heard that one."

"Snard is a Zetithian word," he explained. "I prefer it to…the others." He pushed against my hand again. "It is sweet," he reminded me.

"Yes, it is," I agreed. "*Very* sweet, and under different circumstances, I'd love to have some, but somehow, I don't think Rafe would understand."

"But you have been upset," he said seriously. "It would help you to feel better."

"I'm sure it would, but—"

"Suck me, my lovely witch," he said, punctuating his words with a loud purr, "and I will—"

"Yeah, I know," I said. "Give me joy unlike any I have ever known. Not that I'm disagreeing, mind you, but I don't think—"

"Use your hands then," he suggested, "and I will tell you when I am ready to give it to you."

His cock was already slick and wet with his fluids, and I slipped my hand out from under the blanket to lick a droplet from it. My orgasm followed quickly. "Well, that's one way to get warmed up!" I declared as heat flooded through my body clear down to my toenails.

His eyes were partially closed, but I could see them glittering beneath his lashes, and a soft smile played across his lips. "Better than a fire," he said, then added, "but, as you know, snard is even more effective."

I took a quick look at Rafe, who was still busy with the dinner preparations. "Okay," I said. "Tell me when."

Actually, he didn't really have to tell me, because I'd already gotten pretty good at recognizing the signs. And he was right about one thing, because I was feeling better already, the horror of seeing his nearly lifeless body almost forgotten as I stroked him. My hands were warm by then, and I slid one up and down his shaft while massaging his chest with the other. He felt so good to me—all of him, too, and not only what was in my hand.

Our voices had been quiet, so I doubt that Rafe had overheard us, and had he bothered to look in our direction, he'd have only seen my hand on Leo's chest. I did my best to make it seem like a magic ritual of some kind. I thought perhaps I should be muttering some sort of incantation to go along with it, too—a revival spell, or something of that nature—but what it wound up being was encouragement for him to "Come to me," which would have applied whether I was trying to wake him up or get him to ejaculate.

His purring grew louder as he reached his climax, and I nudged the blanket aside as he let out a growl, just in time for his snard to come shooting out in a long arc to catch me right in my open mouth and land upon my waiting tongue. As sweet and creamy as I remembered from that first time on the floor of my cottage, I savored it and waited for the burst of euphoria and warmth that followed.

Sighing deeply, I said admiringly, "I'd be willing to bet you're one of the few men on this world who could do that after being buried in an avalanche."

"I would not be able to do it, if it were not for you," he purred. "Do you feel better now?"

"Much better!" I agreed. "But then I wasn't feeling all that bad to begin with. How about you?"

"I believe I will survive," he said.

"Very funny!" I growled, giving him a playful slap. "You'd better do more than that!"

"I will," he chuckled. "With my talented Tisana to care for me, how can I not?"

I'm not certain that talent had anything to do with it, because I was pretty sure that any woman alive would have dearly loved to do what I'd just done to him and would have done her very best to give him pleasure. And not just for the snard, either—which was great stuff, mind you!—but because simply watching him come was guaranteed to bring out the raging sex goddess in anyone.

Leo wanted to be caught up on the events of the day he had missed during his little catnap, so I told him about

Craynolt and repeated the creature's cryptic words. "'I am the wind and the desert. The wind will bring you light, and the desert will not fail'—I mean, really, did you ever hear anything so obscure?"

To my relief, Leo didn't seem as stumped as the rest of us. "I believe I know what it means, Tisana."

"Really? That's great!" I said. "Let's hear it."

"The wind is both him and his ability to fly, the light is the information he can obtain, and the desert refers to his reptilian wings, which are strong and will not fail us."

"Uh-*huh*," I said dubiously while trying to work this one out in my head. "Wonder why he couldn't just say: Hey, I can fly pretty well, and I'll do the best I can to help you?"

"It is not his way," Leo replied in a maddeningly patient fashion that made me long to give him a quick elbow in the ribs; but since I was so pleased that his ribs were still intact after the avalanche, I decided against it.

"Well, as long as you can translate for us," I said glumly, "I guess he can help. He's all we've got, it seems—and since you were the one who said we needed a bird, you can deal with him."

By the time I had helped Rafe get our meal cooked, dusk was falling, and the day's thaw was turning to ice. Even Rafe reluctantly agreed that there wasn't much point in trying to travel until the next day. After dinner we divided up the pack so Goran didn't have to carry so much, which would enable us to travel more quickly, but, even without that change, his pack was still getting lighter. We might make better time as a result, but I still worried that we wouldn't have enough to get us home, and I said as much to Leo.

"We may not leave the same as we arrive," he said mysteriously.

I wasn't sure exactly what he meant by that, and I wondered if he'd had another "vision" regarding the boys. Then another scary thought occurred to me. He was starting to sound a bit like Craynolt—a trend that I'd just as soon didn't continue—and I began to rethink having him act as interpreter.

Still, even if he did sound like Craynolt, I enjoyed working with Leo, and we seemed to be falling back into the easy companionship we'd had while we were alone together in my cottage. Now that Leo was free to do or say whatever he liked, he didn't hesitate to offer suggestions, unlike the way he'd been during the first part of our journey. Rafe, for whatever reason, seemed to keep away from us. I didn't know if he was trying to isolate himself, so I didn't have the opportunity to ask him any difficult questions, or if he simply thought Leo and I should have some time alone together. Either way, it was very comfortable.

Craynolt returned, looking like some strange prehistoric bird on the wing, for while his head was like that of an owl, he flew more like a bat. He looked kind of creepy even in daylight, and fluttering around at night, he would have startled anyone, as silent as he was on the wing. Landing near the campfire as though drawn to its warmth, he tucked in his long wings, settling into the snow with strong talons that could have killed Gerald in an instant. I'd have to remember to ask him not to attack my squirrel. Then it occurred to me that I had no idea what otterells ate, so—silly me!—I asked him.

"The fates sustain those who are patient and diligent," he replied.

"Meaning you'll eat anything you can get, I suppose."

Craynolt cocked his head to one side, still following me with his huge, round eyes, but didn't reply.

"So, what did you find out?" I went on to ask. *"Anything interesting to report?"*

He raised his head, staring off into the sky. *"Quiet warmth is upon the land, what is sought is beyond reach, what is desired is no more."*

I decided I was either getting better at understanding him, or he'd driven me nuts, because I had a pretty good idea what he meant, but I went ahead and asked Leo anyway.

"Leo!" I called out. "See what you make of this."

Having heard Craynolt's report, Leo merely shrugged, so I gave him my take on it.

"Well, *I* think it means that while the snow was melting and we've been delayed, they've been moving faster and are in the village now—probably locked up tight and beyond our reach—and if that's the case, how the devil are three of us going to storm the village keep?"

"What's that?" Rafe asked suddenly. He'd been so quiet that day; I'd almost forgotten he was there. "A keep? Who said anything about a keep?"

"Oh, sorry!" I said sheepishly. "I've been talking to Darley. He says the lord of his village doesn't have any children of his own and thinks that's why he took yours."

Rafe looked grim, and I had an idea that the worst of his fears had been realized, but all he said was, "Who is Darley?"

"One of the horses we captured," I said impatiently. "The big bay gelding." Eyeing him suspiciously, I went on, "You know something about that village, don't you? And don't you go telling me to keep my mouth shut again, because it's too late for that! Honestly, Rafe! If we're going to end up tangling with a small army, I think you'd better tell us about it now."

Rafe lifted an eyebrow. "We've already tangled with a small army," he said with a slight grimace. "What we will be facing now is a rather larger army."

"Rafe!" I all but shouted at him. "That's impossible! There are only three of us! We simply can't do it!"

"We can, and we must," he said firmly. "And we have help of a kind which no one will suspect."

My voice was getting higher pitched with each sentence. Pretty soon I'd be screeching like a drakna. "The animals?" I squeaked. "But they can't wield swords or storm the gates! What can they possibly do?"

"They can get inside and gather information, and, perhaps, let us in," Leo said quietly. "I believe sending the squirrel in first would be best."

"Or the bird," Rafe said with an approving nod.

"And they're going to unbolt the gates?" I exclaimed in disbelief. "Come on, Rafe! Gerald is pretty clever, but he probably doesn't weigh enough to push open the door to my cottage! How's he going to pull back a bolt?"

"He wouldn't be capable of that, of course," Rafe conceded, "but he *can* tell us what to expect when we do get in—perhaps even sabotage something for us."

"Like what?" I demanded. "Wedge the door open with a pebble?"

"Perhaps," Leo said, considering this carefully. "We must wait to see what he discovers."

"If someone doesn't kill him first," I grumbled. "The dogs might get him, you know."

"My dog hasn't hurt him yet," Rafe pointed out, "so I'm sure he'll be okay."

"Max hasn't hurt Gerald because I asked him not to," I explained as patiently as I could. "And even if I were able to talk to the dogs inside the keep, there's no guarantee that they would be as cooperative. We're strangers, after all, and they have no reason to trust us."

Rafe stared at me as though he didn't trust me, now, either. "You said you would help me," he said evenly. "And I have paid you with my slave. Don't tell me you're going to back out on me now!"

"I'd sure like to," I declared. "But I said I would help you, and I will. I just don't want anyone else getting killed—I mean, there's got to be a way to do this without any more bloodshed! And besides, while you and Leo might be great fighters, there's a limit to what two men can do against an entire army."

"True," Rafe agreed, "but given what's already happened, if we sent word that we wanted to negotiate, these people would probably kill the messenger."

"I know," I groaned, "it's just that—no, wait! Craynolt could carry a message, couldn't he? We could bluff our way in!"

"How?" Rafe wanted to know.

"Well," I said, stalling for time while I cast about for ideas. "We could…you know…tell them we brought our own army. Those three men they sent after us didn't come back. They may not know how many of us there are."

"That is true," Leo agreed. "We may still have that advantage."

"We may *think* we do," Rafe pointed out. "But they may have known exactly how many of us there were before they planned their attack—after all, we *were* three against three."

I had to admit he had a good point. "But it still wouldn't hurt to ask," I insisted. "I mean, they already know we're following them, so we wouldn't be giving anything away by asking them to be reasonable and at least parley with us."

"We could tell them we have a witch who will destroy their stronghold with a mere glance from her beautiful, smoldering eyes," Leo suggested, with an amused glimmer in his own.

"Aw, Leo, that's awfully sweet of you, but I'm sure they have their own witch, and—who knows?—she might be able to knock us flat just by blowing at us."

"Wish you witches kept better tabs on one another," Rafe said ruefully. "There ought to be a registry of some kind, so you all know where you live and what you can do."

"Well, I've always thought it would be useful," I agreed, "but, unfortunately, no one ever asked my opinion. We aren't that well organized—too much distance between us, I guess." I thought for a moment. "I still think sending in a message would be the best plan. They wouldn't do anything to Craynolt if he just dropped it on a table or something."

"Yes, but what guarantee do we have that anyone will read it?" Rafe asked. "Or that they even *can* read it for that matter! Some ignorant peasant might pick it up and use it to start a fire."

"Then Gerald must go in first," Leo stated firmly, "discover which is the man who ordered the boys to be taken, and then the otterell will take him a message."

We stood there for a long moment eyeing each other questioningly. Obviously no one thought it was a bad idea—though we hadn't, as yet, approached Gerald and Craynolt with the plan. "Okay, then," I said brightly, "we'll give it a shot. Anybody got a pen?" If their blank expressions were any indication, neither of them did. "No? Ink, then? Paper, perhaps?"

"You have those purple feathers," Rafe reminded me. "We could use one of them to write with."

I shot him a scathing glance. "And write in what, blood?"

"That would be effective in gaining their attention," Leo said equably, "but I do not believe we have any to spare."

"No kidding," I agreed. "Okay, then, I guess we can use water mixed with ashes or something like that. And we can use a piece of fabric to write on."

The guys both thought this was a great idea. So, in the end, we used *my* feather, the lining of *my* cloak, (Rafe's and Leo's were both lined with black cloth) and charcoal from a fire that *I'd* started. "You guys would be lost without me, wouldn't you?" I grumbled. "See, Rafe, I told you those feathers would be valuable."

"Well, if you're going to gloat…" Rafe began testily.

"I'm not gloating," I argued. "I'll do that if this works."

It took forever, a circumstance to which anyone who has ever tried to write legibly on a piece of cloth with a quill pen will attest. Meanwhile, since the keep was still a good distance away, we decided that Craynolt would have to fly in with Gerald riding on his back. It took some doing to convince Gerald to get that close to what was clearly a predator, but his innate cockiness and sense of adventure won out. He thought flying was great fun when we had them take a short test flight to see how well Craynolt could carry him, but I think Craynolt would rather have eaten Gerald than given him a ride. As usual, the otterell was philosophical about it.

"This need is but one of many," he said gravely.

So, having established that they could fly together, I coordinated a plan for the two of them, gave Gerald a hug for luck, let them both have a share of my stew, and sent them on their way.

I'd have given a lot to see the expressions on the faces of anyone who happened to see them come swooping in, but had to console myself with waiting for Gerald's report. Craynolt would probably see more than Gerald would, since his night vision was excellent, but, as you know, getting a description of anything from Craynolt was unsatisfactory, at best. Later on, I wished I'd asked him, just to hear what he'd have said, but I didn't bother at the time.

That night, sleep probably would have been the best thing for both of us, but our tent was warm and dry, Leo was purring, and knowing that the morrow might bring untold dangers, I threw a leg over his hip, pulled his cock inside me, and he rocked me for half the night. Well, it *seemed* like half the night—though it might have been longer. It never got old, though, because, if anything, it kept on getting better and better.

As I lay there in a blissful daze while his hot cock drove me into another orgasmic stupor, I tried to keep quiet, knowing that I was probably keeping Rafe awake, but I couldn't help it—I mean, sometimes, you just have to moan out loud—and Leo, himself, was downright chatty.

"Does that feel good, my lovely witch?" he purred. "Do you like the feel of me inside you?"

My reply was a long, sincere, "Mmmmmmmm…"

Laughing softly, he said, "I enjoy giving you pleasure, my love. It makes my own complete." I noticed then that he seemed to linger over the outward stroke, instead of focusing on the inward thrust the way most of my lovers had done. When I asked him why, he explained that the outstroke pulled on the scalloped edge of his cockhead, stretching it back on itself. He withdrew again very slowly, his breath hissing in through clenched teeth. "It feels like nothing else you can imagine."

"I don't know," I murmured as another orgasm shook me. "I can imagine quite a bit." Though in this case, I wasn't sure I needed to, because Leo had a way of making any fantasy I'd ever had seem pale in comparison.

As if to further illustrate this, he changed positions, getting up on his knees to slide inside me once more, pushing in with quick, hard trusts, then withdrawing with an almost painful slowness. My body tightened around him, squeezing him in a viselike grip, making it even harder for him to pull out. I could see his outline silhouetted against the walls of our tent, made brighter from the glow of the fire. Even his silhouette was beautiful.

"Witch," he whispered. "You torment me, making me insane with desire."

I disagreed, since the best I could tell, he was the one tormenting me. He was too much, and I knew I could never love him enough to give him back what he gave to me—but I could certainly try. Still holding his cock as tightly as I could, I reached up to touch him, to feel the smooth warmth of his hard chest. Licking my fingertips, I feathered his sensitive nipples with wet, tantalizing touches.

Leo responded with a tortured groan as I felt his hips curl under me, his balls smacking against my ass. His purring grew erratic, loud, then soft, and then loud again. His hair teased my own nipples until his head snapped back, flinging those golden tresses over his shoulders as he came, filling me with his cream and sending me flying. I had an idea that even if he hadn't been touching me at all, I would have come, myself, for the mere sight of him in climax filled me with ecstasy.

Not that he didn't bother to try. Backing off, he scooped some of his snard out of me with his tongue and laved my clitoris with it. My mind felt like it was blowing apart, and I'm pretty sure Rafe heard me scream, but this time I didn't care.

It must have been late that night when Gerald and Craynolt returned. Having waited as long as he possibly could, Gerald came hopping into our tent very early the next morning with no warning whatsoever, bursting with news, catching me with Leo's cock in my mouth.

"Tisana!" he exclaimed. *"Boy, have I got a lot to tell you!"* He paused a moment before asking, *"Hey, what's that you're doing?"*

One nice thing about my method of communication with animals is that you don't have to stop what you're doing in order to talk—you can literally talk with your mouth full.

"I'm sucking his cock, Gerald," I replied. *"I should have thought that was perfectly obvious."*

Gerald moved in for a closer inspection. *"Isn't he afraid you'll bite him?"*

"If I did, it would be purely accidental," I replied, *"and I believe he considers it to be worth the risk—and besides, my teeth aren't as sharp as yours."*

"Feels good to him, then?"

Gerald must not have been very good at reading facial expressions because, if asked, I'd have said that Leo looked positively ecstatic. *"Yes, I believe it does."*

"But what about you?" he asked curiously. *"Do you like doing that?"*

As I had succumbed to another orgasm at that precise moment, I should have thought the answer to that would be perfectly obvious as well, but I answered him anyway. *"Yes, Gerald. I like it very much. So, what's new?"*

"Well, I found out who took the kids!"

"That's great, Gerald! Did you give him the message?"

"No, but Craynolt did—dropped it right in his plate! I'm glad he handled that part, because once you bite someone, they aren't too inclined to take a message from you." This had been the signal to Craynolt—whomever Gerald bit was the one to receive the message. Painful, perhaps, but an unmistakable signal, nonetheless. After all, it wasn't like he could actually *tell* Craynolt which one it was.

"I suppose not," I replied. Leo let out a loud purr then to let me know he was about to climax. I backed off slightly and took a big shot of snard on my tongue.

"You know," Gerald said thoughtfully, *"you'd get better results if you—oh, wait, I forgot! You're already pregnant."*

"Yes, Gerald," I said dryly. *"I am, so this is a purely recreational activity."*

He watched for a moment or two, seemingly fascinated by the effect a mouthful of snard was having on me. *"Does it really taste that good?"*

"Yes, it does," I replied. *"But it has an euphoric effect, as well. It's not like human semen at all. It's much better."*

"I'll take your word for it," he said hastily. He probably thought I was going to offer him a taste, but he needn't have worried, because it wasn't something I felt inclined to share. *"But listen, Tisana!"* he went on, nearly bubbling over with excitement. *"The boys are there, too! At least, I think it was them. I mean, they looked like they were brothers, but I've never actually seen them before."*

"Neither have I," I said. *"Are they all right?"*

"Yeah, and they weren't tied up or anything. They seem to be fine."

"Well, that's good to know," I said with considerable relief. *"So what did the man do with the message? Did he read it?"*

"Well," Gerald began doubtfully, *"he looked at it, so I guess he did. I don't understand human speech, but he seemed to think it was funny, because he laughed."*

"Not a good sign," I muttered.

"Is there a problem?" Leo asked with an amused expression.

"Oh, not with you—or me, for that matter!" I assured him. "No, Gerald said the man read the message we sent and then laughed."

"That is *not* a good sign," Leo agreed.

"What was that?" Gerald asked. I repeated what we'd said, and he didn't think it sounded good, either. *"I would have watched him longer,"* he said, *"but then Craynolt flew by and picked me up."*

"Was the man alone when he read the message?"

"No, he was at dinner with a whole lot of other people," he replied. *"They all seemed sort of upset when we came flying in."*

"I don't suppose that's something you see every day," I agreed.

"Well, yeah," Gerald said. *"Anyway, I decided this guy was the right one because he was sitting at the end of the table, and he looked sort of important—had on more jewels, at least. Do you think he was the one?"*

"Probably," I replied. *"And we did address the message to the lord of the manor, so if it wasn't, it should reach him, anyway."* I blew out a pent-up breath and shook my head. *"I sure hope that wasn't a mistake."*

"Me, too," Gerald said. *"So, what happens next?"*

"Well, if they agree to talk with us, there should be a white flag hanging above the main gate to the keep when we get there. If not, I'm not sure what we'll do."

And I *wasn't* sure, but, somehow, I had an idea we'd probably wind up getting into a battle with that rather larger army Rafe had mentioned. I certainly hoped not, because if we did, we'd probably have to arm the animals to increase our numbers, and I didn't think we could find a sword small enough for Gerald—not one that would be very useful, anyway. His teeth were pretty effective, though I didn't think he could win many wars with them. Now, if we had a whole army of toothy squirrels, that might have been worth something—but only one? Probably not.

The other option was to turn tail and head for home if the white flag wasn't flying—though, knowing Rafe, that was about as likely as that army of squirrels coming to our aid. Leo seemed to think that getting inside the keep and kidnapping the boys ourselves was possible, but our enemies had to know we would probably try something like that and be ready for us—and unlike them, we weren't nearly as willing to kill. Rafe might have been feeling murderous, but Leo and I were simply there to find the boys. "Well, I guess I'd better go tell Rafe," I said grumpily. "He's bound to be anxious to hear the news." I thanked Gerald for his efforts—he seemed to think he'd done nothing terribly remarkable, though he did admit to having been anxious when the people at the dinner table got over their fright and began brandishing knives, but I could tell he'd enjoyed the adventure.

"Not bored anymore, are you, Gerald?"

"Nope!" he agreed. *"Best time I've ever had!"*

Wish I could've said the same. Sure, there were parts of the journey that had been fantastic, but there were plenty of others I could have done very well without.

Leaving a nice, warm tent and an even nicer and warmer Leo, I pulled on my boots and trudged over to where Rafe slept. Fortunately, it hadn't iced up as much during the night as we feared, and though the weather now seemed set on this becoming a true spring thaw, I could still see my breath and slipped into my cloak as I went. The sky was a bright, luminous blue without a cloud to be seen, and the songbirds also seemed to think spring was in the air, for they were perched in the trees, singing their little lungs out. Craynolt was lurking near the fire, apparently looking for scraps.

"Hey, Craynolt!" I said cheerfully. "Sounds like you did a great job last night! Thanks for all your help!"

Craynolt bowed briefly. "The heart of the wind may be small, but it grows larger with praise," he said, and then went on with his foraging.

"We'll have breakfast in a little bit," I said, feeling the need to bite my tongue trying not to prompt him to say "you're welcome." "It won't take long to get the fire going."

"Simple needs take little time," he said, seemingly unconcerned.

"And by that, I suppose you mean you don't need food that's been cooked," I concluded.

"Truth is like the cool wind which blows on a sultry day."

"Craynolt, I don't want to seem picky or anything, but would it kill you to just say yes?"

"The old ways are familiar, the new ways are not."

I was still grumbling as I trudged over to Rafe, and I'll swear Craynolt was chuckling to himself. At least, I think it was laughter; I heard something from him, anyway, and it made me think he was being deliberately obscure, just to annoy me.

"Hey, Rafe," I called out, shaking his tent. "The guys are back."

Max burst from inside the tent, wriggling with all the exuberance of a young pup. I gave him a big hug and tried to be patient while he licked me in the face. A moment later, squinting his eyes against the sun, Rafe stuck his head out from under the tent flap.

"And?"

"They delivered the message," I reported. "Unfortunately, the man who read it laughed, but Gerald thinks the boys were there with him at dinner. He said they looked okay. Of course, he's never seen them before, so he couldn't be sure it was them, but—"

"That will do," Rafe said shortly, cutting me off. "We must get moving. I'd like to get there as soon as possible."

I made some comment about the nice weather, to which Rafe responded with a grunt and crawled out of his tent. "Get the fire going," he said, sounding even more brusque. "I'll tend to the horses."

"Sure, Rafe," I said, trying not to let my irritation show. The nerve of the man! I mean, I'd gotten an otterell and a squirrel to fly into a well-guarded fortress and deliver a message for him; I thought the very least he could have done was to be civil. He'd been okay the day before, and I wondered why he seemed so angry now that we were so close. Nerves, I decided, and went off to work on breakfast. Leo had already stacked up more wood, so I shot a bolt of fire into it and had it blazing almost instantly.

"Did he anger you?" Leo asked, smiling warily.

With a grim laugh, I replied, "Does it show?"

"I believe it does," he said, coming closer to take me in his arms. "This will be over soon, Tisana, and then you will not have to talk with him again for a very long time."

Cocking a wary eye at him, I asked, "Another vision?"

"No," he replied, pressing his warm lips to my cheek. "A promise."

One I sincerely hoped he could keep, though I wondered how he planned to do it.

"Gonna run him off whenever he comes around?"

"Possibly. Or I may tell him that it would be most unwise to anger my witch."

"*Your* witch?" I repeated. "I like the sound of that, but the funny thing is that I've heard Rafe refer to me as *his* witch before. It sort of made me mad."

"I will make certain he understands the difference in the future."

I smiled at him in gratitude, but went on to grumble, "If there *is* a future! We're getting in over our heads, here, Leo! I hope he realizes that. These people we're dealing with are downright ruthless!"

"I believe Rafe to be ruthless, as well."

"Yeah, but what good will it do us if he gets us all killed?"

Unfortunately, Leo didn't have an answer for that.

Chapter 11

WE MOVED ALONG WITH SURPRISING SPEED THAT morning. The horses seemed to be feeling much more energetic, both from the rest and the improved weather. Max trotted happily alongside Morgana, and Gerald rode in the front of my cloak with his nose peeking out, while Craynolt either flew above us or perched on the cantle of my saddle. Leo and I exchanged sultry glances from time to time, but Rafe's face was a mask of grim determination. It was perfectly obvious that he was going to do this if it killed him—and everyone else, too.

My mind drifted toward thinking what a lovely journey this would have been a month or so from now, with Leo and I traveling alone together in the warm, spring sunshine while flowers bloomed along the wayside. We would lunch together by an idyllic stream, and then make love. Leo could sit in the cool grass at the base of a tree, leaning back against the trunk while I sat in his lap with his fabulous cock, warm and strong inside me, moving by itself, working his magic upon me.

And it *was* magic—more potent than any magic potion I could have concocted, or any power which I might have possessed. His quiet, gentle strength made me feel safe, too, and his love was more powerful than anything I'd yet encountered. To me, he was life itself. I realized I'd only been existing before Leo came into my world—yes, I had my studies and my work, but now, with the miracle of a new life growing within my womb, for the first time in my life, I felt truly alive.

And I had every intention of remaining that way. Having gotten a taste of what life with Leo could be like—and could continue to be like—was enough to make me rack my brains in an effort to find a peaceful solution to the problem facing us. I felt I would have done much better if I'd had all the information at my disposal—Rafe still knew something that I didn't—and it made me angry that he was keeping it to himself. There had been a time when the outcome might not have mattered as much, but I had so much more to lose now.

Darley had not considered the lord of his village to be a bad man, and horses were uncannily good at spotting evil. Looking at it that way, this whole scenario seemed to be one more of desperation than malice—he had wanted those boys badly enough to take them, to kill for them, and to risk their own lives to bring them to his stronghold.

His laughter at our proposal could have meant many things, but the fact that he now had the boys safely behind his own walls might have accounted for that. A sort of, "I have them now, let them try to take them if they will" attitude, which I could readily understand. It was the way I would have felt had Rafe suddenly gone back on his promise that Leo was now mine. Yes, I believe I truly would have killed Rafe rather than let him take Leo from me, and, yes, I would have laughed at the suggestion that he might try it. I would have blasted him off the face of the planet before I'd let that happen. No, this was not a bad man we faced; this was simply a man who had a very good reason to want to keep those boys.

But what was the reason? And how, given the distance between Rafe's village and the one we now approached, could anyone form an attachment to children unknown to them? It was inexplicable, under the circumstances. If this man only needed children to succeed him and could have none of his own, he might marry a widow with children—I tried not to dwell on the probability that there were three new widows in his domain now that we had killed three of his men, and they might have had many fine sons for all we knew. What was it that made him want to take Rafe's sons?

I wished I could have been able to discuss this with Leo without Rafe knowing what was said. It was unfortunate that my mind couldn't reach his the way I could reach, say, Sinjar's. Still, Sinjar was not without wisdom, though as Darley had said, the motivations behind human behavior were often a mystery, and family ties between horses were systematically ignored in favor of our own convenience. Given that fact, it was distinctly possible that Sinjar might have thought it served Rafe right to have his children taken from him.

We did that with most animals—the domesticated ones, anyway. We killed young calves for food, sold young horses to the highest bidder, took eggs from the hens—all with a callous disregard of how the animals themselves might feel about it. Other people might consider their feelings to be insignificant and console themselves with the belief that the animals didn't care about such things, but I knew differently. Even Gerald had said he wouldn't let one of his women near Leo.

I had to laugh thinking that, for the mental picture of scads of lovesick female squirrels hanging all over Leo was too funny for me to keep a straight face for long.

"By the gods, Tisana!" Rafe said angrily. "What can you find to laugh about at such a time?"

"Something Gerald once said," I replied. "And you don't need to be jumping down my throat just because I find something amusing, Rafe. Lighten up a little."

"I will not lighten up," he growled. "And you should be able to understand why."

"Yes, I do understand," I said wearily.

"And are we going the right way?" he went on, as though I hadn't spoken. "Is that damned mare of yours still following the scent?"

"No," I replied. "We're actually following Darley's directions now. He knows the way from here. Craynolt does, too, and if we stray from the trail, I'm sure he'll put us back on the right track." I probably wouldn't have been able to understand anything Craynolt said, but I wasn't going to tell Rafe that, since he seemed to be getting more testy by the minute.

By midafternoon, the trees began to thin out, and Darley informed me that we were getting close to his village. Rafe's response to that information was to draw his sword.

"Remind me not to invite you to a parley again," I muttered. "You're supposed to go in unarmed."

"I'll be damned if I'll go in unarmed, Tisana!" he swore. "We have no reason to trust these people."

"These people?" I echoed with a smirk. "Don't you think it's about time we gave this guy a name? After all, you *have* to know who he is—you big cheeses get together from time to time and flaunt your wealth, so you must have met him before."

"I am not…certain," Rafe replied warily.

"Oh, come on!" I scoffed. "We know he's unmarried and childless! How many lords fitting that description could there be within this distance? And you know very well which direction we're headed. It won't be giving anything away to tell us that much, because we'll find out soon enough."

"Very well," he said, though I could tell it pained him. "I believe his name is…Brandon."

"Brandon," I repeated. "You see? That wasn't so hard, was it?"

Leo chuckled softly, but Rafe was grumbling so loudly I don't think he heard him.

"And what else do you know about Brandon?"

"He is an outlaw!" The words burst from Rafe, as though he'd been holding them in for far too long. "He is responsible for the death of one of my servants, and if either of my boys have been harmed…"

"Yes, yes," I said consolingly. "You'll kill him in a duel or something, won't you? Though, you know, he may hold an even bigger grudge against us for defeating his soldiers and might want to kill you, too." I paused for a moment, thinking I might have inadvertently come up with a way to keep this fight between Rafe and Brandon and leave everyone else out of it. The way I saw it, it concerned them, and no one else. "Tell me something, Rafe, if we could arrange it, do you think you could beat him in a duel?"

"I have no doubt whatsoever," Rafe replied tersely. "He is a much smaller man than I, and besides, I have justice on my side! The gods will be with me."

"The gods do not always favor those whose cause is right," Leo pointed out. "It is not unheard of for evil to triumph over good."

"Yeah, Rafe," I chimed in, "sometimes the enemy is a bunch of badasses who don't always fight fair—and Brandon hasn't exactly been fighting fair, has he?"

Rafe stewed on that until we reached the village, and if there was a white flag flying anywhere, I certainly couldn't see it. Not so much as a bedsheet was fluttering in the breeze, and the entire village was silent, without a single soul out on the street. It was obvious that no one wanted any part of a parley.

When we arrived at the heavily barred door to the keep, there was something white on it, all right. Our message to Brandon was nailed to it with the words, "These children are mine!" scrawled across it in red ink. At least, I hoped it was ink. If it was blood, I didn't want to know whose it was.

Rafe rode Sinjar in for a closer look, though it wasn't necessary, because I could read it myself from six yards away.

"Okay, Tisana," Rafe said quietly as he rode back to Leo and me. "Burn down the door."

I stared at him in frank disbelief. "What? And make myself a target for every archer and swordsman in the place? I don't think so!"

"You are already a target," Leo said, keeping his voice down. "Look up."

Following his gesture, I raised my eyes. Above us, the palisade was bristling with arrows.

"We wish only to speak with Lord Brandon," Leo called out to them.

"Lord Brandon does not wish to speak with you," someone called out from above. "Leave while you still have your heads."

"Well, now, *there's* a nice Utopian spirit!" I said as loudly as I could. "We have always been a peaceful society, with little bloodshed. Why would you change that now?"

"This has never been a true Utopia," another voice answered, this one deep and rasping. "There has always been strife amongst us, else why would each village have a force of fighting men?"

Something told me that this was Lord Brandon speaking. "Good point," I conceded. "Our society is not perfect, as this situation would demonstrate. But, tell me, are the boys unharmed?"

"You may be assured of that," came the reply.

"I can't say as much for the men you sent after us," Rafe put in. "They were all slain. Do we have to kill more in order to take back my children?"

"*Your* children?" the man scoffed. "Prove that they are yours, and I will return them to you."

Rafe was beside himself with fury. "Prove that they are mine?" he bellowed. "When you killed their nurse and stole them from their beds in my house? Stole them from the mother who bore them, and the father who sired them? It is *you* who should have to prove that they are yours, not I!"

"Much of what you say may be true," Brandon said. "But not all, for they are my sons, not yours."

This remark fell like a thunderbolt among our little group. My mind raced, trying to piece together what I knew about Rafe's family. Words that Leo had spoken several days before came back to me then. *"Her heart is not steadfast,"* he'd said of Carnita. *Oh, surely not...*

What did I really know about Carnita, other than what Rafe had told me? Our paths had seldom crossed before this tragedy struck, so I knew almost nothing of her character from firsthand experience. I believed her to be beautiful, vain, and a bit shallow, but still...

"At the last meeting of the cartel," Brandon went on, "I saw these boys and knew they were my own."

"Oh, yeah?" I yelled back. "And how would you know that?"

"Judge for yourselves," Brandon replied.

Slowly, the door to the keep opened, and the two boys emerged, followed by a lean, black-haired man. I could scarcely believe my eyes.

"Rafe!" I exclaimed involuntarily. *"This* was your little secret? Oh, come on! Did you think I wouldn't notice? They look exactly like him!"

And they did. Rafe was big and broad-shouldered, with curly, dark red hair, while Carnita was a delicate blonde. These boys were as dark and slender as the man who stood beside them—they even had his slightly hooked patrician nose, which was as unlike Rafe's as anyone's could be. They were no more Rafe's children than my own child was.

"What lies did your wife tell you?" Brandon asked Rafe. "She told me many—chief among them that she would not conceive when we lay together—that she was barren. But she lied, for it was not she who was to blame for your lack of children, but yourself.

"I later heard that there were children, but they were kept away whenever the cartel met, and I'd never seen them. I assumed, as no doubt others did, that they were your own. But you insisted that they attend the last meeting, didn't you? That was your error. Did she try to convince you not to let them go?"

Rafe's mouth opened, but no sound came forth.

"I thought as much." Brandon's smile was grim and his eyes bleak. "Would you believe that I once loved her?" he asked wistfully. "I did. I loved her beauty and her grace, but she used me, just as she used you, Lord Rafe. She promised to leave you and come to me, but she did not." He smiled bitterly. "My…wealth was not to be compared with yours. She used me to sire her offspring, and she used you for what you could provide. I have—" he paused there, and his mouth twisted, as though the words tasted almost too foul to utter "—waited for her all these years. Now I realize that with two fine sons to assure the succession and a husband with great wealth, she no longer had a need for me, so I have acted."

I almost felt sorry for Lord Brandon—almost. I believed that he could have gone about this a different way, could have confronted Carnita, or confronted Rafe, and no one would have had to die. All it would have taken would have been a panel of impartial observers, for no one looking at them all together could even begin to doubt whose children they truly were.

Then I realized that Rafe would never have given up his sons without a fight, so someone still might have died as a result of any judgment against him. His children meant a great deal to him, for their very existence promised him the immortality which comes from fathering children, leaving them the legacy of his wealth, his name, and his lands.

But they were obviously *not* his, and if Carnita had been questioned, given what Lord Brandon had told us, I doubted that her protests of innocence would have carried much weight. In fact, she'd be lucky if she came out of it alive, which was, perhaps, the reason she had kept her secret and hadn't left Rafe to go to Brandon's village. I doubted that any man would ever trust her again, for, having been unfaithful to one husband, it was very likely that she might betray another. The fact that both of her children appeared to have been fathered by the same man spoke of no other reason than a lack of options, though perhaps she had cared for Brandon a little. Leo hadn't been kidding when he'd remarked that her heart was not steadfast.

Still, I found it difficult to believe that Lord Brandon's heart was as steadfast as he claimed. There were too many other available women, even in this small village. If he was capable of fathering Carnita's children, then he could just as easily have taken a different wife and had more of his own. There was something else going on here—something that no one was admitting to.

Had Brandon hoped to lure Rafe outside his realm and have him killed? The three men we had fought seemed evidence enough of that. They had been trying to kill us, not frighten us away, and they had all gone straight for Rafe, at least initially. Brandon must have wanted Rafe dead and Carnita free to come to him. He still loved her, or at least wanted her—or Rafe's wealth. He was lying.

"Lord Brandon," I said loudly, "why take these boys, who are strangers to you? Are you now incapable of fathering children—or of finding another woman to take to wife? You have taken them from the only home they have ever known. Do you expect them to react to this outrage with love and devotion?"

"They will adjust," he replied, ignoring my earlier question.

"I believe we should ask the boys what they would wish," Leo said evenly. "They should have a choice."

"They have no say in the matter!" Brandon exploded. "I am their father!"

"But Carnita is their mother," I returned, "and has an equal claim to them." I stared at him intently. No, the boys weren't the only things he wanted—perhaps, not even the most important. "You still want her, don't you? When you saw these boys, you knew you still had a chance. You hoped to lure Rafe out and kill him, or else hold Carnita's children hostage until she relented and came to you."

I may have gone too far, for Brandon's fists were clenched, as well as his teeth, and he was drawing his sword. I knew I had to act quickly, or all was lost. With a swift, but intense gaze, I heated the sword in Brandon's hand to an uncomfortable temperature. Unfortunately, the doors to the keep stood open behind him, and he had only to slip back inside with the boys. Dropping his red-hot sword, he began to make for the door, so I did as Rafe had asked initially and ignited it.

Unable to return to the keep and unable to wield his sword, Brandon made a grab for the boys, missing them entirely, because Rafe had called to them, and they came running. Brandon was quick to pursue them, but not quick enough, for I did something then that I'd sworn I would never do—I set him on fire. It was only his cloak, but it was enough to slow him down. Craynolt rose to the occasion and flew at Brandon with his talons spread wide. Brandon had the presence of mind to scream at his archers not to fire at us for fear of hitting the boys, which at least proved that he cared for their safety and said a great deal for his motives.

With all these diversions, the boys had time to scramble aboard our extra horses, and we set off at a gallop through the slushy snow, making for the forest. I looked over my shoulder just in time to see the pursuit come storming through the burning gates—and it *was* a rather larger army than we'd faced before, at least twenty or so mounted men, all brandishing swords or bows. I did a few quick, mental calculations and decided that there was simply no way we were going to be able to elude them for long. Our horses were rested, but not fresh, and we now had the boys to consider. What Rafe or Leo were thinking, I couldn't have said, but Gerald was screaming at me from inside my cloak.

"Can't this bloody horse go any faster?" he squealed, for as I might have expected, the other horses were outrunning Morgana, and we were bringing up the rear. *"We're gonna get creamed!"*

"Shut up, Gerald!" I shot back at him. *"Come up with a plan, and do it quick! I'm fresh out of ideas!"*

"Shoot fire at them!" he responded immediately. *"Lots and lots of fireballs! I've seen you do it, Tisana, so I know you can!"*

"I don't know how long I can keep it up, though," I replied. *"And I don't want to kill anyone!"*

"Yes, but they don't know that!" Gerald reminded me. *"Just scare the pants off them!"*

With a quick word to Morgana to please not make any sudden turns, I looked back over my shoulder again and fired.

The first shot exploded on the ground and took out three of them at once. It was a desperate measure, but it still made me sick to think about it—and the possible repercussions weren't much better. *"Oh, God, Gerald, they're gonna burn me at the stake for this!"*

"Are you kidding?" Gerald said earnestly. *"And risk having you blast them to bits? No way! Keep going, Tisana! You're doing great!"*

I launched another attack, this time bringing down the four lead horsemen who rode abreast of each other. Pretty soon, the trees would become so dense that they would be riding single file, and I wouldn't be able to get many of them at a time, so I knew I had to get them as quickly as I could. I sent another round at them, noting that Craynolt had abandoned his attack on Brandon and was now swooping in and flying right into the faces of the men who were in hot pursuit.

I kept firing, but, unfortunately, I didn't appear to be stopping them well enough, because they were still gaining on us.

"Hit a tree!" Gerald suggested helpfully. *"Make one fall down in front of them!"*

"I don't think I can do that, Gerald!"

"Oh, yes, you can!" he assured me. *"Come on, Tisana! Go for it!"*

Picking a random tree to blast while looking over your shoulder from the back of a horse while galloping through the forest isn't as easy as it sounds, but I gave it a try, anyway, actually managing to hit a branch, which didn't even come close to landing on one of our pursuers, but fell to the snowy ground with a hiss. Gerald was optimistic, however, and kept egging me on.

"Keep trying, Tisana!" he urged. *"They'll get scared and stop pretty soon."*

"You promise?"

"Well...sure!"

"You don't seem very sure," I said darkly. *"I think what we need now is an army of really fierce squirrels!"*

"Sorry, I didn't think to do any recruiting along the way," Gerald apologized. *"You should have said something before."*

We were crossing a small clearing, and I was pretty sure they would catch us soon. "Guys!" I yelled out loud. "We're gonna have to turn and fight! We can't keep up this pace forever!"

"That's what you think!" Sinjar neighed. *"I can go a lot farther!"*

"I thought you didn't want to fight!" Rafe shouted back.

"I don't!" I said. "But we have no choice! You and the boys keep going! Leo and I will try to hold them off!"

If I'd expected Rafe to protest, he would have disappointed me, for he took me at my word and rode on without so much as a backward glance. I looked over at Leo, who was thundering along beside me on Calla. Our eyes met, and on an unspoken signal, we both pulled up our horses and wheeled around to go on the offensive.

"I love you, Tisana," he said.

I smiled back at him with a nod. "And you already know how much I love you, you big, sexy tomcat!"

Taking a deep breath for courage, I said grimly, "Okay, then. Let's do it."

We drew our swords and charged, but we weren't alone, for Max came with us, as did an unmounted Darley. My last round of fireballs had slowed them down, but they were coming up on us fast now. As they broke through the last of the underbrush and came charging across the clearing, I fired volley after volley into their ranks, taking out several of them, but they kept right on coming. One of them reached me, but Leo fought him off, killing him with one swift stroke of his blade. I heated up swords, caught cloaks on fire, but they were a determined lot, which made me wonder what Brandon had promised them in return for all of this valor, because whatever it was, it wasn't enough. Then I realized that they might have been promised a share of Rafe's lands, which would account for their fervor in the face of all the fire I was bombing them with. Of course, in order to get Rafe's lands, they also had to get Rafe…

I'd never kept up the fireballs for so long before—had never needed to—and I had no idea if there was an upper limit to how many I could produce. We'd bought Rafe and the boys some time, but it was still a long ride to safety. We had traveled for three days to get to Lord Brandon's keep, and while weather and traveling conditions were certainly improving, we were no longer the predators, but were now the prey.

A group of riders ventured closer to me, obviously thinking that if they killed or incapacitated me, they could continue their pursuit unhindered. Now that the boys were unlikely to be hit by stray arrows, several archers took up positions and began firing at us as well.

Leo's sword was flashing and spinning as he fought, and
Darley, may the gods bless him, took up a position near
Morgana and was kicking every horse that came near us.
Max went for a few throats before finally being kicked
himself. I heard him yelp, but, in all the commotion,
couldn't see how badly he'd been hurt.

And we still had Craynolt. I have to say, these guys
we were up against must have been pretty tough, because
I believe I'd have turned tail and run if Craynolt had
come after me. His inch-long talons drew blood wherever they struck, and his batlike wings caught the occasional soldier right in the face. He managed to unhorse
many of them in that manner. One man got past Leo and
me to continue chasing Rafe and the boys, but Darley
lit out after him, heading him off before finally running
him into a tree.

I was getting tired, and even Gerald's exhortations
were beginning to lose their effect. I was no soldier
trained to arms, and the best I could do was to get the
other men to drop their overheated weapons when they
got too close. Leo had three of them engaged at once
and was bleeding from a couple of cuts on his shield arm
while he tried desperately to keep them from reaching
me. I tried to help him as best I could by heating up their
weapons, but my initial estimate of twenty seemed to
have been low. There were simply too many of them.
We were losing.

One man finally got through to me while Leo and
Darley were occupied, and I actually had to use my
sword against him. He was a fierce fighter, and I was
therefore surprised to see him suddenly back off with a
look of fear in his eyes. Thinking that Rafe must have

returned to the battle, or that Craynolt was coming to my aid, I took heart and somehow managed to hit the man's sword arm with my blade, sending his own spinning off into the melting snow.

I took a quick look behind me and saw what he had seen, and it scared me, too, for a large, fluttering, purple mass was now flying toward me at a frightening speed. Then Royillis and what must have been his entire clan swept past me and attacked the troops.

I never had the chance to count them, but there must have been at least a hundred huge, purple birds that came flying in to fight along with us. With the numbers now in our favor, we fought on as the birds dove right at our opponent's faces, unhorsing several and sending the rest of them fleeing into the woods.

Then, suddenly, the battle was over, but whether or not it had truly been won remained to be seen, for there was still a good chance that the men would regroup and launch another attack upon us. I sat there on Morgana, her sides heaving from the run, and my own lungs aching like never before. The air was filled with the sound of sizzling as the last of my fire was extinguished in the melting snow. At least I hadn't burned down the forest. My sword arm felt like it was about to fall off, and I had a stitch in my side—only, as it turned out, it wasn't a stitch, but an arrow. I was bleeding and so was Leo. Max was nowhere to be seen, but Gerald was still in the front of my cloak, a little shaken up, but otherwise unhurt.

Royillis flew in to report that the men were being chased all the way back to the village by his cohorts, which, unfortunately, wasn't very far—nothing at all like the road we had ahead of us. What with tired horses, a variety of wounds, and limited supplies, the going would be tough, to say the very least. Speed was something we needed, as well, but I wasn't sure we were up to it.

While the birds kept watch in case of another attack, Leo and I bound each other's cuts—none of which were terribly deep, fortunately. The ointments I'd brought along would help them heal, but, even so, they stung like fire.

Then Max came limping up. Some of his ribs were broken from having been kicked, and being able to run alongside us was clearly out of the question.

"You might have to leave me behind, Tisana," he said bravely. *"I'd just slow you down. I'll follow as best I can."*

"We won't leave you unless we have to, Max," I said bracingly. *"We'll rig up something."*

The trouble was, even a travois would have slowed down any horse we put it on, and in another skirmish, would have severely limited their maneuverability. The only choice, therefore, was Darley, and when I put the suggestion to him, he was optimistic.

"If we have another fight, which I doubt, no one is going to come after us, anyway," he said. *"We'll stay out of the way."*

Considering how much help Darley had been the last time, I hated to have those powerful hindquarters of his pulling a travois rather than kicking the enemy in the teeth, but I honestly couldn't see any way around it, unless we left Max behind, which was something I flatly refused to do.

I prepared a poultice of sage and comfrey for Max's broken ribs and bound it to his side, but time and rest would do more to heal them than anything I could do, and, unfortunately, we were not in a good position to provide either of those things. If we'd been at my cottage, he could have lain by the fire to recover the way Leo had, but here, we were forced to improvise.

Together, Leo and I cut some stout branches—which, according to him, was a shocking use of a sword—and managed to rig up a sling of sorts between them using the bedroll which had belonged to Darley's previous owner. After fastening the branches to the saddle, we laid Max in the sling. Considering that there was still a fair amount of snow blanketing the ground, I didn't think he would get bounced around too much, which might save him further injury. Hopefully, they would catch up with Rafe before we would, but if Rafe had any sense at all, he should have been a long way off by then. It would have been considerate of him to drop off a tent along the way, but somehow, I doubted he would think of it, especially since he would need the shelter for the boys. The horses we'd taken all had bedrolls tied to their saddles, but, unfortunately, no tents.

We transferred what little food Darley had been carrying to Morgana and Calla's saddles, and I sent Darley on ahead with Max, following the trail through the snow that Rafe and the boys had left behind as they made their escape. Since they appeared to be taking the same route we'd taken to get there, it was pretty easy to see, and Darley promised to keep going for as long as he could. Before they set off, I fed him a nosebag full of grain, which wasn't much, but was all we had to spare.

I cupped some snow and melted it in my hands for them both to drink. Max didn't think he could eat anything, and wouldn't drink, either, which worried me. A dog that won't eat is a pretty sick puppy.

As I stroked his ears, he tried to wag his tail valiantly, but I wasn't fooled. *"Sure you won't at least drink something? Alowa bark tea is good for everything, you know."*

"I just don't feel like it, Tisana," Max said. *"It even hurts to breathe."*

"I know," I said gently. *"Darley will take you home. You just sit tight, and you'll be stretched out in front of a nice, warm fire before you know it. I'll come and see you as soon as we get back."*

"If you don't get killed," he whined. *"Without us to help, I'm afraid for you."*

"Don't worry," I said. *"Leo is the best swordsman I've ever seen—and we still have Gerald and the birds. We'll make it. I promise."*

Gerald hopped up on the travois and patted Max on the head. *"Tell him he can chase me all he likes when we get home, will you, Tisana?"* Gerald said anxiously.

Max thumped his tail again when I relayed the message. *"I'll be waiting for you."*

Wiping a tear from my eye, I gave Max a kiss and then left him to confer with the horse.

"Take good care of him, Darley," I said, stroking his neck fondly. *"Godspeed to you both, but don't kill yourself doing it. Stop and rest when you need to, but your best bet for getting anything to eat is catching up with Rafe, because Goran should be with them,*

and he's the one carrying most of the horse feed. Good luck!"

"Good luck to you, too!" Darley said and set off at a steady trot.

"Bye, Max!" I called after them.

Max's reply was faint, but encouraging.

"I sure hope he's okay," I muttered. Turning to Leo, I said, "Well, I guess it's just you and me with Gerald and the birds now. Some wedding journey this is," I remarked ruefully. "I really hope they don't come after us again, but I'll bet they do."

"Yes," Leo replied. "We should ride now as fast as we can."

Craynolt said he'd fly on ahead to find Rafe and the boys—at least, I think that's what he meant, because the word "seeking" was in there somewhere—and Royillis promised to stick around with a good number of his clan in case we were attacked again. When I asked him why he'd come back, he said he'd had a feeling we would need more help than Craynolt could provide alone.

"You were in need," he said. *"I could not leave you undefended, though I cannot explain why."*

"Well, I'm very glad you did, because we couldn't have done it without you!" I said warmly. *"And your timing was excellent! Thank you very much!"*

Royillis only made a soft, whirring sound in his throat in reply, but I could tell he was pleased. Leo gave me a leg up on Morgana, mounted his own horse, and we set off.

"Well," I said, trying to look on the bright side, "at least we know where we're going this time. Now that Rafe isn't here, I can admit I felt like chirping 'Are we there yet?' about a hundred times along the way."

"It is good to see a clear road ahead of us," Leo agreed. "As well as the melting snow."

I thought so too, but I would have been even more pleased to see the smoke curling from the chimney of my cottage and hear Desdemona fussing at me for being gone for so long. I'd even be glad to see the mice.

Chapter 12

DESPITE OUR INJURIES AND FATIGUE, WE WERE ABLE TO move along at a fairly good pace. Royillis reported that most of his clan had now returned from Brandon's village and said that Brandon appeared to be having a great deal of difficulty convincing his men to go after us. This was excellent news, for, with any luck, by the time they caught up with us, we'd be on our own turf with Rafe's men at our backs. I was pretty sure we could trust them, too, because I had a sneaking suspicion that Brandon hadn't told us everything and that Carnita was somehow involved with the kidnapping scheme. Too bad there'd been no reason to suspect her sooner, because it might have made Rafe a little more trusting of his own troops—which he should have brought with him in the first place, instead of Leo and me. Sure, we'd managed to track down the boys and they were now on their way home, but when you're seriously outnumbered, it's a wonderful thing to see the cavalry coming to your rescue.

Precisely what part Carnita might have played in this scheme still had me puzzled, though. If Brandon was telling the truth—and I couldn't be completely sure of that—then she was, at the very least, guilty of infidelity and had also told a good many lies. How much more she had done I could only speculate on, though I had a very hard time believing that she would have killed the boy's nurse and allowed her children to be taken. No one had actually suggested that she had done such a thing, but someone must have let those men inside the keep, and she had been unfaithful to Rafe in the past…

But even if this hadn't been planned with her knowledge or assistance, Carnita must have realized who was responsible afterward—in fact, looking back, I was pretty sure she did—but she hadn't said a word about who she might have suspected, though it's possible that she only remained silent out of fear. It was perfectly obvious now that Brandon had always been the only logical culprit— and Carnita and Rafe both knew him—but Brandon had given no hint that Carnita was involved, and Rafe hadn't seemed to suspect her, either. Brandon had said he didn't want her now, so if they'd truly been lovers in the past, they didn't seem to be too friendly anymore— sort of like Rafe and me.

But if Carnita wasn't involved, then that left some other traitor who lived inside the keep. I certainly hoped Rafe had some ideas, because I didn't know any of his men well at all, or anyone else who worked in his household. I know I'd treated some of them in the past, but I hadn't spent much time at Rafe's house lately, and there could have been any number of new people there. I could talk to more of the animals to see if any of them had any suggestions, but beyond that, I didn't think I'd be much help.

Fortunately, Rafe wouldn't be expecting me to "see" the answer in the fire, and if he wanted any magical insight into the situation, he would have to consult Leo, who seemed to be much better than I was at that sort of thing. The trouble was, Leo wasn't clairvoyant on demand, so we'd just have to wait for it to come on its own.

We rode on until darkness fell, still with no sign of Rafe or his sons. Nor did we catch up with Darley and Max. Craynolt didn't come back, either, which didn't bode well. The horses were getting extremely tired, but we decided to press on even after dark, relying on our horses' (and Leo's) excellent night vision—though with the snow on the ground to reflect the moonlight, I could see remarkably well myself. Leo and I agreed that Rafe and the boys would probably stop for the night, and, if we were lucky, we might come upon their campsite.

The prospect of hot food and shelter was enough to tempt us onward, but pretty soon I was swaying in the saddle. It had been an eventful day, and I had been wounded as well—that arrow in my side hadn't touched anything vital, but it was enough to weaken me. Not surprisingly, Leo was holding up better than I was.

"We can send another bird ahead to locate the others if you wish," he said. "But now, you must stop and rest."

"I'll rest when we get there," I said wearily. "I have no desire to curl up in the snow without a tent."

"We have our bedrolls to sleep in and dried food in our saddlebags," Leo reminded me, "and it is warmer now. We should make camp."

"Wish we'd caught up with Max, at least," I grumbled. "I really should have taken a better look at him. That Darley must have made some serious tracks."

Leo nodded. "He is a big, strong horse, and carries a much lighter burden than either of our horses—but we have been following their trail."

This was true, for even I, who was no tracker, was easily able to discern the marks in the snow that had been made by the travois. "Yeah," I agreed. "At least we know they made it this far, but I hope Darley's being sensible and doesn't run himself into the ground."

"I believe you should not worry so much about the others," Leo said, sounding stern. "You were injured, and we must think of the child. Must I pull you from your horse to stop you?"

"Apparently," I said with a wan smile. "They always say healers make the worst patients, and it's probably true."

I pulled up Morgana and looked about. The sky was murky, as it often is during a thaw, but the moon was nearly full, and the forest was bathed with its luminescent light. It was so quiet and still that even the trees had ceased their whispering, and it wouldn't have surprised me to hear Rafe's voice in the distance, but we heard nothing. Royillis was perched on the back of my saddle, and Gerald had been asleep for hours in the front of my cloak. Royillis had said that the other vultures would be traveling with us, though I hadn't seen much of them along the way, but just then, they descended from the sky in droves, their iridescent feathers sparkling in the moonlight as they fluttered to the ground.

"Well, we might not have a tent to sleep in, but I feel much safer with a flock of vultures around," I declared. "No one in their right mind would attack us now." I wasn't really sure whether or not Brandon *was* in his right mind, but the fact remained that neither he nor his men seemed to have followed us.

"I hope the birds do not get hungry in the night," Leo said grimly.

I did my best to reassure him, but I'm not sure he was convinced. "I think they know we're still alive, Leo,"

I said. "And, besides, they have other things to eat—though with this many of them, there may be nothing left from our first little battle." It still made me sick to think about someone's bones being picked clean by vultures, but there wasn't a whole lot I could do about it at that point. I wasn't sure how many we'd killed in the second battle—most of my fireballs had simply unhorsed the riders or had incapacitated them in some minor way, though there might have been a few burned hands from trying to hold onto red-hot swords—and a good many of the men had wisely chosen to retreat rather than face an army of vultures. It wasn't like I'd actually roasted any of them, and it wasn't my fault that I'd had to fight, either; it was Brandon's and Carnita's.

None of this would have happened if it weren't for them. What Rafe would do or say when he next saw Carnita was anyone's guess, but it was a safe bet it wouldn't be pretty. Rafe was a very proud man, and the knowledge that he was not only sterile but had also been cuckolded would probably drive him to new heights of anger. In a way, I was glad we'd been separated because I would never have been able to keep my mouth shut, and probably would have made him angry enough that he would conveniently forget his agreement to give me Leo.

Apologizing to Morgana for not removing her saddle in case we needed to make a quick getaway during the night, I loosened her girth slightly and melted some snow into a puddle for her and Calla to drink. It was nice not to have to hide everything I did anymore—almost like being at home. Desdemona never held it against me that I could talk with her or keep her warm. Just wish I could have counted on the rest of the world's population to see it that way.

Not having a pot to cook in meant that we would have to eat what little rations we had in their dry form. I tried heating up some dried fruit by laying it on top of the snow and giving it a quick stare, but the snow around it melted too fast and some of it wound up in the mud underneath, so I abandoned that method. Then I got the idea to cook our rations in single servings right in the cups that each of us carried in our saddlebags, and it wasn't too bad—at least it was hot.

Gerald sat perched in a tree, nibbling on some seeds he'd found, and I gave him a bit of Morgana's grain. One nice thing about having a squirrel along for the ride—they don't eat much.

Leo had spread out our bedrolls while I was heating up the soup and had pitched a tent of sorts over them using a blanket and both of our swords as tent poles. Having then gathered up some wood for a campfire, he paused to take a steaming cup from me.

"It is strange not needing fire to cook," Leo commented. "You have it ready to eat even before the fire is started!"

"A useful skill," I agreed. "I just hope it doesn't get me hunted down and killed someday."

Leo regarded me with a solemn gaze. "You will not be hunted down," he promised. "You will live long."

"Another prophesy?"

"Yes."

I considered this for a moment or two, wondering whether I should question him further—just to be sure—but decided that when someone tells you exactly what you want to hear, it's best not to get too nitpicky over the details.

"Thank you, Leo," I said quietly. "That is very… comforting, especially coming from you." After igniting the campfire, we sat down next to one another on the end of the bedroll nearest the heat. There's something very cheery about sitting by a fire, being all cozy and warm—and *not* seeing the future waiting there for you when you stare into the flickering flames! I was perfectly willing to let Leo handle the clairvoyance department. "Any other prophecies come to mind?" I asked. "About Rafe and Carnita, perhaps?"

Leo smiled. "I believe I said that her heart was not steadfast."

"And now we see how right you were about that." I shuddered slightly, and it had nothing to do with the falling temperature, though I snuggled closer to Leo anyway. "I certainly wouldn't want to be in Carnita's shoes when Rafe gets home!" I declared. "If she has any sense at all, she'll make a run for it."

"Do you believe he would harm her?"

"I have no idea," I replied, realizing that I truly didn't. "Rafe might do anything—or nothing at all. Those boys mean an awful lot to him, but I'm sure they're fond of their mother, so doing anything to hurt her would be a bad idea on his part. Rafe has to know that, and it might stay his hand from doing anything rash. Plus, he'll have had time to think before he sees her, which might cool him off a bit. We're still a ways from home yet."

"The time required for the journey may also give him time to become even more angry," Leo pointed out.

"Yeah, that's true, too," I agreed. "Like I said, I have no idea what he'll do. You know, Carnita might have wanted to buy you to improve their family's prestige, but Carnita, herself, did a lot to increase Rafe's to begin with. It's possible that Rafe might consider her worth keeping, even knowing what she did, because from what I hear, she was very sought after. Brandon wasn't the only one who might have been jealous of him for winning her."

"Jealous men can be dangerous," Leo said seriously. "I should be careful, for there are many who would be jealous of me."

Giving him a wry smile, I said, "I don't think so, Leo. Most of my lovers were only curious to see if they could be the one to father my child. It was more of a contest to them than anything. None of them ever truly loved me—or if they did, it wasn't for long—and none of them have been pounding on my door lately. I think you'll be safe."

"I cannot imagine that I will be," he disagreed. "You are a very beautiful and bewitching woman, Tisana. I should have had to fight for you, and I am surprised that I have not."

I found it difficult not to laugh at this. "Uh, aren't you forgetting something, Leo? We've been in a couple of fights, now, and you *did* fight for me—fought very hard, in fact."

"But that was to protect you," he protested, "not to win your love."

"You didn't have to fight for my love, Leo—and you wouldn't have, even if there had been scores of men vying for my attention—which, believe me, there weren't!

No, all you had to do was love me the way I've always dreamed of being loved—all the fighting in the world wouldn't have made the slightest bit of difference."

He smiled at this, but then asked, "And did you dream of being loved by an enslaved alien warrior?"

I shook my head slowly. "It's hard to explain," I began uncertainly. "The things you say and do make me feel loved—but that's not all. When we're together, who I am and what I have to say matters to you, and your desire for me is always evident. I don't ever feel that your mind is somewhere else when you're talking with me. You're really *there,* somehow—I can't explain it any better than that.

"Perhaps it *is* because you've been a slave and don't have a load of possessions or responsibilities to occupy your mind all the time, but when I talk with you, or ask you to do something, I don't feel as if I'm imposing on you. You *listen* to me—and you respond! You aren't just this great lump sitting at the table, waiting to be fed before you go off to slay dragons, or whatever. Being with me and loving me is something you truly seem to want to do, and I don't have to do anything special to try to impress you—or win you!" I shook my head again, still trying to come up with a better description of the way I felt, but I couldn't. It was as futile as trying to describe why something is beautiful, for there is no *why* to beauty. It simply *is*. "I honestly don't know exactly what it is about you that makes you so special, Leo," I said, finally giving up, "but I like it. I like it very much."

"You are very easy to love, also," Leo murmured into my hair. "And you saw me as a man, not as a slave."

"You were never a slave, Leo," I chided him. "A king, perhaps, but never a slave."

He smiled warmly. "I was never a king, Tisana. I was a common soldier—nothing more."

"Well, you may have been a soldier," I said, shaking my head in disagreement, "but there's no way you were ever 'common!' Not in any way, shape, or form!" As I gazed at him, sitting there, his exotic face illuminated by the flames, I knew I would never look upon anyone I loved more. "I love you, Leo."

"And I, you," he said, and leaned in for a kiss—a soft, sweet, bone-melting kiss.

Just then, I heard Gerald give a loud squeak as he leaped from his branch, which was now occupied by two of the vultures. *"Can I get back into your cloak, Tisana?"* he begged. *"Those birds are looking at me like I'm dinner!"*

"They don't kill, Gerald," I reminded him, still kissing Leo. *"Besides, you aren't nearly big enough to feed them all."*

"My, how comforting!" Gerald said dryly. *"Wouldn't stop a pack of warnocks from killing me, but they'd have to catch me first. Slow bastards, those warnocks."*

"Persistent, though," I reminded him. *"I've heard of them tracking their quarry for days until, finally, their prey just gives up and lets itself be killed."*

"Good thing they hibernate in winter, or we'd be in danger from them, too."

"Small comfort if you freeze to death instead," I pointed out. I was hoping to wrap up this discussion so I could focus on kissing Leo properly. After all, I'd just commented on how much I liked the way he

focused his attention on me—it wouldn't do to let my own wander.

"You know, on the whole, I think I'd rather freeze to death than be eaten," Gerald said reflectively.

"But then the vultures would still get to eat you!" I said, my laughter finally breaking off the kiss.

"You find my kiss amusing?" Leo asked curiously, though he didn't seem the slightest bit miffed that I'd laugh at such a time.

"Gerald is debating the pros and cons of freezing to death or being eaten alive," I replied. "Which would you prefer?"

"Neither," Leo said firmly. "I believe I would wish to die in your arms as an old man."

"Oh, I hope not!" I said, shaking my head vigorously. "I'd much rather die in *your* arms as an old woman!"

"And why is that?" he inquired.

"Because I have no desire to watch you die, Leo," I said, caressing his face. "I hope the gods spare me that much."

"And I would not wish to watch you die, Tisana."

"I think you probably will."

"And why would that be?"

"Well, for one thing," I replied, "you're obviously very hard to kill, so you're bound to outlive me, anyway, and for another, that orgasmic cock of yours will probably kill me someday."

"Would that be bad?" he asked slyly.

"I can't think of a better way to go," I said honestly. "So if I'm ever near death, give me a little taste and send me off to the gods in style."

"You are very odd, sometimes," Leo observed, setting down his empty cup to put both arms around me.

"Yeah, I know," I said, leaning even closer to him. "But it's a nice, witchy kind of odd, wouldn't you say?"

"Yes," he replied. "Sitting here by the fire that you started with a mere glance of your bewitching eyes, eating soup which you cooked without fire, and with a flock of vultures, two horses, and a garrulous squirrel for company, I would say that it was."

"But no people," I reminded him. "We're finally alone again!"

Leo smiled and regarded me through eyes glowing brighter with desire. "Yes, we are alone, my lovely witch-wife, a fact which I have not forgotten. And here in the moonlight by the fire, I will show you how just much I enjoy being alone with you."

I couldn't help but chuckle at that. "Most men would say they were too tired, or afraid the enemy would catch them with their pants down or something like that, but you, you're always ready and always willing."

"It is because of you that I am," said Leo, pulling me down beside him beneath our makeshift tent. "My desire is only for you."

Then his lips melted into mine again, and I was lost. "You say the nicest things," I mumbled. "And I do love the way you kiss."

Leo responded with a loud, rumbling purr and delved beneath my cloak to begin seeking my skin to touch. I pushed his clothing aside as well, and soon, he was teasing my clitoris with his slick cockhead. Remembering what had happened the last time he'd done that, I simply lay back and let him send me into orbit.

Oh, yes, this was the way I wanted to die: in Leo's arms with his magic enveloping me like a soft, warm cloud. How could anything possibly feel this good? The pain from my wound was completely obliterated, for this was ecstasy beyond belief. He was both love and loving personified, and I knew I could never get enough of him, could never tire of him, even if I should live out my own natural life and beyond. I could never have hated him—never have even been angry with him—not knowing how he could bring me into such a state of bliss.

As hard cock penetrated wet heat, he groaned softly. "Here is where I wish to be, always," he said, "for this is where love lives."

I didn't know if he meant our child or something else, but it was a nice thought, anyway. He thrust in hard and deep, as though trying to touch the child I carried. It felt sublime. I cried out his name and wanted to tell him that whenever we made love, it was as though it were the first time, the last time, the best time, but calling out his name was all I seemed to be able to do. He had to know how good it was, he had to!

I gasped as he pulled his cock out and stroked my clitoris again. I missed him immediately from where he belonged, but the sensation made me delirious—unable to decide which was better. Just when I thought that outside was best, he drove in again, reminding me that I was wrong about that—so *very* wrong, indeed!

I tried calling out his name again, but couldn't seem to remember what it was. I'd gone mad—would continue to grow madder still, because, unbelievably, each time with him *did* seem better than the last. But how could that be? How could total perfection ever be improved upon?

He pulled out again and went for my clitoris. He was slowing himself down, I realized, putting off his own inevitable climax to prolong my pleasure, driving it to a fever pitch. My orgasms became constant, one blurring into the next—almost to the point where I didn't think I could take it anymore. Then, at last, I remembered his name.

"Leo, please!" I cried out in desperation.

"You wish for more?" he asked.

"No," I groaned. "I've already got it all...every-thing...don't need anything more."

With a satisfied purr, he whispered, "Then I will finish," as he thrust into me again, but this time harder, faster. Pounding into me more deeply than I would have thought possible, the sensations seemed to alter, and what I had thought was ecstasy before now seemed pale in comparison.

"How do you *do* that?" I moaned helplessly.

His purr changed to more of a growl as he slammed into me as deeply as our joined bodies would allow. Gripping him tightly with my slick inner muscles, the rumbling in his chest deepened, and I felt the vibrations throughout my entire body—in fact, I'm surprised the ground itself didn't shake.

With his climax, Leo arched his neck, his head snapping backward while his hair cascaded down his chest. I could see his eyes glowing brightly, and his fangs gleamed in the dim moonlight. His balls contracted in uncontrollable spasms, pouring his snard into me in long, forceful jets. Clenching him as tightly as I could with every muscle I had control of, I waited anxiously for the euphoria his snard would give me. I had to think of it as snard, because semen was something *completely* different, just as he was completely different from other men himself. He was rare, he was precious, and, now, above all, he was mine. I had been of the opinion that I'd never possessed anything of value before, but now, I was the richest woman in the world—possibly the entire galaxy. If Rafe had only known what he'd given up to keep me silent, he'd never have done it. He could have sold Leo for millions of credits on the open market—and I'd gotten him for virtually nothing.

As sleep began to carry me away, I thanked the gods for giving me this great gift and prayed that they would keep him safe, for I wouldn't have wanted to live long if he were not there to share that life with me—whether he was "the one" or not. For his love alone, I would gladly have gone to my grave childless. No, Leo didn't have to be the one. I would have loved him anyway.

The next morning, I awoke amid a huddle of purple feathers. "What the devil?" I grumbled. It seemed that a few of Royillis's clan of vultures had gotten chilly during the night and had opted to share our tent. I started to argue that they were supposed to be out keeping watch, but kept quiet when I realized there were only four of them out of possibly a hundred.

Royillis poked his beak beneath the blanket that covered us all and spoke to me. *"My brood has kept you warm?"* he asked.

I realized then that I *was* warm—warmer, in fact, than I'd been on any night of our journey thus far. I'd never considered feathers to be particularly good as insulation, but I suppose I should have.

"Yes," I replied. *"Thank you for your kindness."* I

remembered Craynolt then, and asked Royillis if he'd seen him.

"He has not yet returned," Royillis reported. *"But I have sent others in search of the humans."*

"I probably should have sent someone other than Craynolt to begin with," I grumbled. *"Who knows what he'll tell us if he ever does come back."*

Royillis made an odd, cackling sound that had to be laughter. *"Have you not discovered the way to understand him?"*

"Well, sort of," I admitted. *"Leo seems to get it pretty well, and sometimes I can, but he does take some getting used to."*

Royillis didn't argue with me on that point. *"I have sent watchers out, but no one seems to be following us."*

"That's not too surprising," I commented. *"You guys scared the pants off those men."*

"We are quite…formidable…when we fly together," Royillis agreed.

"You are, indeed," I said. "Leo," I said aloud. "Royillis says nobody is following us—not yet, anyway. If you were Brandon, what would you do at this point?"

He thought carefully for a moment. "Having come this far, I would not give up easily," he said. "Therefore, I would either follow as closely as I dared, or ride hard on a different route to arrive at Rafe's village ahead of us."

I nodded. "And Brandon knows where we're going, which gives him an advantage we didn't have." One that we *could* have had, if Rafe had only admitted it. I was still convinced that he'd known exactly where we were headed all along. He *had* to have known! He knew

Brandon, and while it might have been painful to admit—
to himself, if no one else—he had to see the resemblance
between Brandon and his sons. He might have tried to
convince himself otherwise, but the evidence was right
there in front of his face—and everyone else's, too! It
was stupid of him not to admit it to us, but it got Leo
freed, so at that point, I thought it was a fine idea for him
to have kept mum about it.

I thought for a moment, trying to think of how they
might get to Rafe's ahead of us, and unless they sprouted
wings, I didn't see how it was possible. The kidnapping
party had to have taken the most direct route, which we
were now following, so there was simply no way they
could do it any faster—unless…

"You know," I mused, "they could easily have kept on
going all through the night. Royillis didn't say whether
his watchers had checked parallel routes through the
forest. They might have missed them if they didn't fan
out enough."

"So, we should try to journey through the night—
again?" Leo sounded unhappy about this plan, and I
couldn't blame him. I was already reaching the limits
of my endurance, and though he was undoubtedly
tougher than me, without adequate sleep we would
be no match for Brandon's men should it come to
another fight.

"Sounds terrible, doesn't it?" I agreed. "But it might
at least enable us to catch up with Rafe. He's probably riding as hard he can, because unless Darley and
Max have managed to catch them, they have no way of
knowing we won that last fight."

"They would know it if the enemy did not pursue them," Leo pointed out.

"True." I sighed wearily. "Well, about all we can do is keep going as fast as we can, but it got pretty cold last night, so it's going to be icy. Wonder how those boys are holding up."

"He did not leave them behind, and he is still ahead of us," Leo reminded me.

"Lighter weight for the horses, too," I mused. Pushing one of the vultures out of the way, I sat up, combing the hair back from my face. "Guess we'd better get up and get moving then. I'd much rather sleep in, but that's not going to happen until we get home."

It occurred to me, then, that I'd never been away from home for so long before—in fact, I'd never been away from home at all! Of course, a pleasant journey in the springtime without armed men attacking us at regular intervals might have been preferable. It went without saying that having Leo with me made it more tolerable, but home and hearth were sounding better all the time.

We fed the horses and then ate a quick breakfast. Gerald found a squirrel nearby who had seen Rafe and the boys pass through, but he couldn't say how far ahead they were. Royillis had some of his clan spread out, but no one saw anything remarkable. I tried not to become too complacent, because Brandon's troops still might have been following us and, knowing that the vultures were on our side, had simply hidden whenever they saw the birds flying overhead.

As we rode, I tried to think of some other way to spy, and, try as I might, I couldn't come up with one, and Leo was at a loss, as well. Gerald seemed to think the squirrels could help, but they weren't nearly as swift as the birds, nor could they see as far ahead. I was worried about Max, too, and Morgana picked up on it, telling me more than once to quit my fretting and sit still.

The day was a bright, sunny one, as the day before had been, but late in the afternoon clouds rolled in and the sky went from clear blue to quilted gray, which meant that the moon wouldn't be lighting our way that night. Still, snow on the ground has a way of improving visibility, whether there's a decent moon or not. Unfortunately, the trail was now quite slick, and we found much better footing by staying just off the path.

Craynolt flew in about the same time the clouds did, and I thought he was reporting that all was well ahead of us, but it was hard to tell, for what he said was, *"The paths of time grow short, all souls are moving."*

"Well, thanks, Craynolt," I replied, though I wasn't completely sure if thanks were in order. *"You want to go see if Brandon is following us? Royillis's gang say it doesn't look like they are."*

"All souls are moving," he repeated.

"So, Brandon is following us?"

"Truth is like the cool wind, which blows on a sultry day."

"Ah, ha!" I yelled to Leo excitedly. "He actually repeated himself! I know what that means now! It means, yes! I should just ask him yes or no questions from now on." My excitement was short-lived, however, because I quickly realized I had no idea what the phrase was for "no." Experimentally, I asked him, *"Is the sky purple?"*

To which he replied, *"No."*

"No?" I echoed in disbelief. *"That's it? Nothing lofty and obscure? Just, no?"*

"Truth is like the cool wind which blows on a sultry day."

Obviously, he didn't consider negative responses to be worth philosophizing over. I tried to remember if I'd ever asked him anything that straightforward before, and if I had, I couldn't remember what it was. I was pretty sure he'd never given me a one-word reply, though—to anything.

"Do you think they'll be able to catch up with us before we catch up with Rafe?"

"Truth is—"

"Yeah, I got it," I said hastily, interrupting him. *"I don't mean to be rude, but if that's the case, we'd better get a move on!"*

Reporting this to Leo and urging Morgana to a faster pace, it occurred to me to ask, *"Hey, how come you could see Brandon and Royillis and his gang couldn't?"* I was pretty sure I'd get a strange reply with that question, and I wasn't disappointed.

"That which is given is taken."

"And by that, I suppose you mean don't look a gift horse in the mouth?"

"Truth is—"

"That's it, Craynolt!" I said, cutting him off again. *"Truth. That's all you have to say when you mean yes. Okay?"*

"Okay."

While I found it extremely difficult to believe that a flying reptile on a planet this far from Earth would have known what "okay" meant, I suppose I shouldn't have been too surprised. It's the sort of word that manages to catch on anywhere it's used, and I hadn't imagined it—it had popped into my mind the same way that Craynolt's other thoughts did. *"You understand the word 'okay?'"* I asked incredulously.

"Truth is like—"

Ignoring that, I went on, *"So, to you, yes, and okay, are not the same thing?"*

"Truth."

Silently thanking every god who ever existed on this planet or any other, I said to Leo, "I think we're making some real progress here. Now if I can just live long enough, I might actually be able to learn to talk to him without wanting to tear my hair out."

"You will live long," Leo reminded me. "And I hope that even if you do not ever understand Craynolt, you do not tear out your hair. I am very fond of it."

"Like to have it tickling your face when I'm on top, huh?" I teased.

"Very much," he replied. "And I will like it just as well when it turns gray."

"Sweet," I said, grinning at him. "No one would ever guess we were, you know, running for our lives here, would they?"

"We are not running," he said sensibly. "The horses are."

"Yes, but have you ever noticed how winded you can get riding a fast horse, even though you aren't running, yourself?"

"Yes," he replied. "But I am not now."

"Want to keep talking?"

"Yes," he replied. "I want to tell you how I long to

be back at the cottage with you, making love by the fire with no one hunting us."

"Longing for the good ol' days, are you?" I said approvingly. "Me, too. Except, once this kid's born, I doubt we'll be doing much of that."

"I will find a way," he said.

"I'll bet you will," I laughed. "After all, sex is your middle name."

"It is not," he said stiffly. "I have no middle name."

"Figure of speech there, Leo," I chuckled. "Don't take everything I say so literally—although sometimes, it is kinda funny when you do."

"You enjoy laughing at me?"

"Nope," I replied. "I like laughing *with* you. And what a hoot it is to think I can do it for the rest of my—and you did promise me it would be long, didn't you?—natural life."

"It will be long," he promised.

I found this difficult to believe when, a moment later, I took an arrow in the shoulder. Craynolt had been right, apparently, for Brandon was obviously much closer than we'd been led to believe. Royillis had some explaining to do.

Chapter 13

I MIGHT HAVE GUESSED THAT HAVING A PACK OF vultures as your lookout was a bad idea. Royillis had said once that it was a pity we weren't more warlike, and I was beginning to suspect that he was doing his best to make us more so. I don't believe he intended that anyone in particular should die, but it was looking more and more like he'd be feeding on one of us before long, rather than any of Brandon's troops. No doubt I should have killed more men in the last battle, so Royillis wouldn't have felt the need to start another one in order to get a few new bodies to munch on.

I managed to hold on to Morgana's mane as she ran, but, unlike the last one that had barely gotten beneath my skin, this arrow had driven in deeply. I managed to get off a few fireball rounds before I passed out, but that's about all, and I have no idea if I actually hit any of our pursuers. The last thing I saw was Leo being surrounded by horsemen and pulled from Calla's back.

When I came to, my shoulder was throbbing, my hands were bound tightly behind my back, and I had a blindfold on that was so tightly padded against my eyes that I couldn't open them at all. Obviously, Brandon didn't want to have to deal with any more fireballs. They'd gagged me, as well, which was okay, because I could still talk with any animals nearby, but what I really wanted to know was whether or not Leo was hurt—or dead.

We were still on the move. Someone's arms were around me, holding me upright in the saddle, but whose they were I couldn't have said. I put a call out to Morgana, and, having received no reply from her, tried Calla and still got nothing. The reply from Gerald was faint, but pursuing. Obviously we were leaving him behind. That left Royillis—who didn't respond—and Craynolt, who did.

"Where's Leo?" I asked desperately. *"Is he alive?"*

"Truth," Craynolt replied. *"But where there was speech, there is now silence."*

Gagged as well, I assumed. At least that meant he was well enough to need a gag to keep him quiet—though I suppose it could have also meant that he was unconscious. *"Did they leave him behind, or is he riding with us?"* Then I remembered I'd best stick to yes or no questions. *"Is Leo on a horse?"*

"Truth," Craynolt replied.

"Is he hurt?"

"No."

I was glad to hear he was okay, but I felt pretty terrible myself. Dizzy, nauseated, and in more pain than I could ever remember being in my life, I wondered what would happen if I vomited while I had a gag in my mouth. Probably drown in it, I decided. What a way to go! Guess it wouldn't be one of those fabulous Leo-induced orgasms that did it after all. Too bad, I was almost looking forward to that…

I mulled over our situation and decided that outrunning Gerald would have been easy enough for a mounted troop, but Morgana and Calla? Surely they weren't dead! Why would anyone kill a horse, if they didn't have to? I asked Craynolt where they were, and all he said was something about darkness and light, which I figured meant that he didn't know. Hopefully, they'd both taken off in Rafe's direction and would somehow warn him that trouble was following close behind.

"Keep out of range of those arrows!" I told Craynolt. *"I don't want you getting killed!"*

"The heart of the wind soars," Craynolt replied. *"The witch heart is true."*

"You're welcome, and thank you, too," I said, unsure of which response was expected there. *"Is Royillis still with us?"*

"No," Craynolt replied. *"The purple heart is no more."*

"Dead?"

"Swift arrows have taken many hearts."

So, they went for the birds, then—and me. Leo posed no real threat, one man against a whole troop, so they'd simply disarmed him and taken him prisoner. Brandon was being much kinder than I would have thought, given the circumstances. Of course, we now had his sons. I knew Rafe wouldn't kill them just to keep Brandon from taking them back, but the thought must have crossed Brandon's mind or he would have been more ruthless. For example, if I'd been him, I believe I'd have killed a witch who could shoot fireballs from her eyes, rather than take her prisoner, though he might have thought to use me as a bargaining chip. It wouldn't work, for the boys meant far more to Rafe than I did, but Brandon might not know that.

I was very sorry to lose Royillis, for he'd come to our aid more than once during this adventure. It might have been a gamble on his part, or it might have been that Craynolt was simply better at spotting our pursuers than the vultures, but whether he'd truly betrayed us or not, I would still miss him and think of him kindly.

Then I remembered Gerald. *"Craynolt,"* I said. *"Would you please go back and get Gerald? We can't leave him behind. You've flown with him before without eating him. Do you think you could do it again?"*

It took a few moments for Craynolt to reply. Obviously going back for a squirrel and not eating him was a difficult task for an otterell. But he *had* done it before.

"I'll give you something else to eat just as soon as I can," I promised. *"Please?"*

"The witch heart is great," Craynolt said finally. *"The wind is strong, and the desert will not fail."*

"Thanks, Craynolt," I said gratefully. I was actually beginning to like the way Craynolt talked. It was downright poetic sometimes.

I didn't even know where he'd been when he'd been talking with me. I could only assume he'd been flying nearby, but I heard no flap of wings as he left; the only sounds I heard were the creak of leather and the hoofbeats of the horses we rode. I felt so alone without anyone to talk with. Leo was there, but, not being able to see or hear him, I had to keep reminding myself of that fact. At least it wasn't too cold, but my arms were killing me—and tied the way they were, they probably wouldn't have felt very good, even if I hadn't taken an arrow in one of them.

Deciding it might be useful, as well as a distraction from my discomfort, I struck up a conversation with the horse I was on. His name was Alton, and, not surprisingly, he was very tired and also a little miffed at having to carry the extra weight—which gave me an idea that might slow us down.

"If you're tired, why don't you stop?" I suggested.

"Stop?" Alton echoed in disbelief. *"Without being told to stop?"*

So, he was one of those born obeyers who didn't take a step without being told what to do. I wasn't sure at that point whether I could turn this to my own advantage or not, for he was obviously used to doing exactly what his rider—the man behind me—told him. Suggesting that he do otherwise might be seen as rebellion, but most horses will rebel when the requests on them are unreasonable and unrelenting.

"Yes, you know," I went on encouragingly, *"just stop and refuse to move any further. And when your rider starts whipping you to make you go on, then you can rear up and let us slide off backward—but pick a nice, thick, snowdrift to do it in, will you? I've already been banged up enough as it is."*

This was apparently an option that Alton had never considered, though I'd seen a good many horses plant their feet and refuse to budge. This guy must have been among the most willing horses I'd ever run across. I hoped that meant he would be willing to take orders from a complete stranger—especially one who seemed so sympathetic to his complaints.

"You could use a break," I reasoned. *"And I'm sure the other horses would be grateful for a short rest, too."* I had an idea the men would, as well—except for Brandon, perhaps—but they probably wouldn't admit it. *"Oh, and act like you're scared of something,"* I added,

"—like there's some horrible monster lurking behind a tree up ahead. And you might tell the other horses that, too."

"You're sure about this?" Alton asked warily. *"It sounds very disobedient to me."*

"That's why you all need to act frightened," I replied. *"That way, no one can blame you too much."*

"Okay," Alton said, obviously willing, though he still didn't seem convinced it was a good idea. *"There's a big pile of snow beside a tree up ahead. Would that be okay?"*

"Sure," I replied. *"I can't see a thing, so I'll have to take your word for it. And, like I said, do it gently. I'm going to have a baby."*

"Really? Why, that's wonderful!" Alton exclaimed. *"But they should not be hunting a mare in foal! It is very wrong of them to do so! And even more wrong of me to throw you off!"*

"Generally speaking, I couldn't agree more, but I don't think they know anything about it. I'm not what you'd call obviously pregnant yet."

Alton obviously thought that my being pregnant was a very good reason to *not* make me slide off backwards, so I had to encourage him.

"And I'll be much better off for having had some rest," I said reasonably. *"Besides, I'll probably fall on top of this man behind me—and it'll be in the snow, too—so I don't think I'll get hurt."* I'd already taken two arrows—what was one little jump into a snowdrift? Then something else occurred to me. *"And please, Alton, whatever you do, don't fall over backward and land on top of us."*

"You think I might?" Alton asked, horrified that this might actually happen. *"I've never thrown anyone before. I'm afraid I won't do it right."*

"Come on, now, Alton," I said soothingly. *"You can do it. It's easy. I've seen lots of horses get rid of their riders, and I'm sure you can, too."* The fact that he never had was obviously the reason Alton had been chosen to carry me. Brandon was at least making sure I made it to the stake alive, which was *so* thoughtful of him…*"How about if you just spook at the monster, and I'll try to go off sideways?"*

"That might be better," he said fretfully. *"I'll jump to the right, and you fall to the left, okay?"*

"Sounds great!" I said, trying to sound as enthusiastic as I could about getting dumped off a horse. *"That way I won't land on my bad arm. Go for it!"*

"All right," Alton said. *"We're almost there…almost there…okay, jump!"*

I'll say this much for Alton, he was quick on his feet. Even if I hadn't known it was coming and taken a dive, I think I'd still have gone off sideways, because one minute he was right there beneath me, and the next, he was gone. Unfortunately, our original plan might have been better, because that way I might have at least landed on my captor. Going off sideways—and jumping first because I knew it was coming—meant that *he* wound up landing on *me*—at least partly. Unfortunately, it was the part that hurt the most, because he hit my right arm when he fell. You know, it's really hard to scream out in pain when you've been gagged, but I managed to do it anyway.

I heard the man swearing at Alton, and Brandon

shouting for the others to halt. There was quite the little fracas for a moment or two as all the other horses went berserk. I don't know if Alton had asked them to, or if the mere sight of the normally unflappable Alton going off the deep end was enough to convince the others to spook first and ask questions later, but I believe they all managed to unseat their riders.

"Are you okay?" Alton asked me, sounding worried. *"I heard you scream."*

"This asshole landed on my arm," I grumbled. *"Other than that, I'm fine, and so is the baby. How about the others?"*

"Pissed off more than anything," Alton reported. *"That man who was with you seems okay."*

"Good," I said thankfully. *"Now, if you guys will keep on acting crazy for a while, the men will have to stop and let you horses calm down. It might help if some of you run off, too."* I wondered if Craynolt and Gerald were back yet. *"You haven't seen an otterell and a squirrel, have you?"*

"Not recently," Alton replied. *"Want me to go look for them?"*

"Not now," I said. *"Just keep an eye out and let me know if you see them."*

Someone took hold of me then and sat me up—none too gently, either. Removing my gag, he held a cup to my lips.

"It is only water," he said when I seemed reluctant to drink. I recognized his voice. It was Brandon. "I will remove your blindfold," he went on, "but if you make any more trouble, I will have my men slit your friend's throat."

I nodded. He had to mean Leo. If he thought he could sway Rafe with me, he apparently thought he could do the same thing with me by threatening Leo—and in this case, he happened to be correct. Once my blindfold was off, I could see he wasn't kidding, either, because Leo was standing behind him, held by two men while a third brandished a knife.

"You have bewitched the horses, haven't you?" Brandon hissed.

I shook my head. "I just wanted to rest," I insisted. "That's all."

"That's all?" he said in a voice dripping with sarcasm. "And I suppose you simply asked them to behave in this fashion?"

"Well, yes," I said lamely. "That's pretty much the way it went. They're tired, too, you know. It didn't take much convincing."

Brandon was right in my face, his eyes narrowed in suspicion. "And I'm supposed to believe that?"

I shrugged. "It's the truth, Brandon. I'm not going to lie to you. I won't risk Leo's life for Rafe, or his children—or anyone else, for that matter."

"They are *my* children!" Brandon seethed. "Even you saw the resemblance!"

"Yeah," I said reluctantly. "I did. So you were Carnita's lover, were you?"

"I should have been her husband," he said, spitting out the words. "She loved me, and we were to marry, but then Rafe made her a better offer."

Ah, yes, the thwarted lover, I thought. *Shouldn't be too hard to play on his emotions.* "I'm sure he did," I said smoothly. "But, you know, he's a bit angry with her right now. He might let you have her."

"I don't want her," Brandon insisted. "I want my sons."

"Now, be reasonable, Brandon!" I chided him. "Those boys don't know you! To them, you're just some slimy bastard who killed their nurse and kidnapped them! They have no loyalty to you! You'd have much better luck raising some other children—more of your own, perhaps. You and Carnita could have other children, couldn't you?"

His face was grim, but he was wavering, I could tell.

"She's still very beautiful," I reminded him. "But you've seen her recently, haven't you?"

"Yes," he said bitterly. "I have seen her."

"Spent a little time with her, perhaps?"

He didn't reply, but judging by the look on his face, I'd have to say he had.

"I don't suppose she's pregnant again, is she?"

"I have no way of knowing," Brandon replied stiffly.

"Me, either," I said. "I don't see her much—don't really like her, either. You see, Rafe and I were lovers once, but he was unable to father my child—which is not too surprising since, as you may know, only certain men are capable of impregnating a witch—and he decided that having sons was more important to him than I was, so he cast me off in favor of someone who could give them to him."

Brandon seemed skeptical about this. "Surely, he knew that witches only give birth to daughters?" he scoffed.

"Yeah, he knew," I said with a weary sigh. "I think

he just wanted to see if he could be the one. He wasn't."
I gestured at Leo. "He is."

"Ah, so you are with child now?"

I could have gone either way, here. Brandon might
think that, being pregnant, I no longer had a need for
Leo, and therefore wouldn't care if he lived or died. I
considered using this option, but abandoned it immediately in case Brandon should decide to call my bluff. I
was taking no chances with Leo's life.

"Yes, I am," I said grimly. "And, make no mistake,
Brandon, if you hurt him, then you'd best kill me, too,
because I swear before all the gods this world can muster
that I will hunt you down and burn you to ashes where
you stand."

I must have sounded pretty serious, because Brandon
sat back on his heels, his eyes much wider than they'd
been a moment before. "I believe that," he said quietly,
then motioned to the men who held Leo. They still held
him, but the knife disappeared into a sheath.

"So, what do we do now?" I said briskly, trying not to
let my relief show. "Go after them, and possibly end up
killing one of the boys? I think that's a bad idea, myself.
Really, Brandon, your best bet is to have other children.
Would it be so difficult? While you've been waiting for
Carnita to come to you, haven't you at least *looked* at
another woman?"

I could see he hadn't, and it was paining him to have
to admit it. My goodness, he was smitten!

"I think you could get an excellent deal on a slightly
used wife if you play your cards right."

"How?" Brandon demanded. "If she hasn't come to
me in all these years, why would she come now?"

I stared at him as though he'd gone mad. "Brandon, if your wife had done to you what Rafe's did to him, and you just found out about it, how would you feel?"

He laughed grimly. "Worse than I did when I found out she'd lied to me," he admitted.

"Right!" I concurred. "So, unless I miss my guess, she might be needing a new home...if he doesn't kill her, that is," I mused.

Brandon's expression grew fierce. "He wouldn't dare!"

"Well, why not? You killed someone to get those boys—or, if not you, personally, at least someone did, but it still amounts to the same thing." I paused there to reflect upon one of the more questionable aspects of our society. "You know, we did a bad thing coming to this world and electing to police ourselves," I said with a rueful smile. "It hasn't worked out so well, has it?"

"Crime is rare here," he reminded me, "—especially murder. We hadn't intended to kill anyone, but it was... unavoidable."

I thought he should try telling that to those who died, but did my best to soften my retort. "Should have thought about that before you acted, then, shouldn't you?"

"I...regret the deaths," he said slowly. "It was not meant to happen as it did. The woman who was killed—Rafe's servant—was simply in the wrong place at the wrong time. The man responsible for her death was one of the three that were sent back to slow you down and is now dead himself."

"Convenient, isn't it?" I remarked acidly. "But that

still doesn't excuse you, Brandon. You were still the one in charge."

"There was a...miscommunication," he said. "I truly doubt you'll believe this, but I gave no orders to kill."

"Those men came after us with swords drawn and engaged us in battle!" I exclaimed. "There was never the slightest hint that they meant to leave us alive."

"They were told only to slow you down," Brandon reiterated. "Those were the orders I gave."

"Slow us down?" I scoffed. "Come on, Brandon! They were out to kill us! Those may have been the orders you gave, but someone took it upon himself to interpret them rather liberally. We were engaged in a battle for our lives!"

"I am truly sorry for that," he said, and he seemed sincere. "Perhaps if Rafe had not been so quick to anger—"

"Now, don't you go blaming all this on Rafe!" I said, wishing I'd had my hands free so I could have shaken my finger at him. "You took his sons, Brandon, and he wanted them back! Does it surprise you that he was out for your blood? What the devil did you think he would do? Give them to you with his best wishes?"

"No," he replied. "I didn't."

"And if he was conveniently killed in battle," I went on, "no one would ever question your decision to marry his widow and adopt his sons, thereby acquiring his land, now, would they?"

Brandon was looking more uncomfortable by the moment and was undoubtedly regretting the decision to remove my gag. I probably shouldn't have pressed my luck, but I still had one more question I needed to ask.

"So, tell me something, Brandon. Who let you into Rafe's house?"

When he didn't reply, I came to my own conclusion.

"It was Carnita, wasn't it?"

To his credit, he wouldn't come right out and admit it, but I was sure I was right. Regarding him closely, I decided that he was a remarkably handsome man—in a swarthy, rakish sort of way—and different from Rafe in most respects. It was distinctly possible that Carnita *did* love Brandon, which might have been why she'd never been able to make Rafe particularly happy.

"Did she at least know why you were there?" I prompted him.

Brandon shook his head and sighed, giving me reason to believe I would now be hearing the truth at last. "I sent her a message that I wanted to see her," he said. "We arranged a time when the gate would be untended. She didn't know I was there for the children."

I nodded. "You do still want her, don't you?" When he didn't reply, I went on to suggest, "Why didn't you just take her instead?"

"Because she'd told me she wouldn't stay with me!" he exclaimed vehemently. "And I begged her, believe me, I begged!"

"So, when you took the boys, did you think she might be the one to follow instead of Rafe, perhaps?" I, for one, couldn't see Carnita doing anything of the kind, but men have some strange ideas sometimes—and women, too. At the very least, taking Brandon as her lover had been foolhardy, but Carnita must have been out of her mind to let Brandon into Rafe's house.

Brandon shook his head. "No, I knew he would come. I thought perhaps they both would come and I—"

"—would kill Rafe and then take his wife?" I suggested. "*Not* a good plan!"

"I don't know *what* I thought would happen," he said shaking his head—and I believe he was being honest about that. "But I knew that if I had the boys—"

"—you'd be that much closer to getting her," I finished for him.

He nodded silently.

"That little speech of yours back at the gate about not wanting her anymore," I said gently. "That was because she *didn't* come, wasn't it?"

"*Whoa!*" Gerald exclaimed as he and Craynolt swooped by. "*Who do you want me to bite first?*"

"*Hey, guys! Good to see you both!—but don't bite anybody yet,*" I replied, "*You might chew on the ropes, though…*"

"*Yours, or Leo's?*"

"*Either one—although I may be talking our way out of this, so hold off on that for now.*"

"*Righto! Hey, thanks for sending the big bird back for me.*"

"*Don't call him a bird, Gerald. He doesn't like it.*"

"*Can't hear me, though, can he?*"

"*Probably not, but you never know with otterells. He's probably hearing my side of this conversation and can guess at what you're saying. He already wants to eat you, so I wouldn't tease him too much—you might regret it.*"

"*I'll be careful,*" he promised quickly.

"*See that you are,*" I said warmly. "*I don't want to

*lose anyone else on this trip—and speaking of which, I
don't suppose you know what happened to our horses,
do you?"*

"Went on ahead, I think," Gerald replied. "Maybe
they're bringing back help."

"That might be interesting," I commented. Depending
on who they brought, of course. There had been a time
when I couldn't imagine Rafe following two riderless
horses back to our aid, but times had changed considerably since then. Now, if they could just bring back
Carnita...

I realized I'd carried on an entire conversation with
Gerald while, in the meantime, Brandon still hadn't
replied to my query—possibly because he didn't feel
the need to, so I altered my question.

"Which would you truly rather have, Brandon?
Carnita, or the boys?"

"I should have taken her years ago," he said quietly,
"—despite her protests! But I always thought she would
come to me. I was wrong, obviously. I never knew the
boys were mine until that last meeting. I think I went
slightly mad, knowing that another man was calling my
sons his own—a man whom I've always regarded as an
enemy of sorts, because of her...I don't know now."

Brandon seemed to be at a loss as to what to do next,
so I decided to help him out. I was going for broke, and
I knew it, but the way I saw it, it couldn't hurt to try.

"Okay, then," I said briskly, "here's what you're
going to do. You're going to let us go—or at least take
off Leo's gag—and then we'll try to talk some sense
into Rafe—or Carnita—or both. But we can't do it
while we're waving swords at each other and—if it's all

the same to you—I'd really like our hands untied, too, because my shoulder is killing me."

Brandon was eyeing me warily, so I went on to add, "And if you don't, I'll get loose somehow, but you won't like what I'll do, then—what I *could* do right now, even with your men holding Leo, and even with my hands tied." Brandon had no idea what the extent of my powers were, so it was a bit of a gamble—a little nudge, actually—to get him to see things my way.

"You'll tell all the horses to run off home if I don't, won't you," he said with the first smile I'd ever seen from him—which was quite charming, actually. No wonder Carnita liked him so well.

I smiled back at him, thinking that this might work out after all. "Wouldn't take much to get them to do that," I said. "They're tired, hungry, and they'd much rather go home than stay here—and so would I."

And I *would* go home, too, but not without giving that little bitch, Carnita, a really big piece of my mind before I went, because this whole mess was starting to look as though it was her fault—and hers, alone. These men would never have fought if it hadn't been for her! Rafe might have put her aside, if she'd never given him sons—which may have been the motive driving her—but she could still have gone to Brandon after that. She might have had to swallow her pride to do it, but I was sure Brandon would have welcomed her with open arms. Things might have worked out much better that way, though it would have left Rafe with no one to succeed him, which had been his driving motivation through all of this.

I know that having heirs meant an awful lot to him, but—and you may think this selfish of me—looking at

it from my own perspective at that moment (sitting in
a snowdrift with my hands tied behind my back while
someone else held Leo prisoner), I'd have to say I really
didn't give a damn.

Chapter 14

I KNOW WHAT YOU'RE THINKING; I HAD ONE TINY little thing to be grateful to Carnita for, and that, of course, was Leo. If she hadn't been such a social-climbing little hussy, I'd never have found him. I'd have to keep that in mind, so I wouldn't allow my gut instincts to overrule my better judgment and deck her with a fireball.

I kept these thoughts to myself, because if Brandon had known what I was thinking, he would have been much less cooperative—but it made me feel better. Perhaps, years from now, I could get together with Rafe, and we could discuss all the dire fates that Carnita deserved, but that was best left for another time. Right now, I had to get this adventure wrapped up, so I could go home with Leo, have his baby, and live happily ever after.

By the gods, I liked the sound of that!

Brandon seemed to be taking his sweet time to consider my suggestion, though I couldn't see that he had much choice, but you know how these guys get when they're on a testosterone high.

"Come on, Brandon," I urged. "Let's get this over with and then we can all go home and forget it ever happened."

I had a strong suspicion that there were some things that none of us would be able to forget, but the idea was still very appealing.

"Kiss and make up?" he suggested with a wry smile.

"Something like that. Of course, Rafe won't have anyone to kiss but his kids, but he'll get over it. He's pretty tough. And it's the boys that he cares about. Carnita just makes him crazy."

"You really think it will work?"

"Never know 'til we try," I said honestly. "Just remember that *your* solution to the problem has been one big, fat fiasco after another, so it couldn't hurt to let me give it a go. One witch against another, as it were."

"Carnita is not a witch," Brandon objected.

"Well, maybe not in the strictest sense of the word," I admitted, "but there are plenty of people who would hear her story and come to that conclusion."

"You don't think much of her, do you?" he observed.

"I really don't know her well enough to answer that question," I said—and this was true—"but Leo says her heart is not steadfast. Are you sure you want to deal with that?"

"It has always been steadfast for me," Brandon replied. "Not strong, perhaps, but steadfast. I believe she still loves me."

"And I believe she never loved Rafe," I said agreeably. *The shallow, two-faced bitch!*

Gerald heard that and snickered from a nearby tree. It was good to hear his laugh, but I'd really have preferred to hear Leo's at that point.

"Will you please untie Leo now?" I prompted. "I promise he won't hurt anybody."

"I believe he has hurt quite a few of my people already," Brandon said grimly. "He is a good fighter."

And an even better lover, I thought, but didn't voice that opinion, since guys don't like to hear that sort of thing. Girls do, but there weren't any around at the time. Well, Morgana might have been around somewhere, but she didn't like hearing stuff like that, either. I needed to get home to Desdemona. Then it occurred to me that she might not join in the discussion of Leo's sexual prowess with a great deal of enthusiasm, either. Damn! I needed a girlfriend! Maybe I should try to strike up a friendship with one of Gerald's women.

"No!" Gerald said vehemently. *"You should not! I don't want them hearing anything about him!"*

"Coward!" I shot back at him, trying hard not to laugh.

Brandon saw me smiling anyway, but he misinterpreted it, giving it my original meaning instead. Signaling to his men, he said, "Loose him, then. Seems the witch covets him for some reason."

"If you only knew," I said with a knowing shake of my head. "He was Rafe's slave before—well, actually, he was Carnita's—but he's my husband now. And, trust me, Carnita would *never* come to you if she still owned him!"

"Well, then, let's make sure that never happens," Brandon said briskly, getting to his feet. "Now, if you would be so kind as to tell our horses to return and behave themselves, we can be on our way." Pausing for a moment to consider, he added, "I believe I will still have someone ride with you. Forgive me for not trusting you completely, but…"

"I understand," I said graciously. "But Alton will be *so* upset."

"Another horse, then," he said, taking my meaning

immediately. "I wouldn't want you to end up in another snowdrift."

"Me, either," I declared. "I've had enough snow on this trip to last a lifetime!"

Brandon grinned hugely. "You can thank my witch for that," he said.

"She can control the weather?" I squeaked. "Wow! That's really impressive!"

"Oh, she is," he agreed with another smile. "She's also very…useful—and beautiful," he added.

"Should Carnita be concerned?" I inquired carefully.

"Not really," he replied. "I may have fathered her daughter, but that was a long time ago—before I met Carnita, in fact—and she'll have none of me to wed." So, there *had* been at least one other woman in his life… I'd thought as much.

"Smart girl," I said approvingly. "It's best not to fall in love with 'the one.' "

"But you did," Brandon pointed out.

"Yes," I replied. "But since Leo doesn't have any property for sons to inherit, it won't matter to him that he has only one daughter."

A shadow of a doubt crossed my mind—Leo was a warrior, that much had been made clear to me on this journey. Would he be content to settle down on a primitive planet with an herbalist witch and help me brew potions? And would he be satisfied with only a daughter to raise? All the other men I knew valued sons so highly—would Leo be any different in this regard? Wouldn't he want sons to carry on his prowess with the sword and bow, his skill as a tracker?

His gag removed, Leo grinned. "It would not matter to me if we had no children at all," he said. "But we will."

"Only the one, Leo," I reminded him.

"You may be surprised," he said mysteriously.

"I doubt it," I said, dismissing the subject with a wave of my hand. We witches never had more than one daughter—never!—though it was very sad that Leo would have no sons because they surely would have driven all the local girls wild. Then I remembered all the turmoil that one extraordinarily beautiful woman had caused and decided that perhaps it was best if he didn't...

The ride from there on was much more pleasant. In addition to Gerald sitting snugly in the front of my cloak, I had a charming young man named Kyle riding behind me, who held me on the pommel of his saddle with such strong arms and kept me laughing to the point that Leo scowled at him from time to time. Turns out he was the one who'd fired that arrow into my shoulder— and the one in my side!—something which he seemed to regret, for he kissed me on that shoulder a few times while we rode.

I made a point of complimenting him on his marks-manship and thanked him for not actually killing me either time. I had an idea he might have only been attempting to placate a witch whom he knew could blast him off the face of the planet, but since he hadn't needed to tell me anything at all, I decided that this was yet another reminder to me that I really should travel more and meet new people. After all, it's much harder to wage wars with your friends than with people you've never met.

I really wanted to meet Brandon's witch, too. We needed to form a network! With my abilities and hers—she might be able to do a lot more than make snow!—we could probably whip the place into shape in no time—perhaps even get slavery abolished. I'd have liked to learn how to control the weather, too, but doubted that I ever could, because witches are born with their own set of innate abilities. We can develop them more as we grow, but they aren't something that can be taught. I mean, I couldn't even begin to guess how to teach someone to talk to squirrels!

As we neared the village, it became perfectly obvious that Rafe had heeded my advice and hadn't stopped or probably even wondered what had happened to Leo and me—though he might have decided we were dead and spared no more thought for us than that. This was unkind of me, for he'd only done exactly what I'd told him to, but it would have been nice to think he cared enough to wonder what had become of us.

My shoulder ached like the devil, and the one night we spent out on the trail was one of sheer torment. I slept very little, and though Leo was allowed to sleep with me, we weren't what you'd call intimate with one another for obvious reasons—one of them being that Gerald and Craynolt shared our tent, and we also had a guard or two close by. Anyway, by the time we arrived at Rafe's doorstep, I was tired, hurting, and horny as hell—in no mood, therefore, to put up with any crap from anybody.

But, of course, the gates were shut fast against us, and it was obviously going to take a good bit of persuasion to even get Rafe to come out and parley.

Brandon signaled to Kyle, who, right on cue, produced a knife that he held tightly against my throat.

"Forgive me," he whispered softly, "but I have to make this look good."

"Oh, go right ahead," I grumbled. "What's one more wound?"

"That's the spirit," Kyle said with genuine approval. "We'll get the bastard out here—you wait and see. Brandon's got quite a mouth on him."

"Come out!" Brandon roared. "Or the witch dies!"

"My, how dramatic!" I commented acerbically. "Might I remind you that Rafe probably doesn't give a damn whether I live or die?"

At another signal from Brandon, Kyle pressed even harder with the knife. It was going beyond mere discomfort into the realm of actual pain now, and, so far, there was no indication that Rafe was paying any attention at all. Leo was, though, because I could hear him growling—presumably at Kyle.

"Do you want her blood on your hands, too?" Brandon shouted. "She means nothing to me! However, I would hope that the witch of your realm might be of use to you and your people. Perhaps they might have a say in this?"

Despite the fact that a troop of armed men stood ready to kill anything that moved, a crowd was beginning to gather. Not exactly an angry mob, but there were a few grumblings amongst them. I recognized many of the faces, for they were people I had cared for in the past. Looking further, I saw the woman whose child I had once found, and she was being pretty vocal on my behalf. I hoped Rafe was listening, because having a knife pressed against your throat is not a pleasant experience, even if a charming fellow like Kyle was involved.

Brandon shouted at Rafe a few more times—his deep, raspy voice sounding more like a roar than ever—and the crowd began to take up the chant as well. I was in the process of telling Kyle's horse to *please* stand still and quit fidgeting, lest I inadvertently lose my head, when the gates opened at last. Kyle lowered the knife, but didn't loosen his grip on me.

Rafe and Carnita were flanked by what was probably each and every one of Rafe's men, right down to the stable boys. All of them were armed and ready, though I wasn't sure if their intention was to win a fight, or merely to deter one. Rafe stood there glaring at us defiantly, holding a nervous Carnita tightly around the waist, as though he was afraid she might escape. If I hadn't known better, I'd have said she was a hostage herself. Rafe and Brandon were wasting time staring daggers at one another when, to my delight, Max trotted out, happily wagging his tail. He looked a little stiff, but seemed otherwise okay.

"Max!" I exclaimed. *"It's so good to see you! I was so worried! Are you all right?"*

"I'm fine," he replied staunchly. *"Want me to bite someone?"*

Good old Max! *"No, if I need anyone bitten, I've still got Gerald in my cloak,"* I said as Gerald stuck his nose out to watch the show. *"And Craynolt is around here somewhere."*

"Morgana is in our stable," Max reported. *"She's fine, too. And the boys are glad to be home. They didn't like being with that other man."*

When Rafe finally said something, it was to inform me that if Morgana gave birth to a live foal, I owed him a stud fee. Sinjar had scored at last!

"Sorry I can't pay you right now, Rafe," I apologized. "I'm...occupied at the moment. If it's not too much trouble, would you please talk to Brandon and try to calm him down? He's rather...testy."

"I will not!" Rafe seethed. "I have nothing to say to him."

"Yeah, well, he has plenty to say to you," I said. "Tell him, Brandon."

Brandon still sat on his big, white stallion and was looking down at Rafe from that superior height, as though he were an insect to be stepped on. "You may keep my sons in exchange for your wife," Brandon said. "Those are my terms."

Which sounded reasonable to me, but just because Brandon wanted Carnita, Rafe now seemed to want to keep her at all cost. It was probably only to save face, but the townspeople had seen Rafe's boys, and were now looking at Brandon with some degree of interest— and recognition. I heard a few murmurs in the crowd about the resemblance. Rafe himself had never admitted that he believed it, but the fact that—according to Leo, whose insight was very helpful at this point—Carnita was pregnant again was now a factor. This child was also his own, or so Rafe claimed.

"Bullshit!" I exclaimed with disgust, completely losing the guard I usually keep on my tongue concerning the use of swear words—in public, that is. "She and Brandon got together when the cartel met! He told me so!"

"He would say anything!" Rafe spat out. "The poor, childless wretch!"

Brandon appeared to be too tongue-tied with anger to even respond to being called a poor, childless wretch, so I went on, "Come on, Rafe! Admit it! You don't believe those are your kids! You can't possibly! No one believes it! The only one you're fooling is yourself." I looked at Carnita. "Tell him, Carnita. You know the truth better than anyone."

"Don't say a word to that scum!" Rafe warned her, tightening his grip around her waist. "He stole my sons, killed my servant, and sent armed men out to kill us," Rafe shouted to the crowd. "Tisana, I can't believe you've been taken in by him!" Then his eyes narrowed, taking in the fact that Leo was also being held captive. "Oh, I see," he said grimly. "He's threatened to kill the slave if you don't cooperate. Well, I'm sorry Tisana, but I am not giving up what is rightfully mine. Not for you, or anyone else."

I heard a gasp from someone in the crowd, but didn't have the opportunity to notice who it was, though it was obviously someone who thought Leo was pretty neat. I looked over at Brandon, rolling my eyes before turning back to address Rafe. "It still comes down to property and ownership, doesn't it, Rafe? Is that all you care about? That, and saving face? Because you won't be, you know. Everyone in the cartel must know the truth."

Rafe ignored this. "I keep what is mine," he said firmly.

"What about Leo, then?" I asked. "You gave him to me just to shut me up! You knew!"

"But you haven't shut up, have you?" he said nastily. "So I guess the deal's off, then."

I looked over at Carnita. "Spend five minutes with Leo, and you'll never let Rafe—or Brandon, or anyone else, for that matter—touch you again. Believe me, he's a better lover than any mere human could ever be! One taste of him, and you'll be having orgasms 'til you can't see straight."

"I'll second that," a female voice called out from the crowd.

I was dying to know who that was, but couldn't take the time to check it out just yet.

Carnita seemed momentarily diverted by this. "Oh, really? I just thought he looked interesting."

"Trust me, Carnita. He's much more than interesting!" I said earnestly. "I wouldn't trade him for any other man on the planet—all of them, in fact. And that's aside from the fact that he's the only one I love."

"And love is the only thing that matters in this life," Leo said gravely. "Whatever else we may possess, love is the one thing that cannot be bought." His gaze sought Carnita's. "For all of Rafe's wealth, you do not love him," he said simply. "It is plain to see."

Carnita's eyes reflected her indecision. It was apparent that she loved Brandon, not Rafe, but it was very hard for her to admit to it. Honestly! She and Rafe deserved each other! Brandon would be much better off going back to his witch, even if he *never* had any sons! Rafe was making me mad, too, and just when I thought he'd made a change for the better! I wanted to slap them both!

"Rafe, I'm surprised at you!" I snapped. "She plays

you false, passes off Brandon's children as your own, and now she's pregnant again! You wondered how anyone could have gotten in there without making a stir the night the boys were taken, well, this is why! She let him in! She's the enemy here, not Brandon! He's as much her dupe as you are."

"I am no one's dupe!" Rafe roared. "And she is not the enemy! She is my wife!"

"She did let me in," Brandon said quietly. "And we have been lovers since before you were wed. I loved her then, and, despite everything that has happened, I love her still."

"Which is a lot more than you deserve!" I spat at Carnita. Fireballs were forming in my eyes, and it took everything I had not to fire one at her. "People have died because of you! And you aren't worth it!" I said disgustedly, "Best give it up, Brandon. She's not worth the effort. Go back to your witch and try to be happy."

Inadvertently, I'd said exactly the right thing. "Your witch?" Carnita exclaimed in disbelief. "Your *witch?*" Her voice became more high-pitched and screechy with each repetition. "You said you were faithful to me, that you'd never looked at another woman!"

Brandon must have seen this as his best weapon, because, God love him, he gave it his all. With an insolent smirk, he said, "That does not include witches." His smile became more pronounced as he added, "There's a difference." He sat his big horse with a casual arrogance, obviously very sure of himself now. He had her, and he wasn't going to have to beg, either. "She was a good lay," he said, glancing over at me. His lust-filled eyes raked my body with such a fierce heat, I could almost feel his gaze ripping my clothes off as it went from my head to my toes. "Most witches are, you know—as is this one."

He was very convincing, and, by the gods, if I hadn't known better, I'd have believed him myself. Even Leo, who knew it to be a lie, was growling again, and that Carnita believed him was evident. Kyle was chuckling softly in my ear and whispered, "I'll bet you are, too," as his arms tightened possessively around me, pulling me back against him. He was enjoying this immensely, and if I wasn't mistaken, it was making his cock hard.

"Her too?" Carnita squealed, her face flushing with anger as she stomped her foot. "Oh, you cad! You swore you'd be faithful to me forever!" She squirmed out of Rafe's hold and started toward Brandon, her fists raised in fury.

Rafe grabbed her arm. "You are not jealous of him?" he demanded.

"You bet your sweet life I am!" she swore, wrenching away from him. "Just let me get my hands on him. I'll kill him!" Ordinarily, I wouldn't have thought she'd had it in her, but if I'd been Brandon at that moment, I think I'd have been just a tiny bit afraid, because from the way she was glaring at him, it was a wonder he wasn't dead already. I'm pretty sure if I'd looked at him that way, he'd have been reduced to smoldering embers in no time at all.

Brandon obviously wasn't afraid of her, for he never flinched, but simply let her approach, still with that provoking smirk on his face. Seizing the bridle above his horse's bit, Carnita spun the poor thing in circles around her while she screamed at Brandon like a banshee. I didn't catch everything she said, but

I know that ripping Brandon's balls off and feeding them to the dogs was in there somewhere. Finally, she managed to get the stallion off balance enough that he fell over in a tangle of thrashing hooves and frothy white tail. Brandon jumped clear and then stalked toward Carnita menacingly, stripping off his gloves as he came. Striking her full across the face with one of them, he snarled, "Shut up, bitch!"

She might have been surprised, but it didn't stop her—barely slowed her down, in fact—and she launched herself into him, fists flying. Brandon stood it for a few minutes, then he did what he should have done all along and, pinning her arms to her sides, kissed her fiercely, right on her wide open, screaming mouth.

"Damn, this is getting me hot," Kyle swore against my neck as he thrust his hips forward against my ass. "Are you *sure* that cat's really that much better than the rest of us?"

"Kyle, my friend," I said, smiling as Carnita finally began to return Brandon's kiss, "you have no idea."

"How about three or four of us together?" Kyle persisted. "He couldn't top that, could he?"

"Bound, gagged, and standing on one foot," I replied absently, still watching Brandon and Carnita. Rafe snarled and went back inside, slamming the gates on the scene, as though the mere sight of it made him physically ill. He was going to be better off without a wife who didn't love him, of that much I was sure, even if he wasn't used to the idea yet. It really was the boys who held a place in his heart. Maybe now he could find a nice local girl who wasn't quite as beautiful and provoking as Carnita and finally get some peace.

"I've got a really big cock," Kyle assured me. "You'd like it."

My voice was firm. "Not as much as his, Kyle. We are talking deluxe model now. You might as well give it up."

"But I've always wanted to fuck a witch," he said wistfully. "Are you sure you wouldn't…?"

"Absolutely. And besides, if you'd wanted to fuck a witch, you should have done it before now," I scolded him. "I've been sitting in that cottage all alone for years and years! You could have come to visit me anytime."

"But I didn't know where you lived, or how…sexy you were."

"I wasn't," I replied, smiling at Leo, who had dismounted and was now heading our way. Oh, wow, did he ever look like the man of my dreams! Glowing eyes, fanged smile, pointy ears, curly hair, and all—and I couldn't even *see* his cock at that point. "*He* did that to me," I said firmly. "Made me what I am today. He's the one."

Leo came closer and, reaching up, he took my hand, pulling me from Kyle's grasp, who he took no more notice of than he did the horse we sat upon. Entwining my arms around his neck, my feet never touched the ground as my dear Leo kissed me.

And, yes, he was *my* Leo—now, forever, and always.

Chapter 15

I WASTED NO TIME IN LOCATING THE WOMAN IN the crowd who'd seemed so knowledgeable about Zetithians—and she wasn't too difficult to locate, because she had four of them with her! Three of them were children, but that they were Zetithians was undisputable—and also that the adult male knew Leo.

"Leccarian!" he called out.

Leo's head spun around so fast, I thought he would pull a muscle. "Cark?" he said in a voice that sounded nothing like his own.

The tall, dark-haired Zetithian grinned, revealing his fangs. "I thought it was you," he said. "But I did not wish to interrupt. You seemed…occupied."

I'd never seen Leo cry, but if he didn't have a few tears in his eyes at that point, I'd have thought much less of him. The rest of what they said to one another must have been in Zetithian, because I didn't catch a word of it.

"You two *know* each other?" I exclaimed. "I'd heard the galaxy was getting smaller, but I never *dreamed*…"

The tall, dark-haired woman with him responded with a smile. "Me either! Cat said there might be others, but, honest to God, finding another one is like finding a needle in a haystack—one helluva big haystack, too." I couldn't have agreed more, since Zetithians were obviously pretty rare. "What are the odds of finding two of them?" she marveled. "Must be about a hundred quadrillion to one!"

The man she called Cat looked up from hugging Leo, "I believe it would be more."

"Probably would, at that," she agreed. "Allow me to introduce myself. I'm Captain Jack Tshevnoe of the starship *Jolly Roger*, and this incredibly sexy fellow is my husband, Carkdacund Tshevnoe—otherwise known as 'Cat'."

Bending down, she herded three pint-sized versions of her husband toward me. "And these guys are Larry, Moe, and Curly. They've got Zetithian names, of course, but they're as unwieldy as Carkdacund; I had to call them *something* for short! I wanted to name them Larry, Darryl, and Darryl, but Cat wouldn't let me—thought it would be too confusing."

Cat rolled his eyes and laughed. There was a joke there somewhere, but I didn't get it. No doubt I would be enlightened at some point.

I shook Jack's outstretched hand, staring at her in awe. What a woman! Tall, lean, and muscular, she looked tough enough to take on Rafe and Brandon at the same time and beat them both in a fair fight. And what a man! He could have been Leo's brother, except for their coloring. And she'd introduced herself as captain of her own starship, no less! My wanderlust returning with a vengeance, I thought, now here is a woman who really *has* spread her wings to fly! Other women might have envied her the man standing next to her, or her adorable children, but all I could think about was her ship.

"Must be great to have your own ship," I remarked. "You can go anywhere you want, can't you?"

"Well, yeah," she agreed. "Most of the time. We've had a few close calls, but mostly we haven't had too much trouble." She glanced around suspiciously. "You haven't got any Nedwuts on this planet, have you?"

"Never heard of them," I replied. "But that doesn't mean there aren't any. I haven't traveled much."

Jack eyed me speculatively. "They said you were a witch. Just what kind of witch would that be?"

"A good witch," I replied. "I'm a healer...nothing more," I added out of habit. Then I thought, well, since everybody else already knows... "Though I *can* communicate with animals...and...start fires with my eyes," I added lamely.

Jack just looked at me for a moment, then scratched her head. "Got to be a way to make a profit with *those* talents!"

Shrugging my shoulders in an offhand gesture, I said, "Not really. At least, not around here."

"Well," answered Jack, "I wasn't thinking of 'around here.' It's a big fuckin' galaxy, you know."

"Yes, but I'm sort of stuck here," I said. "I have a responsibility to the people of my domain."

Jack viewed me with open skepticism. "Listen to me—what's your name?"

"Tisana," I replied.

"Well, Tisana, I'm sure they could find someone to take your place—and besides, it's not every day that two of the last remaining Zetithians find each other. It'd be a damn shame to split them up now, wouldn't it?"

My mouth fell open. "You mean you'd take us with you?" I whispered hoarsely. "On your ship? Through space?"

"Do bees be? Do bears bear?"

I felt like I was talking to Craynolt. "Huh?"

"I mean yes," she said, laughing. "And don't worry, Cat doesn't get that one, either." Rolling her eyes, she added, "He's still got *so* much to learn!"

I must have looked like I was about to faint, because Gerald wanted to know if I was having morning sickness.

"No, Gerald," I replied. *"It's not that. She just offered to take us with them."*

"Where to?"

"Into space! Into the sky!"

"Go for it, Tisana!" Gerald urged. *"This is one chance you may never get again as long as you live! You took me with you, remember? You gave me a chance to prove myself, now it's your turn!"*

He was right, but my head was already spinning with the possibilities. To travel to other worlds! To fly past the stars! What could be more exciting than that?

"But how could I leave you guys?" I asked him. *"And Morgana and Desdemona?"*

"You can take the cat with you," he said reasonably. *"But I think the horse had better stay here."*

"Yeah," I replied. *"I guess it would work."*

"What about me? Can I come, too?"

I looked down into Max's soulful eyes. What *is* it about dogs that can make even the toughest person want to cry?

"You'd take me with you, wouldn't you?"

"Max," I said gently. *"You need to stay here with Rafe and the boys. You belong to them."*

"But I don't want to," he said stoutly. *"I can run away. Dogs do it all the time."*

"But would you like to be on a ship all the time? Never get to chase squirrels anymore?"

Max shook his head so hard his ears made a snapping sound. *"Chasing squirrels isn't all it's cracked up to be,"* he said. *"I want to stay with you. It doesn't matter where we live."*

"So, what about it, Tisana?" Jack was saying. "Want to go where no witch has gone before?"

I looked over at Leo, who was obviously overjoyed to have found his old friend. Jack was right; we shouldn't split them up so soon. I didn't even have to feel like I was being selfish, because I was sure he wanted it every bit as much as I did. But still, I thought it best to ask.

"What do you want to do, Leo?"

"I want to be with you, wherever you go," he replied. "I will remain here if you wish."

"She *doesn't* wish," Jack said knowingly. "So you'd best be packing your bags, Bucko."

"Um, that's *Leo,*" I reminded her.

"Figure of speech," she said with a casual wave. "Don't get your panties in a wad."

Seeing my puzzled look, Cat remarked, "Yes, Jacinth is very odd, but it is not difficult to become accustomed to her ways."

"Hey, if I can understand an otterell, I'm sure I can figure her out, too," I declared. "Might take a while, though." I looked down at Max. Housebreaking him would be no trouble at all, since I could talk to him. Desdemona might not like the idea of leaving my cottage, but I knew her pretty well, and I was sure that as long as she had plenty to eat and a warm place to curl up, she'd be happy. "Um, Jack—er, Jacinth—which is your real name?"

"It's Jacinth," she said grimly. "But Cat's the only one who says it the way I like to hear it."

"Jacinth," Leo said experimentally.

"Damn, he can do it, too!" Jack exclaimed. "Must be a Zetithian thing. I guess you can call me Jacinth, too, Leo—but no one else is allowed." Returning her attention to me, she went on, "Now, what were you going to ask?"

"Can I bring along a dog and a cat?"

"Sure, my ship's pretty big. That dog there?" she asked, pointing at Max.

"Yes," I replied. "He says he wants to come along. I'll have to ask the cat, but she probably will, too." Desdemona might hate Max for a while, but I was pretty sure she'd get used to him. If I could get a squirrel and an otterell to work together, a dog and a cat should be a piece of cake.

"That's settled, then!" Jack said. "And don't worry about paying passage or any stupid shit like that. We'll make *millions* off of your ability to talk to animals!" She paused a moment, as though considering our other options. "Might not be a good idea to market the fire-starting thing, though. Might make people a little nervous."

"That's what I've always thought," I agreed. "Maybe we should keep it quiet."

"But it would be useful if we meet any more Nedwuts," Cat pointed out.

"Oh, no shit!" Jack exclaimed. "She could roast their hairy little asses, couldn't she?" Jack seemed terribly pleased with this idea. She must have really hated Nedwuts, whatever they were.

"And Leccarian is a very good fighter," Cat added. "He was the best swordsman in our company."

If anyone expected Leo to disclaim, they'd have been disappointed. He just nodded and smiled.

"Ha! Those fuckin' Nedwuts won't stand a chance!" Jack declared. "With a few more of us, we could take on their whole damn planet!"

"Excuse me," I said meekly. "What are Nedwuts?"

"Just the nastiest, slimiest bastards in the galaxy!" she replied. "They're the ones who destroyed Zetith!" She eyed me speculatively. "Don't suppose you could blow up a planet just by looking at it, could you?"

"Well, no," I replied. "At least, I don't think so."

"Hmm," she said, tapping her chin. "Maybe with a little practice…"

"She will not," Cat said in a firm tone. "We will not destroy an entire world."

"Oh, all right!" Jack grumbled, though it was obvious that she would have liked to see me try it.

"I don't believe in killing people," I said.

"Is that right? What if someone threatened Leo?" she asked.

"Well, that's different," I said. "If it was a choice between him and the Nedwuts, I'd blast 'em!"

"Good girl!" Jack said approvingly. "Oh, and by the way, we need to talk!" The look in her eye left no doubt as to what it was she wanted to talk about.

By the gods, I'd found a girlfriend at last!

Epilogue

IN THE END, I LEFT MORGANA WITH RAFE AND SINJAR. Seems she decided stallions weren't so bad after all, but it didn't do to tease her about it. You know how mares are.

Leo and I had a lovely daughter with my green eyes and dark hair, who is the most beautiful girl in the galaxy! I realize that I may be somewhat prejudiced in my opinion, but Desdemona thinks so, too, and, as you know, she is perfectly impartial! Max absolutely adores the baby and hardly ever leaves her side—except when we visit other planets. There aren't squirrels living on all of them, but he manages to get in a good run now and then. Speaking of squirrels, parting with Gerald was tough, but I have a feeling it wasn't long before he found someone else to throw nuts at. He's just that kind of guy.

I finally figured out what Craynolt meant when he said there were more souls now—not two, or four, but more. Apparently Zetithian snard is good at overcoming lots of obstacles—not the least of which is the witch tendency toward single births. I don't know how it works, but that made little difference to me, because I had sons! Two of them! And, best of all, they look just like Leo!

Leo and I have been traveling with Jack and Cat for a number of years now, and it's been quite an adventure! We found some other Zetithians along the way—those two brothers are *really* hot, and what happened to Lynx will make you cry your eyes out! As for the others, well,

I'd love to tell you more, but Leo doesn't want me to spoil the rest of the story.

So I won't.

Acknowledgments

I WOULD LIKE TO THANK:
My husband for keeping me sane;
My friends for their enthusiasm;
My dog for letting me listen in on his thoughts;
And *The Green Witch Herbal* by Barbara Griggs for providing me with information and inspiration.

Read on for a preview of

ROGUE

Book #3 in The Cat Star Chronicles by Cheryl Brooks
Coming from Sourcebooks Casablanca
in March 2009

AFTER DINNER, SCALIA SENT ZEALON OFF TO BED, telling her that she needed to rest well before embarking on her new career as a concert pianist. I seconded that and was then left alone with the Queen, who wasted no time in introducing a new topic for discussion—one which she probably considered unfit for young ears, just as the wine was for young palates.

"I will not keep you much longer." She paused, calling out to a servant in the next room before taking another delicate sip of her wine and continuing, "But before you go, you must see my cats."

"Your cats?"

Nodding, she said, "I'd like your opinion of them."

That sounded odd. What did it matter what I thought of her pets? The little toad creature was told to fetch the cats, so I had a little time to think. Okay, if this was a desert planet with intelligent life forms that looked for all the world like dinosaurs, what kind of cats would they have here? Saber-toothed tigers?

On that thought, the door opened again and the two cats entered—but they weren't cats, at least not in the ordinary sense. They were tall male humanoids—undoubtedly more of Scalia's "exotic slaves"—and they certainly were exotic! Separately, each one would have been stunning; but together, they took my breath away—would have taken *anyone's* breath away, even Nindala's. For myself, I was just glad I happened to be sitting down when I saw them for the first time. Staring back at them in awe, I had barely managed to take another breath when one of them turned his startlingly blue eyes on me and, no doubt noting my open-mouthed expression, lowered his eyelids ever so slightly and sent a roguish smile in my direction.

And I had an orgasm.

Scalia probably thought I'd choked on my wine, but that wasn't it at all! I felt a fire begin to burn deep inside me when I first laid eyes on him, and his smile sent me over the edge. I'd never felt anything quite like it before in my life—nor had I ever seen anything to compare with him.

"They are my most prized possessions," Scalia said. "Very beautiful, are they not?"

I'm not entirely sure what I said in reply, but it was affirmative, though undoubtedly inarticulate.

Scalia smiled. "I'd hoped you would like them."

I took another sip of my wine—actually, it was more of a gulp than a sip—and asked, "W—where did you find them?"

"The slave traders in this region know of my penchant for interesting specimens and brought them to me," she replied. "You would not believe what I had to pay for them! The trader said that there had been a bounty placed on them, which, of course, meant that I was required to pay about twenty times that amount in order to get them—and also to keep him quiet as to their where-abouts! Apparently someone holds a grudge against their kind and set out to exterminate them entirely—which would have been most unfortunate, as I am certain you will agree."

I think I nodded, but sitting there trying to imagine a whole planet full of these guys nearly made my uterus go into another spasm. I decided that a group of jealous men must have gotten an army together and plotted against them, for certainly no female in the known universe would have gone along with such a scheme. I mean, Scalia was a lizard and even *she* liked them!

"But they are safe here," she added firmly. "They are kept under lock and key at night, and no one beyond the palace walls knows they exist. And, unlike my other slaves, even my daughter has never seen them."

The fact that they were both entirely nude except for jeweled collars around their necks and genitals might have been one reason Zealon had never been permitted to see them. She was much too young for such things, though I didn't think that anyone under the age of—oh, I don't know, *a hundred*, perhaps?—could look at them and not be affected.

"These two are brothers," Scalia went on as though she were truly talking about a pair of pet cats who happened to be litter-mates. "I would dearly love to breed more of them, but they are a mammalian species and will not cross with our kind. Nor are they... aroused...by our females."

Which, of course, made me wonder whether or not they liked humans. I, for one, certainly liked *them*, especially the one who'd smiled at me. The other one didn't seem terribly pleased to see me—not quite scowling, but certainly not smiling.

As they had positioned themselves on either side of Scalia's chair, across the table from me, I had an excellent view of them both. They didn't seem particularly shy, either, not minding a bit that I couldn't take my eyes off them. The blue-eyed one had perfect, pale skin setting off the most spectacular hair—jet black with a thick streak of white running through it near his temple—hanging to his waist in perfect spirals. The other also had black hair which curled to his waist, but with a similarly placed orange stripe, green eyes, and more tawny skin. They both possessed up-swept eyebrows and pointed ears, as well as vertical pupils that seemed to glow slightly. The green-eyed one yawned just then, revealing a mouth full of sharp white teeth and canines that looked downright dangerous. All in all, they put me in mind of Earth's tigers—the one Bengal, and the other Siberian—but they had body hair more like that of human males, not the fur you would expect to find on a cat. Neither of them had beards, but I wasn't close enough to determine whether or not this was natural. Both were tall, broad-chested, and lean, with smooth, rippling muscles and perfectly proportioned limbs. It was no wonder Scalia had paid a fortune for them!

All of this possibly wouldn't have mattered if they hadn't had one other notable attribute: they were both hung like horses. A crass description, perhaps, but it was accurate, nonetheless. Unfortunately, they were not, as Scalia had mentioned before, aroused. The mere thought of what they might look like if they *were* aroused made my mouth go dry, and I attempted to take another sip from an empty glass.

"My guest needs more wine," Scalia said, crooking a finger toward the Siberian tiger.

Nodding, he collected a flask from the sideboard and came around the table. When he leaned over to pour the wine, his cock was just below my eye level, but as my eyes were slightly downcast, I had an excellent view of it. Among other things, I noted that the jewels on his genital cuff were every bit as blue as his eyes. Scalia, it seemed, was not the slightest bit color-blind and had paid attention to detail when decorating her slaves.

"Thank you," I said hoarsely.

"You are very welcome," he replied. "It is my pleasure to serve you."

His deep voice was like melted butter and, even though polite, his choice of words had me envisioning all manner of pleasurable things—none of them having *anything* to do with food or drink. I couldn't help but look up at him, and when our eyes met, he smiled again and blinked slowly. Then I watched, fascinated, as his nostrils flared with a deep inhalation—and his smile intensified, as did the hot blue of his eyes.

"Oh, excellent!" Scalia said in hushed tones.

Yes, he is! Excellent, perfect, amazing, unbelievable— and just about any other superlative you'd care to use. Still gazing up at him, I felt as though I were about to melt into a puddle and slide off my chair. Honestly, if

I'd ever felt a more overwhelming sense of desire for any other man in the galaxy, this one would have made me forget it.

I felt something wet drop onto my hand. Glancing down to see if I was indeed melting, I saw what Scalia had undoubtedly been referring to, for the tiger's penis was now fully erect. As thick and long as a well-endowed human's would have been, it also had a wide, scalloped corona at the base of the head that was obviously there for one reason only: to give the greatest possible pleasure to any woman fortunate enough to be penetrated by it. Looking closer, I noted that the clear fluid that had fallen on my hand appeared to be coming, not from the opening at the apex, but from the star-like points of the corona.

I tried to swallow and couldn't. I looked up at him again with what must have been an expression of raw hunger mingled with guilt written clearly upon my face. In return, what I saw on his face was the most open invitation to partake of anything I'd ever seen. His mesmerizing eyes beckoned, his full lips promised sensuous delights beyond my wildest imaginings, and his provocative smile assured me of his knowledge of every possible way to drive a woman wild. He was offering himself to me—completely—without saying a word.

Unfortunately, just as I was about to take a taste of him, I suddenly remembered where I was. We were not alone, and he was a slave who belonged to the lizard queen sitting across the table from me. Reaching awkwardly for my wine glass, my sleeve slid across the head of his cock, soaking it with his fluid and drawing a barely audible groan from him.

Trying desperately to ignore his reaction, I looked away from him and saw that Scalia was watching us intently, but she had her hand on the Bengal tiger's thigh, stroking him, though without any erotic response on his part whatsoever. I would have thought that such a pornographic vision right across the table from him would have been enough to stimulate him, but apparently it wasn't.

Then I remembered the blue-eyed tiger inhaling as though he was taking a whiff of me. It was something to do with scent, then—though it was surprising that I was clear-headed enough to figure that out at the time. What was also surprising was the fact that my "scent" hadn't reached the other man, because if the way I was feeling was any indication, it had to have been pretty heavy with sex pheromones.

Breaking the silence, the Queen's voice was now brisk and businesslike. "You will require a personal attendant during your stay with us," Scalia said. "I believe he will suit you very nicely."

"Who? Him?" I gasped. As I sat staring at his cock, I decided that if anyone could "suit me," it would have been him, but he was far more…*man*…than I'd ever so much as touched in my life! He could turn me to mush in a heartbeat—and, of course, in that state, I'd never play piano again… "Oh, but I don't really need—" I protested before she cut me off with an imperious wave of her hand.

"Yes, you do," she said firmly. "You are new to this world, Kyra. He will be able to help you…adjust."

Adjust. What an interesting choice of words! He probably could have helped me adjust to just about anything—even daily torture—if only he were to hold my hand for the duration. And speaking of hands, I wondered if I'd be able to keep mine off of him when we were alone together. Having been within a hairsbreadth of licking his cock just moments before—and in full view of two other people, I might add—I thought I'd probably have some difficulty with that. I also wondered if he'd go running to Scalia to complain if I did something of that nature—or what he would do if I didn't.

To be honest, I doubted that I needed a servant of any kind, though due to the scarcity of water and fabrics, it was a given that there wouldn't be any easy way to wash my clothes. I wondered if my bed would have sheets on it, or if I'd be sleeping on a bed of stones or sand. Hopefully, Zealon had done some homework in that area as well.

My tiger was still standing next to me, flanking my chair just as his counterpart did for Scalia—quite slave-like behavior, despite his persistent erection—and it occurred to me that he might like to have some say in the matter.

"What about you?" I asked, looking up at him curiously. "Do *you* think I need a personal attendant?"

"Absolutely," he replied, his luscious lips curling in a smile. "There are a great many things I can do for you."

I'll just bet you can, I thought grimly. "But do you *want* to?" I said aloud. For some reason, I felt it was important that his service to me be voluntary. Not that he wouldn't have done whatever he was told to do by his owner; after all, he *was* a slave, though a very valuable one. What would happen if he refused? I doubted that Scalia would punish him—doubted that she ever had, for neither of them had a mark on him, nor did they have the cowed expressions of people who were habitually abused or bullied. In fact, they appeared to have been well cared for, if not cosseted, by their owner—truly more like cherished pets than slaves.

"I can think of nothing I would like more," he assured me.

"Because you have been told to." I said this not as a question, but as a statement.

He seemed uncertain about how to reply to that, glancing at Scalia out of the corner of his eye as if for direction, but she gave him none that I could see.

"Because you smell of desire," he said finally. "Being near you pleases me…and I have no doubt that I can please *you*."

"An honest answer," Scalia asserted. "You may believe what he tells you. They are both very truthful."

I nodded. "Yes, I can believe that much," I said. This man undoubtedly could please the most stone-cold woman imaginable, but I secretly wondered if it was my desire which pleased him, or if any woman's desire would do.

Sighing deeply, I relented, knowing that while I might regret my decision in the end, if I refused, I'd regret it even more.

"It is settled, then," Scalia said to my tiger. "You may escort Kyra to her rooms." Turning to me, she added, "Your quarters have been adapted to suit human needs. I believe you will find them to your liking."

"I'm sure I will," I replied, "but, if you don't mind my asking, how are you going to keep him a secret if he's with me? The Princess, or someone else, may see him."

"We will take that risk," Scalia said with conviction. "I believe it to be worthwhile."

And her word was law. After all, she *was* the Queen.

About the Author

CHERYL BROOKS IS A CRITICAL CARE NURSE BY NIGHT and a romance writer by day. She is a member of the Romance Writers of America and lives in Bloomfield, Indiana, along with her husband, two sons, five cats, five horses, and one dog. She is the author of *The Cat Star Chronicles: Slave*. *Warrior* is the second book in The Cat Star Chronicles series. You can visit her website at http://cherylbrooksonline.com, or email her at cheryl.brooks52@yahoo.com.